"Erica Sand spins a wonderful story - a hopefully romantic anecdote, part coming masterful prose paints an empathetic picture t .... with the richness of her details and the quality of her exposition. She describes the emotions of the moments that bind us all as creatures looking for meaning, for acceptance, for individuality, and for love. You'll literally feel the grit of the Middle East - you can feel the lights and hear the tempo of the music as she embarks on what would become the adventure of a lifetime, leading to a pain the likes of which she'd never experience, ecstasy far beyond anything in her wildest dreams, and ultimately an inner peace that very few of us encounter. You won't be able to put it down." Jason Salas, KUAM News Anchor & Author

"Each time I picked up *Handful of Smoke*, it was as if the world around me disappeared and I was right there, feeling everything right along with Jenny. Thank you for sharing your story so beautifully. I can't wait for the prequels!" Pika Fejeron, Restaurateur

"Reading the novel, *Handful of Smoke*, was like binge watching a series on Netflix. It kept me wanting to read just a little more to see what was going to happen next and before I knew it, I had finished the book and was left wanting more. It has a storyline that is unique with lots of romance, seduction, betrayal and lies. It is an easy read and would be a great book to throw in your bag and take on vacation." Jerilyn McLeod

"Seduced all at once by the glitz and glamour of Abu Dhabi's nightlife, Erica Sand takes us from the intoxicating buzz of swaying hips to the treacherous terrain of the heart. Vivid, by every means of the word, *Handful of Smoke* captivates until the very last page." Amber Word, Artist & Jewelry Store Owner

"The book is wonderful. A great read about exotic places. A story about love, travel, and life choices." Bea Hernandez Arcilla, Student

SOJOURNING SOUL

HANDFUL OF
SMOKE

A NOVEL

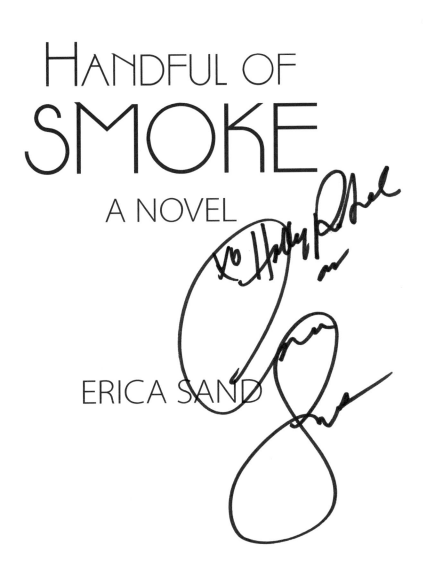

ERICA SAND

ISBN: 978-1-4834-6041-3 (sc)
ISBN: 978-1-4834-6042-0 (e)

Library of Congress Control Number: 2016917375

Lulu Publishing Services rev. date: 11/08/2016

For Isabella. May you always have a voice.

PREFACE

Jenny glanced at Matthew out of the corner of her eye. This was not an easy task, considering the amount of alcohol in her system. His image seemed to quake slightly in this awkward side glance. Seeing him in double was not the only awkward thing about tonight. This was one of the few times they had seen each other since the notorious breakup—the whirlwind romance that had become too intense too quickly and had situationally ended too soon. Graduate school abroad took only one year, which was great for getting a quick master's degree but shitty for sustaining foreign relationships. Still, Matthew had shown up at her going-away party seeming both agitated and sad that there was a crowd.

She faced him head-on with a confident smile. His handsomely chiseled face and cold blue eyes softened when he saw her looking at him.

"I'm going to miss you," he mouthed across the noisy room. It was a sentiment only the two of them noticed.

Jenny's heart sank. She was going to miss him in ways he would never know. The party that bumped around her quieted with this connection, as if in slow motion. A melancholy seriousness filled the gap for a sacred moment. Then time jolted back to its normal cadence when the ever-chipper Emma jumped in front of Jenny, blocking her view of Matthew, and shouted, "Jenny, drink up!"

Giggling, the brown-haired girl handed Jenny a margarita and instantly the room filled with music as hip-hop flooded Jenny's ears again.

"Thanks, girl," Jenny said, taking the glass and clinking it against Emma's drink. Jenny was grateful for this return to time and sound, since she and Matthew were going different directions within the next twelve hours. So the best thing to do was to drink her margarita, enjoy this night, and not dwell on what-ifs. There was no point in trying to conjure up a distracted Cupid.

Kourtney stumbled over, and the three girls who had been inseparable all year—except by their boyfriends—hugged. Soft hair fell against Jenny's shoulder, and she sighed. She was going to miss these girls. Even though they swore they would meet up again, fate wasn't on their side. Getting together would be a bit of a logistical nightmare, since they were all heading in different career directions around the globe. Kourtney was heading back to Canada, Emma was going to some country in Latin America, and Jenny was on her way to a small village outside of Abu Dhabi. They'd be worlds away from one another. Jenny pulled her halter dress a little higher with one hand while taking a drink of her margarita. *Mmm, Emma's specialty*, Jenny thought as she felt the cool, sour drink working to calm the butterflies in her stomach. She hated goodbyes.

Fuck Cupid. Taking a deep breath, Jenny started to walk over to where Matthew was standing. She wanted to feel his strong arms holding her once more. Trying to resurrect her confident smile, she took another deep breath. *You can do this.* But by the time she finally got through the little crowd, he was gone already without a goodbye. They were more alike than she had thought.

PART 1

CHAPTER 1

"For fuck's sake! You slept with Dan? I don't mean to laugh, but what? He is such a loser. And what about your fiancé, John?" Jenny laughed.

"I know. I know. I *know!*" Veronica was a natural blonde, a little chubby in that cute way where all of her features were full and healthy: large blue eyes, cupid lips, and a bubbly personality. Her laugh matched her shape—round and full. The doors to the elevator opened and they stepped out. "I drank way too much, and John was in New Orleans, and I was so far away. I don't know what I was thinking."

Jenny had been ecstatic when her friend Veronica, a teacher with whom she had taught in Kuwait, e-mailed to say she would be in Abu Dhabi on holiday to see her father. Her dad stayed at a residential, posh hotel on the outskirts of town. Jenny smiled from ear to ear, walking next to Veronica, and she let out a giggle when she thought about her friend's very bad choice for an affair. Jenny had missed girl talk and her friends from this part of the world.

For the past month, Jenny had been working and living in Talefa, a tiny fishing village that was a ninety-minute drive from Abu Dhabi. For the entire time in Talefa, Jenny had fantasized about living in Abu Dhabi. Since she had no car, she had only two ways to get to the city. She could use her work angle to guarantee rides to Abu Dhabi with a Pakistani company driver. Or she could hitch rides with her younger German coworkers, nearly all of whom were staunch alcoholics and partied every weekend (although the drive took only an hour when they drove). So Jenny desperately needed a girls' weekend out.

Walking through the hotel lobby, Jenny and Veronica entered Clover's Bar, a stylish sports bar. Because it was St. Patrick's Day and ladies' night, the bar was packed.

The main bar was in the center of the room and entirely carved out of deep mahogany. Flawless accents of the same wood were artfully spaced around the room and seemed to absorb the sound of the room into a softness that, for some strange reason, reminded Jenny of drinking Hennessy on a snowy afternoon.

Taking a deep breath, Jenny followed Veronica toward the large center bar. Feeling a slight warmth on her cheek, Jenny glanced to her right. Instantly and magnetically, her eyes connected with an extremely handsome Arab man who sat at a table a little way from the bar. He had dark eyes, a beautiful heart-shaped face, and lips and chin framed by a trendy goatee. She knew by the intensity of the feeling that this moment would forever remain fixed in her mind and body. He looked slightly surprised, with lips pursed in a small O that fell into a sexy smile. Tilting his glass of beer toward her, he nodded. It was so natural, as if they had been together for a lifetime. In that moment, she imagined them clinking champagne glasses together on their honeymoon and his eyes warming her again with that same intensity.

Jenny couldn't hold back a smile. *Damn, he's hot.*

"Hey, what's free for ladies' night?" Veronica asked the Indian bartender as Jenny walked—more like floated—over to her friend.

"Wine or beer," he said, with a heavy accent.

"Two glasses of your house red," Veronica said. The bartender nodded and walked away. She then looked over at Jenny. "Why are you smiling like that?"

Jenny opened her mouth to reply, but before she could say anything, the Arab guy was at her side.

"Can I buy you ladies a drink?" His accent was almost perfectly American.

Tall and muscular, he was typically Arab except for his nose, which was rounded and small. This difference seemed to give him originality and confidence. Altogether, he was very handsome, but Jenny didn't care for his eagerness. Although she had lived in the Middle East previously, she had never dated an Arab. All of her friends who had dated Arabs had ended up with broken hearts. Also, Arab men were so forward that it was clear they were after only one thing. Nevertheless, in that instant, the undeniable chemistry she had with this guy was *amazing.*

"Well, our drinks are free tonight." Jenny was proud of herself for saying a coherent sentence. Her skin tingled when his arm brushed softly against her own.

His slightly round cheeks reddened, and he let out a laugh that immediately danced around inside Jenny in little electrical movements. "That's why I was asking." He had turned it into some kind of line while simultaneously making fun of himself. *Clever,* Jenny thought.

"No, seriously," he continued. "At least join me and my friends for a drink." He pointed over to the corner, where two middle-aged white guys and one Asian woman sat talking.

"Um, maybe. Give us a minute to get our drinks." Jenny was charmed by his good looks, but she wasn't impressed with his companions. She also didn't want to be stuck to the first man who approached them. She hadn't even had a chance to look around the bar yet—magic eye meeting or not.

"Okay." He gave her a disappointed smile, then looked her up and down before heading back to his table.

Veronica grabbed the wine that the bartender had placed before them and handed a glass to Jenny. "Cheers!" They raised their glasses.

"So what do you think?" Veronica asked, grimacing, as the guy walked away. "Tacky pickup line."

"No kidding." Jenny looked around the room without really looking. *I could eat that laugh,* she thought. "Do you see any other cute guys?"

Veronica took a deep drink from her wineglass. "Nope. Up to you. No one else interesting in here yet."

Jenny felt someone squeeze her shoulder from behind. She whirled around. It was the Arab guy—tall, dark-eyed, and looking a little pissed. He probably wasn't used to someone saying no to him. She looked into his eyes and couldn't believe she'd been thinking of going to a different table that night. His eyes seemed brighter now, and his personality was emerging. He seemed like the cocky type of asshole to whom Jenny was—unfortunately—attracted.

"I thought you ladies were going to join us." He was smiling, but his eyes narrowed. Without waiting for an answer, he pulled at Jenny's elbow and led her toward his table. His touch was warm yet rough, causing Jenny to bite her lip. She looked back at Veronica and shrugged as a broad smile erupted on her face. Veronica shook her head, giggled, and followed closely behind.

After they sat down, there were polite introductions around the table. Peter was probably in his fifties, a very tall man from Louisiana. Veronica talked with him for a while, since she was from New Orleans. He was working in the oil fields like Veronica's dad and living long term at the hotel. Randy, also in his late fifties, had a pinched, sunburned face and squinted when he spoke. He was from Nevada and seemed to have one of those "small-man" egos. He worked at the American Oil Company near Dubai. His girlfriend, Lin, was from Thailand. She had amazing skin and yellow teeth, and did not speak English well.

The Arab, Ghaith, was a Palestinian/Jordanian raised in the Middle East. He owned an IT company and was trying to get contracts with the American Oil Company. He had spent nine years in the United States while earning two degrees, which explained his good command of English.

"Sorry to call it a night, but we've got to get going," Randy said. He looked over at Lin, grabbing her inner thigh.

"Yes, I need to call it a night, too." Peter rubbed his eyes. "It's a good life, but an early one. I have to be out in the field by six."

"Nice meeting you all," Veronica said.

"Good night." It was the only bit of politeness that Jenny could muster up. She was not the least bit interested in the sleeping habits of old men, and she was starting to feel the effects of the two glasses of wine she'd sucked down on an empty stomach.

As if Ghaith understood that Jenny was losing interest, he waved the waitress over and ordered both Jenny and Veronica a third glass of wine.

"This flows too easily." Jenny giggled, her head becoming light. She felt more relaxed now that it was just the three of them. Ghaith was handsome, but there was something else that drew her to him. She thought about the way their eyes had connected when she first entered the bar and how he had raised his glass to her immediately, as though their actions were magnetically intertwined. She felt the pull between them intensify while they sat across from each other. She pulled her chair a little closer.

"As many as you want. I can afford it." They all chuckled at his cheesy pickup line. "I still can't believe I offered to buy you a drink when they were free!" His laugh was deep and something Jenny wished she could put into a bottle.

CHAPTER 2

Ghaith hadn't seen a prettier face in a long time. This girl was exactly his type: blond hair, green eyes, round face, small nose, perfect mouth, and gorgeous body. She was small and petite, yet there was something powerful about her. When she'd walked in, it had been like a slow-motion movie—everything went quiet, his heart stopped, and a spotlight appeared out of nowhere just to shine on her face. He'd been captivated. He had to have her.

His phone lit up, indicating a text, and he tilted the phone back to check the message. He blew out a circle of smoke, a cocky habit he had picked up in America.

"Baby, please pick up some diapers on your way home." It was from his wife, Laila.

"Excuse me for one moment, ladies. Work never stops. I am going to leave my wallet here." He winked at Jenny, knowing that leaving his wallet would mean she wouldn't leave. American girls were too polite. He did make sure to grab his cigarettes, though, and walked out of the bar to call Laila.

"Hey, babe," he said over the phone. "I can't come home tonight. I'm sorry, but I have to go back to Sharjah to fix a work order."

Laila protested, of course, and they argued back and forth in Arabic until she started to whine. Then Ghaith made cooing sounds of apology, trying to sound as miserable as possible. That always helped.

"Okay, *habibi*," Laila said, eventually easing up. "I love you."

Grinning ear to ear, Ghaith hung up the phone triumphantly. *What will I have to do tonight to get into bed with Jenny?* He took a deep breath, stretching his hands over his head while he walked back into the bar. Then he dropped his hands and slapped his thighs with excitement. He was ready. Jenny and Veronica had two fresh glasses of wine on the table in front of them and were laughing, obviously a bit drunk. Ghaith picked up his beer.

"You guys are getting ahead of me," he said, and laughed. Looking over at Jenny again, he noticed how toned her calves were and wondered if she was a runner. She certainly worked out, but she wasn't as tight as some of the personal trainers he had dated. None of them had an ounce of flesh on them to squeeze. Jenny was toned and fit, but she still had curves. He wanted to cup his hands around her waist and squeeze her flesh softly. The mere thought of doing that made him grip his pint glass more tightly.

"Well, we were thinking about opening your wallet, since you didn't seem to miss it," Jenny said. Her smile was meant for him, as was the mischievous look in her green eyes. She tapped a perfectly manicured fingernail on top of his wallet and then, relaxing her hand, stroked her index finger down the soft leather, tracing little circles. The movement was small, but Ghaith felt himself harden.

"You were gone forever," Veronica said. She took a long drink of her wine and put it on the table. They both started giggling again. "We need to go dancing!"

"Oh yeah! What's close by?" Jenny uncrossed her legs and put her elbows on the table. He could see the top of her cleavage and the thin pink lining of a bra.

Ghaith licked his lips and looked up at Jenny, and their eyes met. Her eyes were so green, like an oasis of date trees in the desert. He was used to the brown eyes of Arab women and the blue eyes of expat women. But green eyes were rare, especially on a woman like this. Without taking his eyes off her, he drank the remainder of his beer.

"Come with me," he said.

He put down his empty glass, as Jenny and Veronica emptied their wineglasses. Jenny locked eyes with him while she slowly swallowed her wine. Laying a few bills on the table, he then stood, cocking his head to one side for the ladies to follow him. As he walked out of the bar, the girls semi-stumbled after him, still giggling. *Tonight is going to be easier than I thought*, Ghaith said to himself.

His car had been shipped over from the States: a silver, tinted Porsche Panemera, decked out with all the new options. Grabbing Jenny's hand, he opened the front passenger's door, making sure she sat next to him. He wasn't disappointed with Jenny's reaction as her eyes widened and she let out a little whistle. Then he held a door open for Veronica to sit behind Jenny.

Hurrying around to the other side, Ghaith got into the driver's seat and put his phone on silent. He did not want any further interruptions tonight. Even though Laila was pacified now, she could change her mind in an instant and the whining would ensue. That was how things went with her; she got mad at him and threatened to leave, and then he calmed her down. If that didn't work, he would tell her to go ahead and leave. That good old reverse psychology trick worked, even though it was messier, louder, and took longer to resolve issues.

Laila had fallen in love with Ghaith long before he gave her his heart—and before he had any money of his own. She had been needy back then, and that hadn't changed. But she was the only woman who had given him children, so he was committed to remaining married to her and providing for her. Nevertheless, he still wanted more. Ghaith lived for the experience of loving someone because he felt electrified, not because of obligation.

"This is the nicest car I've *ever* been in," Veronica exclaimed, pulling Ghaith out of his own head. He glanced at her in the rearview mirror. She looked so young, probably not even thirty, and her big, bright eyes danced around, making her appear even younger. But Jenny ... Ghaith glanced at her in the passenger seat. She had settled back in the leather seat, more at ease than Veronica and easily a couple of years older. Jenny looked back at Ghaith evenly, meeting his eyes. She was classy, but he also saw a little bit of edginess in her. Her legs were crossed, and a sly smile came over her face when she saw him looking.

He could get used to that smile. Looking at her exposed thighs, he noticed her dress was riding up slightly, and he ran his tongue over his top lip. As he looked back up, she was still wearing that confident smile.

"You can start the car now," Veronica said from the back.

Ghaith and Jenny laughed.

"Okay, okay. Now, I have very little English music," he warned, fiddling with his stereo to find his one English-language song. His first wife, the American, had given him the CD because she despised the Arabic music he listened to.

He still remembered the long drive they had made to New York when she, finally fed up, had actually ejected his Elissa CD in the middle of her heartfelt lament of "Aa bali habibi" and thrown it out the window. He had been so shocked that he had laughed, laughed hard at the tenaciousness of this American woman. As his tears of laughter dried, he finally asked, "Why? Why didn't you just take it out?" She had sat there, completely deadpan and unaffected by his laughing fit, and said, "All they do is whine. I can't stand it anymore. Your language just whines, whines, whines." He knew then that his marriage was over, especially when she made him this CD with one English-language song—which actually was much worse than any earnest love song in his own beautiful language. But Ghaith was sentimental, so he had kept the CD, and now this other American woman would listen to it. *When I make love to her, will it be romantic, or will it be just a lustful booty call akin to this English crap?*

Juvenile's "Back That Ass Up" blared out of the speakers, and Veronica and Jenny immediately started car dancing and singing along.

CHAPTER 3

"You look good." Jenny flicked the sweat from her forehead and changed the speed on the treadmill from a jog to a run.

"Thanks," Veronica said. "I'm feeling better too, *and* I've lost fifteen pounds! As soon as I finish the half marathon, I'm gonna eat a big bowl of ice cream."

Jenny smiled—then winced. She was still feeling the effects of her last drink at four in the morning, which was only about six hours ago. "When is it?" she asked.

"It's in six weeks."

"Well, you do look great."

Tapering her treadmill to a stop, Jenny took a drink of water and swished it in her mouth, fending off the copious amount of red wine that kept wanting to resurrect itself. Veronica brought her treadmill to a stop too.

"Okay," Jenny said when the room was quiet. "Let's go to the pool. I'm starting to taste the merlot again."

"I know what you mean." Veronica pulled off her shirt, revealing a bikini top underneath.

Jenny let out a laugh. "Well, you sure are prepared! I'm just going to go change."

ଔ

Now wearing her bikini, Jenny walked out to the pool and sat on a sun lounger next to Veronica.

"Kim Kardashian is so hot," Veronica said as she flipped through a *Star* magazine. She had been reading it off and on all morning.

"Why is it that all the really hot girls are brunettes?" Jenny asked. She pulled back her hair and untied the string on the top of her bikini in an effort to forgo any tan lines. Folding the strings carefully behind her, she let out a small sigh.

"Right? We might as well stop highlighting our hair and go dark."

"If you're going to go dark, do it while you're still young." Slipping on her sunglasses, Jenny looked at Veronica. "I went a dark chocolaty brown a couple of years ago, but the only white hairs I had popped right out." She sighed again, but this time she wasn't as relaxed. Apparently white hair emerges in the late twenties. Jenny still remembered that day when she saw a single white hair kinkily poking out at a foreign angle as if it was an alien intruder. She had examined it so closely in the mirror that it had made her eyes cross. That had been her rite of passage, going from regenerating to degenerating, and it had depressed her. She still had hardly any white hairs, but she didn't like to have the fact of any random white hair advertised. "Okay, so tell me, what else is happening in the celebrity world?"

"Well, Heidi Montag went through *ten* cosmetic surgeries in *one* day." Veronica looked up, and Jenny pulled up her sunglasses and arched a brow.

"For fuck's sake. I'd just like to have *one* of those surgeries." Jenny nodded down at her B-sized breasts. "But *ten*? What do you even get for ten surgeries?"

"Apparently, enough to make her look like this." Veronica flipped the magazine around for Jenny to see the before and after pictures. The before picture showed Heidi's cute, girl-next-door look, and then the after picture depicted an overly-made-up, grotesquely large-breasted Hollywood girl.

"She was cute before. I don't understand why she would have so many surgeries." Jenny took a long drink of cold water and inwardly sighed, feeling the chill evaporate inside her body. Rehydration was proving to be a bit of a challenge. She was still dehydrated from the previous night out and the five-mile run this morning—not to mention all the water she was losing just being out in 100-degree weather.

"I think she's doing it only to be famous," Veronica said. "These reality TV stars have no talent. They have to do extreme things to get noticed."

"I guess so."

At that moment, a couple walked out to the pool, and Jenny and Veronica both looked up. The short man, probably in his late fifties, sported a crunched-up face with a downturned mouth and plenty of wrinkles in the same direction. His large potbelly was in direct contrast to his sticklike legs, reminding Jenny of an older version of Humpty Dumpty. The European woman with him couldn't have been a day over thirty and had a svelte figure for which even Heidi Montag would probably go back into surgery.

Jenny and Veronica glanced at each other. "This is an … interesting resident hotel," Jenny said. "Seems like this is the place to stay for old guys who make good money."

"No shit." Veronica let out a groan. "I can't believe my dad and Anna are engaged."

Jenny regretted her insinuation about trophy wives. But it was probably timely that she and Veronica talk about Anna, now that the shock seemed to be wearing off.

"Sorry, I didn't mean … Well, how are you doing with all of it?"

"I don't know. I mean, I'm just coming out to visit my dad, right? All he said on the phone was that he had a girlfriend he wanted me to meet." Veronica took a deep breath and adjusted her sunglasses. "I didn't even know they were living together. I was just getting used to the idea of him having a girlfriend. And then I get here and—*Bam!*—there's a diamond ring on her finger. So now I'm staying with *them* in *their* place. It's just so weird."

Veronica sighed and closed her magazine. "I mean, I am glad he isn't alone, but she's only a few years older than me. And is this sexy chick from Russia? Like, what is he thinking? I mean, an Australian guy in the oil industry—*of course* she's going to marry him. But he's like twice her age, and she barely speaks English. What can they possibly have in common?"

"I'm so sorry." Jenny's own dad was on his third wife, who was a couple of decades younger than him and from Brazil. So she could understand how Veronica felt. "At least she doesn't have kids."

"That's true, but I think they want to have one. My God, if my dad has a baby, I'll scream." Veronica balled her hands into fists and pressed them against her temples.

"Can you imagine if they had one after you do?" Veronica and Jenny both laughed.

"Oh, fuck! We'd be one of those weird families where the uncle or aunt is younger than the niece or nephew," Veronica said. "Ahhh!"

"Well, your mom is from Louisiana, and your dad is from Australia. It kind of makes sense." Jenny laughed, and Veronica let out a snort.

"I guess all I can do is laugh about it."

"Yeah. She's really trying, though. I mean, she made sure your dad had bought all the food and liquor you like, and she's planning your birthday party."

"Except she's inviting all of the 'younger' guys at the hotel. So there's gonna be, like, a bunch of forty-year-olds there tonight."

Jenny stood. "Come on, birthday girl. It's crazy hot out here. Let's go swimming now and worry about your party when it gets here."

"Okay, okay." Veronica stood and readjusted her bikini top. She skipped ahead of Jenny. "Here's to turning twenty-eight!" As her friend dove into the deep end of the pool, Jenny smiled.

ꝏ

Veronica's birthday party ended up being quaint but fun. Anna made sure there were shrimp cocktails, chicken empanadas, a lavish chocolate specialty cake, and—most importantly—plenty of wine, vodka, gin, and brandy. Jenny knew that Anna was trying to win Veronica's affection, and she realized that she actually liked Anna. Even if she was just after a green card and a better life, Anna was trying to make allies. And if she really was in love with Veronica's dad—while also enjoying the fringe benefits— then more power to her for really trying to spoil her stepdaughter.

Anna had persuaded a few of Veronica's dad's coworkers to come to the party, including Tate, who was in his late thirties and from Houston, Texas. She even managed to quickly push Tate toward Veronica, and the two of them hit it off immediately, both being from the South. That seemed to happen to expatriates—they would navigate back to people who shared and understood their own regional idioms and subcultures. Somehow this familiarity would bond them, even if they had completely different personalities. As more wine was poured, the conversation between Veronica and Tate became more intimate.

Now that she had a healthy buzz and her friend was entertained, Jenny grabbed her clutch and headed into one of the empty bedrooms. Standing in front of the vanity table, she opened her purse and took out her phone, lipstick, and Ghaith's business card. Ghaith had given her his card the night before, or rather early this morning, when he had dropped the girls off at the hotel. Jenny smiled to herself, remembering.

They'd danced together at the club, and he had put his arms around her, nuzzling his nose into her neck and saying sweet nothings of Arabic-infused English. They hadn't been able to keep their hands off each other all night. Surprisingly, she had felt more nervous later, an hour before dawn, as she stood a few inches away from him in front of the hotel. It was as if his touch had grounded her. Without it, gravity evaporated and left her to float away. The fading darkness of the night and the bright hotel lights had exposed soft dark circles under Ghaith's eyes. She had felt raw and ready for his touch, but he'd only reached into his wallet and handed her his card.

"Call me," he had breathed into her ear while he leaned toward her, reducing but not eliminating the distance between them. Teasing her with this small space, he lingered for a moment with his warm breath on her neck. "Mmm … You smell so good."

When he had pulled away, still looking at her intently, she'd felt swallowed up in his dark, Arab eyes. His eyelashes were long and thick. She'd felt the oddest desire to brush her fingertips across them, closing his eyes and kissing them gently.

"Call me tomorrow. Any time. I want to see you before you go back to Talefa." He pursed his lips. "I mean that. Any time." He cupped his hand gently under her chin and rubbed his thumb over her lips. "Any time," he said again, so quietly that she only saw him mouth the word as he walked backward to his car.

He was still standing there with one hand on the driver's-side door when she and Veronica went upstairs in the glass elevator. The brush of his thumb over Jenny's lips and the way he'd waited at his car, watching her every move until he could no longer see her, had made Jenny blush.

She decided on a text invitation. "It's any time. Why don't you join the party at the hotel?"

She wasn't to be disappointed. Her phone lit up with a reply not more than thirty seconds later. "I'm on my way."

Drinking the remainder of her wine, she felt the smooth cabernet warm her, and she put on another coat of lipstick. Her confidence crept back in as she looked at her reflection in the mirror. Both the wine and the anticipation were making her cheeks flush.

"You can do this, Jenny. It's just a fun night with your friend for her birthday. If you make out with a hot Arab man, so be it."

Winking at her reflection, she put her phone, lipstick, and Ghaith's business card back into her clutch and grabbed her empty wineglass. The main room of the hotel suite was getting louder, and people had started pouring their own drinks—signs of an actual party. Anna sat on the couch, with Veronica's dad's arm around her, and nursed a glass of vodka. She was slurring something at one of her husband's coworkers, and she seemed to be the drunkest person in the room. Veronica, still standing next to Tate, glanced up at Jenny and gave her a thumbs-up.

80

Ghaith showed up thirty minutes later, in a white suit and holding a tower of Arabic chocolates for Veronica, clearly remembering it was her birthday. Sweat formed across his forehead, as he seemed a bit uncomfortable around the already inebriated crowd. He clicked with Veronica's dad when they began talking about Ghaith's car. Within five minutes, he'd gotten a hug and a nickname— "Porsche." Fitting, Jenny thought, for this smooth, apparently rich guy.

As they sat on the couch next to Anna and Veronica's dad, Jenny slowly crossed and then uncrossed her legs. This was a habit she had picked up to draw attention away from her small breasts and to her toned legs. Her black-and-white dress always made guys' jaws drop, and it didn't fail with Ghaith.

"Wow." He looked over at her exposed thighs and smiled.

Shrugging off Veronica's dad's arm, Ghaith sat up and rolled his eyes at Jenny as though sharing some private joke. She couldn't help but smile back at him.

"Aren't you hot in that jacket?" Jenny asked. Beads of perspiration were now slowly making their descent down Ghaith's temples.

"I don't think that's what's making me sweat." He slowly let his eyes scroll down her body, and then picked up a tissue to blot the sweat from his face.

Unable to wipe the grin from her face, Jenny bit her lip. She wasn't used to such bold advances, and it was fun being so forward in return. Reaching over, she took the tissue out of Ghaith's hand and held it to her mouth, blotting her lipstick and tasting the salt of his sweat. He raised his eyes at her gesture and ran his tongue over his lips.

"Let's go party!" Veronica's dad yelled beside them, shaking Ghaith and Jenny out of their intimate moment. The people in the room erupted into little chuckles and started throwing back their drinks.

"Come on, birthday girl." Jenny stood and walked over to Veronica, grabbing her hand. "Let's lead the way, twenty-eight."

It took another ten minutes for everyone to stop talking, go to the loo, and finish their drinks—as it goes with a group of drunken people when trying to change venues. Ghaith was the only person taking his time in finishing his glass of wine. Standing in a small crowd of people chattering around him, and getting the occasional shoulder pat from Veronica's dad, Ghaith looked over at Jenny. Shrugging, he grabbed an opened bottle of merlot off the table, filled his glass, and drank it down quickly. Jenny giggled, shaking her head. She could literally feel the electricity in the air between them, even though they were almost thirty feet apart.

Ghaith finally took off his jacket and unbuttoned the sleeves of his shirt, rolling them up to expose his muscular forearms. Jenny bit her lip. There was just something so attractive about muscular forearms, as if they were an indicator of how muscular a guy was all over. Ghaith headed toward Jenny through the crowd. When he reached her, Jenny blushed, realizing she was still staring at his forearms.

"Hey, beautiful. What are you looking at?" Ghaith gazed down at Jenny while she finished her drink.

"Ah …" She cleared her throat. "At a very sexy man standing in front of me." They looked at each other while the rest of the party filed into the elevators and headed down to the bar.

"I'm a lucky man if there's a beautiful woman saying that in front of me." They both laughed. He was smooth, but he also made fun of himself, and Jenny really liked that trait.

Veronica grabbed Jenny around the waist and started walking with her to the elevator. "Come on, bi*a*tch! We were supposed to be leading and now we have fallen behind!" she said, her voice drunkenly loud, with Tate following at her heels.

Looking back, Jenny cast a smile at Ghaith, who had been looking at her backside. Tate was too busy staring at Veronica to notice.

When they got down to Clover's Bar, Veronica's dad and Anna waved them over to the bar, where six B-52 shots were lined up.

"Happy birthday, my girl," Veronica's dad said. He waved Ghaith over. "Hey, Porsche, you can get the next round."

Jenny noticed Ghaith's eyes narrow subtly.

"Nothing I would like to do more," he said tightly, and picked up his drink. "To Veronica, may God bless you this year."

A live DJ was spinning at Clover's, so it was already crowded. As soon as Jenny and Veronica finished their shots, they headed out onto the dance floor. A group of guys at the bar joined in, circling around them. Jenny felt the effects of the alcohol. The music seemed to flow through her, so that it felt like her body was guiding the music instead of the other way around. She opened her eyes and saw Ghaith staring at her from the bar, drinking what now looked like whiskey.

One of the guys from the bar grabbed Jenny and started salsa dancing with her. "Hey, gorgeous," he said in an Australian accent.

"Hey there, ah—"

"Mike." He had a familiar look, with a dusting of freckles across his nose and sandy blond hair. Mike seemed to be one of those guys who got cuter and cuter, the better you got to know him. "And you, gorgeous, what's your name?"

"Jenny."

"American?"

"How'd you guess?"

They danced and talked for a while, and Mike even twirled Jenny around a little. He was a great dancer, and she learned that he was a pilot. Man, he was getting cuter already.

All of a sudden, Jenny felt someone poking her back. She dropped Mike's hands and turned around. It was Veronica's dad.

"You're letting Porsche get away!" His face was red from the alcohol, and he began pointing toward the bar, where Ghaith was indeed gathering his stuff and talking on his phone.

"But—"

"But nothing. Go and get Porsche to stay." He squished up his face even more. "He's got *money*."

"Okay, okay." Jenny felt defeated. Even though Ghaith was handsome and seemed to have her heart in his hands, she hadn't forgotten he was an Arab. The likelihood of their connection ever turning into a relationship was nil. She turned back and tossed Mike a limp wave, feeling a pang of regret when he gave her a small salute accompanied by a frown. He was probably used to ex-pat girls running after the Arabs. She knew then, turning toward the bar, that Mike would be much less forward but probably more honest.

CHAPTER 4

Ghaith wanted his first weekend with Jenny to be distant from Abu Dhabi. They couldn't go to her apartment because she lived on a compound at the oil company, but they obviously couldn't go to one of his houses either. So he had told Jenny to book a room at the Emirates Golf & Yacht Resort and to make reservations for anything else she wanted to do. He would pay for it all.

She'd already ordered a bottle of pink Moet champagne to be ready in the hotel room when they arrived. Ghaith smiled at himself in the rearview mirror. This combination of a three-day weekend, luxurious resort, and alcohol guaranteed sex. He was getting hard just thinking about it.

He parked and waited in front of the Loft Mall, since Jenny had arranged for her company driver to drop her here during the day. Fifteen minutes later, she walked outside and stood next to the main doors, holding her roller suitcase in one hand and looking at her phone in the other. Her hair was up in a casual bun, and her tanned skin shimmered in the heat. Ghaith knew that she couldn't see him through the opaque tinting on his windows, so he reapplied his cologne and checked his teeth in the mirror. He looked good. He had just come from the barber, and his goatee was very thin, in a vaguely flame-like design on his jawbone.

You can do this, he told his reflection. He put on his aviator sunglasses and opened his door, his heart racing. Taking a deep breath, he waved at

Jenny when she looked up from her phone. An immediate smile warmed her face when she saw him, and she put her phone in her purse. *Fearless of her emotions*, he thought.

He could feel the air become more and more electrified, the closer he got to her. *Wow, this is some chemistry.* He leaned over and gave her a hug and a kiss on the cheek. She smelled like lavender with a hint of muskiness, and he knew he would associate that scent with her from now on. Pushing his sunglasses on top of his head, he looked her up and down.

"You look ten times more amazing than the last time I saw you, if that's possible." He really meant it. He didn't know how she could look so good in casual weekend clothes, but maybe that was what it was. She looked comfortable. Ghaith imagined this was what she would look like a year from now, if they were in their own apartment and being lazy for the day. For some reason, the thought comforted him.

Jenny smiled back at him and slid her hand up to his jawbone. "Nice design." She continued her fingers toward his left ear and traced the top part of his ear with her index finger. The tingling of her touch reached his very core.

"Fresh from the barber?" she asked as her finger brought back some mousse.

Ghaith blushed. "Ah, yeah, you caught me." He laughed at himself. "Wanted to be looking my best when picking up such a beautiful woman."

She smiled broadly, and he grabbed her luggage and walked toward the car. He was always incredulous at how much luggage girls took on these weekend getaways, and Jenny was no exception. Her carry-on was stuffed to the max and looked three times the size of his duffel bag. His hands were sweaty from the excitement of being with her again—and alone this time. As soon as he got in the car, he wanted a cigarette, even though he had smoked one while he was waiting for Jenny.

"Do you mind if I smoke?"

"Not at all," Jenny said. "I was just going to ask you if I could have one."

Ghaith immediately relaxed and took out two cigarettes. "I thought you smoked only when you drank."

The first time she had asked him for a smoke, he had been relieved, since he didn't want her looking down at him. More and more these days, Western girls didn't like it when he smoked and refused to kiss him when he did. Before he handed her a cigarette, he grabbed her face and kissed her hard. She tasted like honey and responded passionately to him.

"I've been waiting the entire week to do that." He handed her the cigarette, then held up the lighter. "I am going to just make one stop before we go. You are going to have the best juice in the entire world."

He settled back into his seat, took a drag from his cigarette, and exhaled deeply. This was going to be an epic weekend.

CHAPTER 5

The juice *was* good. Blended avocado, mango, and strawberry swirled with honey and sweetened condensed milk. For good measure, pistachios were sprinkled on top in a little cloud of whipped cream. Jenny sucked the juice down and tried not to think about the calories. She had had a great week with her workouts, so she was determined to let loose this weekend and not feel guilty about *anything*. She had actually stopped smoking cigarettes while she was in Europe, but since smoking was so prevalent in this country, she had resumed the habit. As soon as Ghaith had lit up in the car, she realized she had been craving another cigarette almost as much as the kiss he had just given her.

Jenny was surprised that their conversation flowed as naturally and effortlessly as the yummy juice. They hadn't really had a proper conversation yet—just talk scattered between crowded bars or in the car with Veronica and blaring music. Come to think of it, they hadn't actually been alone except that first night, and then it had been only for a few minutes while Veronica waited for the hotel elevator. Their interactions had mostly been innuendos, silent gestures, and deep-eyed gazes. Still, Jenny was surprised it was so easy to talk to Ghaith. They spoke a bit about family, but not the same rote getting-to-know-you chats she'd had with previous dates— "A sister and a brother. My dad left when I was two." Instead, she and Ghaith talked more about contemporary subjects and their opinions on current affairs.

Ghaith was as cocky and opinionated as he'd been the first night, and she couldn't decide if it bothered her or turned her on. He told her all about Hamas, since she knew he was Palestinian/Jordanian and wanted to know where he stood on the issues on Gaza. She couldn't really follow his history lesson though. She was too busy thinking about the way he looked—those little flames on each cheek were so smooth. *Does he have a lot of girls on the side or is he married, or both?* She might never find out. *At least I can have fun this weekend, and it gets me out of that village,* she thought.

"But I would never want to be a fighter," Ghaith was saying. "My ultimate goal in life is to be in power. I only want to fund movements. That way I can really be influential."

Another egotistical remark, Jenny thought as she watched him take a deep drag off his cigarette. He reached for the radio, which reminded Jenny. "I made some CDs!" She began to search through her purse.

Ghaith laughed. "What, you don't like my *one* English song?"

"Not five times in a row! That song is from the nineties! I've been hearing it my dreams, after it was on repeat for like an hour last time." They both laughed.

Kanye West belted out "Gold Digger" from the speakers, and Ghaith turned it up.

"I love this song," he said, and they both began singing while he opened the moon roof on the car.

Jenny lit another cigarette and began dancing in her seat, lifting her hands up through the moon roof. *I'm going to get laid this weekend!* She felt a combination of nicotine, sugar, and primal chemistry rush through her body. She barely knew him and she realized that sex with him might not be a good idea, but she was going to be as bold and outgoing as possible. She wanted to have fun before she got her senses back, so she was determined to take the bull by the horns.

When they arrived at the Emirates Golf & Yacht Resort, a bottle of champagne was chilling in an ice bucket in the room just as she'd asked.

Ghaith popped the cork, and they both laughed when it shot up to the ceiling and then bounced off the wall. Pouring two glasses of champagne, Ghaith handed one to Jenny. She noticed the gleam in his eyes, and she could swear that she could see his heart beating underneath his shirt.

The room itself was painted a soft pink, and French doors opened onto a large balcony overlooking the pool and the Arabian Gulf beyond. Jenny wandered toward the balcony. But before she could open the doors, Ghaith's arms were around her and he kissed her neck softly. Moaning slightly, Jenny spun around and navigated hungrily toward his lips.

"Let's have some champagne and enjoy the view," Jenny said as their lips separated.

"I am enjoying the view," Ghaith said, smiling. A silent moment passed, while they held each other's gaze. Then Ghaith let out a small laugh and reached past Jenny to open the door to the balcony. She turned around and walked out onto the balcony, with him following closely behind her.

Jenny smiled at him, then looked out at the gulf, resting against the railing. Ghaith, standing next to her, followed her gaze. The water sparkled in the waning sun—the perfect backdrop to what she hoped would be the perfect weekend. She took a sip of her favorite champagne and held it in her mouth for a moment before she swallowed, savoring its tangy sweetness.

Ghaith leaned against the balcony, placing one of his hands on the railing. "Very nice." Ghaith made the statement more to himself than to Jenny, and he nodded once.

"Yes, it's very beautiful here."

As they stood there, the sound of the gentle waves on the sand and people swimming in the pool drifted up to them on the gulf breeze. Jenny tilted her head toward the sky, drank in the fading light, and closed her eyes. The breeze intensified as if trying to cool her, and she felt content. The near-awkward silence between them pleasantly and quickly turned into a comfortable one.

When she opened her eyes, Ghaith had disappeared. Jenny looked back toward the room just in time to see him walking back out to the balcony with the bottle of champagne and a pack of cigarettes. He was gorgeous, especially with the orange-and-pink light from the sunset reflecting on his olive skin. Smiling at her, he filled her glass, then put down the bottle and picked up a cigarette, lighting it before he handed it to her.

"Thanks." She hoped the hungry gaze would return to his eyes and he would kiss her again.

As if he had read her thoughts, Ghaith stepped away and looked out at the sea again. The rapidly changing colors of the sunset now made him appear a darker brown, compelling her to touch his skin and feel its velvety softness. "What would you do to have all of this?" He opened his arms widely as if he could hold their surroundings in his strong arms and hand it over to her.

Jenny hesitated. For all she knew, this resort could all be his.

"What would you do to have this resort?" His eyes danced with a hint of sarcasm.

"I don't know." Taking a sip of her champagne, she let her thoughts wander. She actually didn't know what she would do for this place. She had never imagined owning anything except a house and a car, and even that was a scary place of commitment for her. "What would *you* do?"

Ghaith smiled at the setting sun. "One day I *will* own a resort like this. Then I will let you know what I did for it." He laughed and filled her empty glass.

"Well, you let me know if it was worth it, and I might just follow your lead." Jenny grinned and took a deep drag off her cigarette.

"Maybe you will be there along the way." He said this so matter-of-factly that Jenny sucked in her breath. Then he let out a laugh, the one that warmed her even more than the champagne.

The sky was now completely dark, and they could see only the lights of the pool and the lit-up date trees that layered the grounds. "I'm starving!" Jenny said. "It's almost time for our dinner reservation. Let me take a shower and freshen up, so we can go eat."

"All right. But, you know, I could just eat you." He grabbed her for a kiss, and she settled herself against him. As his soft tongue pressed against her own, she melted into him, merging into his essence. Then she winced when she realized she was still holding her cigarette, which had burned down to the filter.

Pulling away, Jenny stubbed out her cigarette on the railing and sashayed toward the room. When she reached the patio doorway, she looked back to see Ghaith leaning on the balcony, his back to her. She could hear him singing in Arabic while he sipped his champagne. He was so handsome, even in shorts and a T-shirt. She was looking forward to what was underneath his clothes, to what she had felt when he had pulled her close and kissed her.

℞

By the time they finished their meal, Jenny and Ghaith both were wasted. They had nearly finished off the entire bottle of champagne before dinner, and during dinner they'd consumed a different wine with each course.

Any shyness Jenny had was gone. She was ready.

Ghaith's hands seized Jenny's waist, as she stumbled into the elevator. She let out a giggle when he turned her around, and he pushed her against the elevator wall when the doors closed. His lips crashed down onto hers, and she could taste the Riesling in his mouth, the wine they'd had with dessert. Ghaith pulled back briefly and hit the button for their floor, then looked at her—and for the first time in her life, Jenny wished the elevator would get stuck. When the doors opened, Ghaith playfully lifted Jenny and carried her, as a groom carries his bride, over the threshold.

"The key is in my back pocket," Ghaith said when they got to their door.

Jenny reached down into his pocket and found the key, but it took a few clumsy tries to get the key into the slot.

"I hope other things aren't this difficult." She giggled, having fun being so blunt about their impending sex.

Inside, Ghaith gently put her onto the bed and kicked off his shoes, then unbuttoned his shirt. Leaning down he gently took off her heels, one at a time, and stood back and looked at her. His pupils were huge, and she was still staring at them when he crawled on top of her.

It was as though his body was casting a larger, warmer shadow of herself, and she felt safe, hidden beneath him. She felt his muscles flexing softly as he propped himself up on his elbows and took her face in his hands, kissing her deeply.

CHAPTER 6

Even with the alcohol, Ghaith had been nervous. By the time they got to the hotel room, he was ready to take Jenny. But the booze made his thoughts wander, and he thought about Laila and the girls. They had come down with the flu, but he had left them anyway because Jenny came into the city only on certain days, and he needed to see her. Also they had this exciting weekend planned at this amazing resort. Still, he couldn't help but think about how sick Aminah, his eldest daughter, had looked before he left for the barbershop. Her words went round and round inside his head. *Do you have to leave for the weekend?*

"I feel so alive," he said. It was nearly one o'clock in the morning, but he wanted to see how Aminah was doing. "I need to go for a walk and get some air."

"What? It's late. Lie down next to me." Jenny drowsily patted the bed next to her.

"Oh, *habibti,* I will lie down next to you and breathe in your magical scent all night." Ghaith leaned down and kissed her cheek gently, then sat up. "But not right now. I feel so alive right now." He stood and smiled at her, flaunting his dimples.

"Seriously?" Jenny didn't look impressed, but her eyes drifted shut while he got dressed.

"You need to rest, and I don't want to bother you." He pulled the comforter around her shoulders, but she was already breathing deeply.

Smiling, Ghaith began to hum the same song he'd had stuck in his head all day. He grabbed his cigarettes and smiled at Jenny lying on the bed. Maybe he didn't need to call home. He could just lie down next to Jenny. Then, as if Laila had been reading his mind, a text arrived: "Wishing you were here."

CHAPTER 7

"Where did you go last night?" Jenny asked. Snuggling closer to Ghaith, she rested her head on his chest. The soft comforter felt cool against her skin, in stark opposition to Ghaith's warm body.

"I just needed to walk. I was so excited to actually make love to you because you are so beautiful." Ghaith kissed her head. "I'm starving. Let's go for breakfast."

"Okay, but first I need to go for a run."

"Are you serious?" Ghaith let out a disbelieving chuckle.

Kissing him on the cheek, Jenny got out of bed and began to unpack her running clothes.

"Our lovemaking gives me energy, too. It makes me want to go for a *run*." Turning to smile at Ghaith, she was pleased to find him staring at her naked backside. Grabbing her clothes, she headed into the bathroom.

She needed to be by herself for a bit, to think more about why he had left the night before. She had heard him whistling softly when he returned, and the clock on the night table had read two thirty in the morning.

Now it was half past nine and the hotel breakfast buffet ended in one hour. She didn't have much time, but she needed to run at least twenty minutes to get her blood going.

"I can't believe you are going for a run," Ghaith yelled from the other room.

When Jenny walked out of the bathroom, now wearing her pink-and-black running clothes, she put her headphones in her ears so that he couldn't argue with her. Her eyes scanned the room, which was a total disaster with clothes, blankets, and towels strewn across the floor. The sultry scent of smoke, alcohol, and sex filled the room.

Ghaith had gotten out of bed and was sitting in a chair by the balcony with a thick white towel around his waist, smoking a cigarette. Arabic music wafted from his phone—a melodic, heartfelt lament. He was so handsome, sitting there halfnaked. She was lucky to have this weekend. He sang along with his music, looking at her with a slight smile on his face.

She smiled back at him, then blew him a kiss. "I'll meet you downstairs in forty-five minutes."

ঝ

The late morning sun was already hot, and she didn't know the area or what the best routes were. She ended up on the long, twisty driveway to the famous golf course and Emirates Golf & Yacht Resort that ran adjacent to the course.

The beautiful fixtures, waterfalls, and greenery were more magnificent than any other Middle Eastern resort Jenny had visited. Halfway down the driveway, she stopped dead in her tracks when she saw a peacock in the middle of the road. *Is this some kind of omen?* She pondered the idea while looking at the bird. The peacock ran behind some shrubs before she could have a better look at it, but she thought about the picture on her wall of a peacock spreading its wings. The round "eyes" on the peacock's feathers were similar to the evil-eye amulets that some people put on their doors for protection.

Resuming her jog, Jenny wondered about the symbolism of the amulets and their similarities to Ghaith. She was still a bit drunk, so this train of thought seemed poetic and sentimental. She let herself settle in this melodramatic feeling while her feet beat against the pavement, a soothing slow beat that was in contrast to the Black Eyed Peas booming through her earphones. She paused the music and let the slapping of her shoes on the road direct her breathing. Then she was able to think about the matter at hand.

Ghaith seemed very westernized because he drank, made love on weekend getaways, and spoke in a very American accent. But there was something more about him. She wondered if they could ever truly understand each other, being from different cultures and religions, and speaking different languages. She let her mind drift, but then she started feeling depressed. So she turned her music back on and shrugged off the feeling that was no longer enjoyable. On the drive to the resort, they had confided in each other about their separate religions—Christian and Islam. Nevertheless, they both were loose with the word *religion* and, even though both said they loved their God, they also respected each other's views. And anyway, this was going to be nothing more than a fun, titillating fling.

With alcohol still in Jenny's veins, the world vibrated a bit with each step. She could feel the remnants of smoke in her lungs, and that sense of conflicted longing was familiar—hating that she had smoked, while also craving a cigarette, coffee, and morning nip to take the edge off. *I am probably reading too much into symbols because of this alcohol,* she thought, glancing down at her watch.

It had already been fifteen minutes, and she needed to return to the hotel quickly to make it in time, even if she was going to have only a cappuccino and a cigarette for breakfast.

CHAPTER 8

Ghaith sat at the breakfast table, irritated. He didn't like to pay for an expensive holiday and then eat breakfast alone. Breakfast was his favorite meal, but he rarely ate it because of his busy schedule running an IT company. But his frustration evaporated the moment Jenny walked through the door. Her freshly washed hair was still damp, and she was glowing in immaculate makeup and a short, sleeveless white dress. Ghaith smiled as she approached, then shoved another bit of French toast into his mouth. He had taken a bit of everything from the buffet, and ushered Jenny to join him in his meal. She smiled at him, then sat and waved down a busy waiter who was putting away empty plates.

"Cappuccino, please," Jenny said to the waiter.

"How was your run?" Ghaith asked.

"Slow, but it was good to get out and see some of the grounds." Jenny leaned down, picked up her purse, and pulled out a plastic bag. "Look what I found on my way downstairs." She pulled out a disposable camera.

Ghaith laughed. It was the last thing he had expected to see.

"I forgot my camera, and your phone doesn't have one."

She snapped a picture of Ghaith before he could pose. With a half-smile, he finished chewing his French toast. He didn't really want to be in photographs, which provided hard evidence of their weekend getaway together.

"So they have water sports, horseback riding, golf, parasailing—you name it," she said. "What do you feel like doing?"

"I'm thinking of the pool," he said. "You can arrange anything you like, but first let's just enjoy this feast." He took another bite of French toast, now able to enjoy the way the maple syrup warmed his mouth.

CHAPTER 9

Later that morning, they walked hand in hand out to the pool. Taking off her sundress, Jenny exposed a brand new hot-pink bikini, and she could feel Ghaith's eyes on her. Climbing down the pool ladder, she swam over to the pool bar and sat on a submerged bar stool. Then she looked up at Ghaith, who was wearing an awkward pair of swim shorts, something between board shorts and Speedos. During their time together so far, she hadn't been able to really appreciate looking at his naked body, because she had been too busy touching him. He was a beautiful man! All six feet, two inches of him. She let her eyes roam across his naturally muscular body, which was a bit soft, and bit her lip. *Damn.*

Ghaith dove into the pool and swam across the length of it toward Jenny. When he popped up, he scooped his hands over his face and tiny ringlets of water scattered around him as if a halo. "I should swim more," he said. "I want to be in shape like you."

"Start running with me and stop drinking with me."

Ghaith laughed and sat on a stool next to her. "I'm not ready to stop drinking with you, but I'll think about starting to run with you. So what do you want to drink?" He winked at her.

"How about a strawberry daiquiri?"

"Two strawberry daiquiris," Ghaith called to the bartender. He looked at a small group of guys on the other side of the bar. They were looking at

Jenny, speaking to one another in Arabic, but immediately changed their tones when they caught Ghaith sizing them up.

"Those guys over there are Kuwaitis," Ghaith finally said. "You can always tell because they are the most stylish of all Arabs."

Sure enough, all the Kuwaiti guys had some variation of a modern Mohawk, designer aviator sunglasses, and brightly colored board shorts.

"Ha, I never noticed before, and I even lived in Kuwait," Jenny said. "That's really interesting."

Ghaith responded with a funny comment, which then turned into a couple of hours of conversation while they sat at the bar drinking strawberry daiquiri after strawberry daiquiri. Jenny wasn't prepared for Ghaith to be so interesting. Since they hadn't been able to have such deep and intimate conversations the first few times they had hung out together, this was a pleasant surprise. Just like in the car, she was astonished by how their conversation flowed naturally and that they laughed so much together. They really did have the same sense of humor; they just clicked and had a connection between them. All that said, Jenny was surprised when Ghaith reached over and squeezed her thigh, excusing himself.

"I need to go make a quick work phone call." He swam back over to the ladder before Jenny could respond, and she sighed. This weekend was a very good booty call, and it might be the start of something else if these frequent disappearances were really just work related. But she didn't understand why he had left the room last night or why he was leaving her now. He ran his own business, but it was Friday afternoon. No one worked on Friday afternoons in the Middle East. Fridays were akin to Sunday mornings in the West, where people might even get offended when someone takes care of work matters.

"Go ahead and relax for a bit," Ghaith yelled over to her as he picked up his towel and dried off.

"Okay," Jenny said quietly.

Not more than five minutes after Ghaith had taken his cigarettes and phone and disappeared, the group of Kuwaiti guys swam over to Jenny's side of the pool.

"Let me buy you a drink," said the cutest one in the group. As he nodded toward her, his Mohawk bounced slightly. "You don't mind if we join you, do you?"

"Ah …" Jenny's gaze followed to where Ghaith had disappeared, and anger rose up in her. She turned back to the attractive but slight Kuwaiti. "Please. I think I do need some company."

He smiled at her and looked over his shoulder at the bartender. "Another drink for the lady."

It turned out that they were all from Kuwait, but they also had flats in Dubai and were just at the resort relaxing for the weekend. Jenny liked their energy. They weren't overly flirtatious, and they laughed a lot and had good fun.

Ghaith returned an hour or so later. He didn't look happy when he saw the Kuwaiti guys sitting with her.

"Ah, there you are," Jenny said as he climbed down the pool ladder and swam back over to the bar. "Everything okay at *work*?" The last word sounded sarcastic, though she hadn't intended that.

"I see you got comfortable." He put himself between her and the leader of the pack. "Thanks for keeping my girl entertained." Ghaith slid his arm around her waist and took a sip of her daiquiri. "Mmm."

"Of course," said the Kuwaiti who had been talking to Jenny the most. "Such a beautiful woman should never be alone. *Yalla*, boys, we need to get dressed for dinner." He glanced over at Jenny once more and added, "We'll be down at the beach later playing volleyball and having *shisha*, if you guys want to join us."

"Of course," Ghaith said, waving them off.

Jenny turned toward him. "What took you so long?"

"There were some complications at work." He picked up her drink and finished it off in one deep swig. "Let's go upstairs and continue what we started this morning."

Not that she minded, but she had hopes that they would actually do something besides drinking and having sex. She already missed the

Kuwaitis' fun energy and laughter, and she wanted to take them up on their offer of a game of beach volleyball.

"Okay," she said. "I really could use a shower."

"Now, that sounds like a very good plan." Ghaith grinned at her, and she couldn't help giggling. For the moment, the long phone call was forgotten.

ॐ

They did make it down to the beach bar that night, and luckily there was no trace of the Kuwaiti boys.

"Why is there no music?" Jenny asked. As they sat down at the beach bar, Ghaith noticed it was eerily quiet. No music or other people.

He looked up at the television mounted behind the bar and started to read the closed caption. "A sheikh has died." Ghaith pointed at the television, and Jenny followed his gaze. The bartender was also looking at the television.

"Oh, wow, he died in an accident in Africa …" Jenny read the English subtitles aloud. "Three days of mourning? So that means no music?"

"It'll be like Ramadan. No clubs or bars will have music." It also meant work would be shut down, so he would have a couple more days at home with Laila and the girls. Ghaith reached into his pockets and pulled out a pack of Marlboro Reds for himself and Marlboro Lights for Jenny, since she liked those better.

"You've got to be kidding me. The one weekend I get away from Talefa, and it's quiet here, too."

Ghaith felt like she had slapped him. Maybe she was just using him to get out of Talefa. At least when he dated girls living in Abu Dhabi, he knew they already had other activities and chose him because they actually liked him. Ghaith snapped his fingers to get the bartender's attention. The Indian man walked over with the remote control in his hand. "Yes, sir?"

"What are we having?" Ghaith asked Jenny.

Jenny winked. "We're having shots followed by a strong drink."

They discovered over the weekend that she knew much more about alcohol than he did. She had worked as a cocktail waitress, so she knew about martinis. She also had a love for wine, so she knew about pairing. And after spending the last year partying in Europe, she definitely knew about shots. This was good news, because their evening of lovemaking and subsequent five-course dinner had significantly sobered him up. They had had a different wine with each course, but he had entered into that state of sobriety induced by all-day drinking.

"Two blow jobs and two Crown Royals on the rocks," Jenny told the bartender.

"A blow job, huh?" Ghaith laughed. "I thought I already had one of those today." It was something he normally didn't care for, but with Jenny it had been nice.

"You've never had one at the *bar*?"

The bartender brought their drinks. Ghaith looked at the shot, topped with whipped cream. It didn't look familiar. "I don't think so," he said.

"You have to put your hands behind your back and use only your mouth."

Ghaith followed her instructions. Clasping his hands behind his back, he leaned down and cupped the shot glass with his teeth, then tilted his head up and back. In one gulp, he swallowed the shot and then set the shot glass down with his hand. It was very sweet and immediately warmed his chest.

"Good job! You're better at it than me, so I am going to cheat." Jenny used her hands to pick up the shot glass. Knocking back the liquor, she then licked the whipped cream from her lips in an exaggerated manner. "Mmm ... What did you think?"

"Sweet. Just like you."

Jenny had put back on the white dress that she'd been wearing earlier that day, even though she'd clearly brought enough luggage for more than one dress. But the white dress showed off her fresh tan and made her legs all but disappear when she crossed and uncrossed them. The strong shot had brought back Ghaith's buzz, reviving his intense sexual feelings toward her.

"Where is the craziest place you've ever had sex?" she asked. Then she took a drink of the smooth whiskey, their second drink.

Ghaith was caught a little off guard by the question and her seductive gaze, so he picked up his Crown Royal and took a long sip.

"You tell me." He gave her a half smile, wondering where this conversation was going.

"Well, I was thinking a walk down the beach might be a good place to start." Jenny smiled, unhooking her legs from the bar stool and standing up.

"If we are caught, we could get into a lot of trouble. You did hear about the British couple last week in Dubai?" He had heard on the news that a couple had been caught having sex on a beach in Dubai. Even though they were married, they were arrested and deported.

"Well, then. Doesn't that make it one of the craziest places to have sex? We'll get a good story out of it even if we don't serve jail time," she teased.

Once again, she had made him feel nervous and excited at the same time. Arab girls did anything and everything he wanted, and Eastern European girls asked him what he wanted. But American girls did whatever *they* wanted, and he just followed along. Something about being taught things by a strong, attractive woman made him feel powerful.

Jenny reached for Ghaith, and he followed her while they walked away from the bar and toward the dark and deserted beach. His eyes quickly adjusted to the night. The tiki torches were out of view, but a full moon lit up the sky. The oversized bean bags on the shore were usually occupied by partiers. The Kuwaiti boys from the pool earlier probably would have been out here if there hadn't been a sheikh who had passed away. But now it was dark and empty, with only the full moon as a witness.

Jenny led Ghaith to one of the large bean bags and sat down. Straddling her, he put his mouth firmly against hers and could taste the syrupy whiskey on her tongue. A primal feeling came over him, and he flipped Jenny onto her stomach and gripped her bare shoulders. As he entered her, he felt drunk all over again.

∞

When they got back to the room, Ghaith noticed that the back of Jenny's white dress was smeared with pink. "What's this?" He lifted the white fabric belt, and Jenny twisted around to look.

"Of course. I started my frickin' period while wearing a white dress."

As she folded the belt in one hand, a deep blush spread across Jenny's cheeks. Watching it, Ghaith had the most interesting sense of animalism. He had felt like a lion when he mounted Jenny out on the beach, and that feeling was still fresh. He was still high on that power. Never had he felt so alive making love to someone, and now this? An irresistible yearning and a simultaneous sensation of raw satisfaction stirred in him. He felt an overwhelming desire to get this girl pregnant, to make her his.

"Well, I guess we need to take a shower." He clicked his tongue and chuckled.

CHAPTER 10

Jenny went for a run again the next day, despite another hangover and painful cramps. She hadn't had this much sex since she was with Matthew, her ex-boyfriend in Belgium, and that had been a while ago. Jenny could see why women fell for Arabs, wealthy or not; they were charmers and loved to have lots of sex and please women. Jenny and Ghaith had really done absolutely no other activities at this beautiful resort. The disposable camera had caught only glimpses of them either hungover or wasted, only documenting debauchery. They ate like kings and had sex like teenagers—but at least it was done on a champagne budget.

Her run eventually became a walk, and then a stroll that took her past the spa. She went in and inquired about appointments, but everything was booked for the day. She regretted not being more proactive about activities. Ghaith had told her to book whatever, but beyond ordering the welcome bottle of champagne, she had been a little nervous about doing that. He didn't seem to want to do anything besides drink, have sex, and eat.

Her route took her out to the beach, where she looked at the kayaks and snorkeling gear rentals. *What will I remember from this trip?* They got along, but he wasn't into doing activities. That bothered Jenny, who liked adventure. Her idea of a holiday had often included activities such as sunrise surfing at some internationally known location or biking from Brussels to the coast. Nevertheless, going to a luxurious resort near Dubai with a handsome, rich Arab man was an adventure of its own. At least she was getting a different kind of physical workout, she mused. And she liked him. She liked how naturally their conversations flowed, and she liked the way his deep, throaty laugh warmed her to the core. But what was he doing all the times he left her to "check my phone about work"?

She sighed and continued walking toward the water's edge. The wind had calmed, and the water lapped lazily against the shore, reflecting her mood. She looked back at the massive hotel, which reminded her of a huge curved Lego set on the desert, complete with foreign flags at half-staff in reverence of the deceased sheikh. It certainly was impressive, and she knew this was going to be a memorable weekend. But she wondered if it would be just another story to tell her girlfriends—*the time I went to that resort with that rich, sexy Arab and we had sex like rabbits*—or would it end up being something more?

Jenny's thoughts were jolted back to the present when a little girl ran out to the cabana, grabbed a snorkel, and then ran down to the beach. Jenny smiled. She was glad they were keeping the watersports open during the mourning period. At least this little girl could have a great time.

CHAPTER 11

Ghaith woke to the fresh smell of Jenny's soap and the sound of running water. Her running shoes and workout clothes lay crumpled on the floor near the main door. She had run again this morning. This time it didn't bother him, since he had slept through it. Instead he was secretly proud of her discipline and her independence. As she opened the bathroom door, the fresh scent of Saturday mornings wafted into the room.

"Hey, gorgeous," Ghaith said in a sleepy voice as Jenny emerged.

"Hi there, handsome."

He spread his arms out. "Come here."

"This towel won't stay white for long if I walk all the way over there." Jenny smiled at him. She shook a small towel out of her hair and picked up a brush.

"Ah, yes, *that* situation. Well, it's a good thing those aren't our towels. And I am pretty sure we spent enough on this room to pay for that one, plus more." He patted the empty bed next to him and grinned. "Come here. Now."

Giggling, Jenny walked over and sat next to him on the bed. Ghaith kissed her tenderly and then paused, pulling his face a few inches back from hers. Opening his eyes, he gazed down at her. In response, she opened her eyes and looked up at him, lips still pursed.

"You are so beautiful." He looked into her eyes. "Absolutely beautiful." Her green eyes were shining brightly, and her cupid lips were a natural rouge.

ॐ

Later that morning, as Ghaith looked across the breakfast table at Jenny, he thought of that same tender moment. They had actually made it downstairs earlier today. As soon as he had finished making love to Jenny, she had screamed out how hungry she was. He had laughed and kissed her hard. She was finally opening up to him and exposing the real Jenny, the sober Jenny.

"I'm not going to lie—you look good without makeup. Of course, you look better with it," he added with a wink, "but you look really good without it, too."

"Thanks." She gave him a small, apprehensive smile. She had a bit of everything stacked on her plate and wasn't holding back like she had yesterday. French toast, eggs, toast, bacon, fruit, and two cappuccinos. Ghaith smiled. He liked a woman who could eat, as long as she wasn't fat. If she was fat, then she should be eating salads. But Jenny wasn't fat, and he wondered if their lovemaking had made her appetite grow like his had grown. They had been binging on everything. Binge eating, binge drinking, and binge sexing.

"Let's go down to the beach today," Jenny said. "I went down there this morning. It was so nice and quiet."

"Sure." Ghaith took his napkin from his lap and wiped his mouth. Then he lit a cigarette and blew out a circle of smoke. "Anything you want, sweetheart. You know ..." He paused and took another drag off his cigarette. "Last night ..." He paused again for emphasis. "I felt like a lion!" His laugh rumbled freely. "Like an animal that had conquered the world. You really are something else."

Jenny blushed. "Anytime." She reached for one of his cigarettes, and he held the lighter for her. As she took a deep drag, her color returned to normal and she winked at him.

After breakfast, they went to the beach and found some chairs not far from where they had been the night before. Feeling his phone vibrate in one of his pockets, yet again, Ghaith knew it would be Laila. He had already felt that sobering vibration five times on their walk down. Jenny took off her sundress, revealing a purple bikini underneath. Ghaith took out his phone and put in his earbuds. He sang in Arabic to make it appear he was looking through his music. He had fifteen missed calls and five text messages, all from Laila.

"Aminah's been throwing up all morning. Where are you?"

"Omar said you weren't at the office. Where are you?"

"Ghaith, I need you!"

"Baby, come home!"

"What the fuck, Ghaith?"

Ghaith moved to the edge of his chair. Jenny was lying just a few feet away. As he looked at her, he felt—not lust, but irritation. He should have left hours ago. He still needed to drive all the way to Talefa to drop her off and then back to Abu Dhabi.

Jenny sat up, as if sensing his agitation. "Let's go down to the sea," she said, getting up and taking his hand. Ghaith dropped his phone into the chair, with the earbuds still plugged in to mute any more phone calls.

As they stepped into the waves, the gulf already felt like bathwater. When summer came, it would be nearly too hot to swim in.

"You want to see my party trick?" Jenny asked.

Before Ghaith could answer, she took his hand and opened his palm to the sky. Tracing the lines on his hands with her index finger and thumb, she studied them intently.

"Are you reading my palm?" This woman kept surprising him, and for the moment, he forgot about Laila and the girls.

"You are spending your life in a series of relationships. Have you been married many times?" She closed his hand and tilted it to the side. It looked like she was counting the sharp little horizontal creases in the fold of his fist. "Are you still married?" She looked up at him with a slight sneer.

Ghaith let out a *tsk* and shook his head to the side, as a way of saying no and being offended at the same time.

Jenny opened his hand back up and continued to look at his palm. "You are very educated and will live a long time." Apparently satisfied with herself, she shut his hand and released it.

"Who taught you how to do that?" Ghaith's hand, now warm and tingling, suddenly made him feel exposed. Had she seen more than what she'd told him? Maybe she could see Laila yelling *"What the fuck, Ghaith?"* in a cloud above his head.

"My grandma's a gypsy. She reads crystal balls, too, but I never learned that one very well. Only palms. Even at that, I'm only an amateur, but it makes a great party trick." She lifted her hair off her shoulders and looked out at the sea. "We should probably get going."

Ghaith, awestruck, stared at Jenny for a moment while her words sank in. It looked like she was trying to shake off something. *She must know more than she said, but she's trying to convince herself she didn't see it.* Spooked, Ghaith leaned down to dip his prophetic hand into the ocean, as though wiping it clean.

"Yeah," he said. "That's a good idea. Let's go pack."

∾

The drive back to Talefa passed quickly, and Ghaith felt his anxiety lessoning with each kilometer. There was a safe and comfortable lack of conversation, very much in contrast to their chatty drive on the way out. They listened to the CDs Jenny had made, stopped for cappuccinos, and smoked cigarettes with the windows and sunroof open. When they got to Jenny's apartment on the compound, Ghaith took her luggage to her door and quickly kissed her goodbye. Then he leaned over and whispered into her ear, "Come to Abu Dhabi next weekend. Not seeing you all week is going to hurt, habibti."

When he'd left her apartment, he took out his phone and dialed Laila. "Yes, habibti, I will be home in an hour."

48

PART II

CHAPTER 12

It was almost time for Chloe to get back to Premiers, the hottest nightclub in Abu Dhabi. Even people from Dubai went there for a night out, and she was just happy to be considered enough of a local ex-pat to have gotten a job at a MasterCard in Abu Dhabi. Dubai had been the trendiest destination, but it hadn't been isolated from the 2008 global economic crisis the way Abu Dhabi had been. Overnight, the view out her window had gone from hundreds of half-completed buildings in Dubai to the wealth and glitter of Abu Dhabi, a city built on oil money.

Chloe was still at the Blues Lounge, and she had been getting bored—until she found a beautiful blonde. Chloe looked into the mirror, smoothing her red lipstick while the toilet flushed. The blonde she had been scoping out walked out of the stall and started washing her hands in the sink next to Chloe. Chloe glanced sideways and then turned to look directly at the girl. The blonde was in a striking gray dress, which fanned out her cleavage nicely and showed off her sexy legs. Chloe smiled.

"Darling, you are gorgeous," she said in her light British accent.

The blonde glanced up and smiled. "Not as pretty as you."

"Oh, you're *American*. Wonderful! I'm Chloe."

"Jenny."

She was getting good at picking out girls Mohammed would like. He loved blonde Americans the best because they were forward yet vulnerable—and this girl looked perfect. Chloe had known it even from across the bar, and she had said so to Salim.

"Who are you here with?" Chloe asked. Her next task was to get Jenny away from whatever gorgeous man she might be with.

"Just a couple of acquaintances, an old American guy and his Asian girlfriend. That's how lame I am tonight."

Chloe shook her head and tsked. "Come sit with me and my friend."

Closing her lipstick, Chloe grabbed Jenny's hand and led her out of the restroom. Chloe was confident and graceful at five feet eight, though she wore low heels so that she wouldn't be too tall. As they entered the club, she scanned the room, trying to spot the couple Jenny had mentioned. It had gotten more crowded in the last few minutes, and Chloe wasn't too worried that Jenny's acquaintances would see her.

As they neared the table at which Salim was sitting, he shot Chloe a disbelieving look. Chloe sat down, leaving the only empty seat between her and Salim so he could get a better look at Jenny.

"This is Salim," Chloe said. "Salim, this is Jenny from America."

Salim raised one eyebrow at Chloe, as if to say *not bad.*

When she had too much to drink, like tonight, Chloe was able to admit to herself she was falling for Salim. And the more she hung out with him, the more attractive he became. His Lebanese good looks and stereotypical five o'clock shadow just did something for her, but he was off limits. Salim was part of the warrior crew who found girls for Mohammed and his friends. He was an ally—someone with whom she must not sleep or, worse than that, fall in love. Besides, Chloe was determined to be with an emirate, because they were richer than Lebanese. She wanted the top dog, so she was annoyed to find herself falling for something else.

Watching Salim look Jenny up and down, she felt a tinge of jealousy, but that was soon replaced by pride when Salim glanced at Chloe and gave her a slight nod. She really was getting good at this.

"Let's grab a drink." Chloe flagged down the waitress. "Three shots of …" She paused and looked to Jenny.

"Patron."

"And three vodka cranberries," Chloe added.

Now for phase three—getting three main pieces of information from Jenny. (1) Are you married or do you have a boyfriend? (If so, there were a few more questions pertaining to ethnicity and whereabouts of lover.) (2) Do you have any children? (3) Are you American? (Already done, for ten points.) Jenny was a perfect match. She had no husband, no kids, and she was American.

When Chloe first started this pastime with benefits, she had thought it would be easy to find women who answered yes to all three questions. In Abu Dhabi, however, that was surprisingly rare.

After downing her shot of Patron, Chloe looked at her phone and noticed time was slipping away. Glancing at Salim, she quickly drank the rest of her vodka cranberry. He followed her lead, then placed a few bills in the bill holder to cover their drinks. But Jenny was only a third of the way through her vodka cranberry, and she looked at Chloe curiously.

"Let's get another drink," Chloe said. "But please, not here. It's so drab. I've got a special treat for you tonight, Jenny. We're taking you to the Castle."

"Sounds good." Jenny emptied her glass and smiled slyly.

Chloe smiled. "You can ride with us."

CHAPTER 13

When Chloe said "the Castle," Jenny hadn't realized she meant an actual castle. Jenny had driven past this iconic landmark many times and even remembered once seeing it featured in a movie, but she had never been inside. The Castle was actually a hotel, but the rooms were far beyond Jenny's means. The twisting driveway was a mile and a half long, and they had to pass through two security checkpoints on the way in. The architecture was even more amazing up close, with dramatic arches, glass chandeliers, and marble floors. Once they got inside, Chloe skipped arm in arm with Jenny through the lobby to the entrance of Premiers, the trendiest nightclub in all of the United Arab Emirates (UAE).

"You know, the last time I brought a friend here, she was so happy that she kept saying, 'I can't believe it, I can't believe it.'" Chloe let out a bubbly laugh.

Jenny arched her brows. "Really?" Tall arching windows, decadent fresh flower arrangements, and thick richly colored drapes. Jenny knew it was extravagant, but through her drunk-colored vision, she just saw jumbles of money not much different from the jumbles of money she saw everywhere else in the Middle East. Yes, she thought, the architecture was amazing, but it was strange that Chloe was clearly showing off.

They reached the front of Premiers, where two large bouncers immediately recognized Chloe. Smiling at her, one bouncer unlatched the velvet red stanchion so that Chloe, Salim, and Jenny could enter the club ahead of the long line. As they passed through, the same bouncer leaned over and whispered something in Chloe's ear. Even though Jenny was right next to Chloe, still arm in arm, she couldn't hear anything, as loud Latin music drifted out of the club. Chloe nodded at the bouncer and unlinked arms with Jenny. Then she grabbed Jenny by the hand and ran into the club. Obviously, Chloe was a little drunk, too. But this was already ten times more fun than sitting next to Randy and Lin at the Blues Lounge.

The only reason Jenny ended up with the two of them tonight was that she had thought Ghaith was going to be meeting them. But then he had texted her some lame excuse, which he seemed to be doing more often lately. Jenny had been in Abu Dhabi nearly every weekend in the last month, but she saw Ghaith only half the time, if even that much. So Chloe was a refreshing breath of fresh air—and so was Premiers.

The dance floor was circular with built-in VIP booths of red plush leather. On an upper deck was another circular room, which was an entire VVIP section. The club might as well have been entirely VIP of different levels. There was also an entire floor that circled the top of the dance floor in a balcony. The DJ's area was sectioned off, while the rest of the balcony was glassed over what appeared to be a private room. *Must be a VVVIP room*, Jenny thought. She had never heard of double and triple *Very* before she came to the Middle East. The extravagance always amazed her in a nonchalant way that felt snobbish, but was really her way of dealing with sensory overload.

When they reached the dance floor, Jenny was whisked into a dance by Salim, who had been following right behind Chloe and Jenny. He started to salsa, and Jenny followed along as best as she could, just as she had when Mike, the pilot, had twirled her around at Clover's. She didn't know how to salsa, but she could feel the offbeat of the music. Salim spun her around, and she confidently landed on a beat and then step one, two, three up and one, two, three back. She fell into a groove while Salim looked intently into her eyes and smiled slyly at her. *Damn, he's sexy.*

"How long have you been into salsa?" he asked, pulling her close.

Jenny could smell his musky cologne as her face brushed against the short bristle of his five o'clock shadow. She inhaled deeply.

"Um, since tonight." She giggled.

Salim stepped back in surprise. "Never before?"

Jenny shook her head back and forth with a small smile on her face, while Salim whirled her around.

"Wow, you are good." Salim grabbed Jenny and pulled her close to his chest again, putting one hand firmly on her lower back.

This time it was Chloe who tore them apart, when she grabbed Jenny's hand and led her across the dance floor, through the flashing lights, and to a VIP table in a corner of the dance floor. On the table was a spread of bottles of alcohol and mixers. A bouncer, or possibly a bodyguard, stood tall on the side.

"This is Jenny." Chloe shoved Jenny in front of a bald Emirate guy who had a welcoming smile. He reminded Jenny of a guy she had known in college, with whom she always had an easy time talking. Of course, he had ended up being gay. "She's from Hawaii," Chloe added with a smile, as though presenting a trophy.

Jenny had done only her undergraduate degree in Hawaii, but apparently that had stuck with Chloe when Jenny talked to her earlier at the Blues Lounge.

"Hello, Hawaii," Ahmed said.

Jenny smiled at Ahmed, as he poured vodka cranberries for her and Chloe. Then she looked around to find Salim, since she had enjoyed their dance, but she didn't see him anywhere. So she accepted the drink from Ahmed and sat down. There were a few Eastern European girls at the table who appeared bored. They smiled politely at Jenny but then began talking amongst themselves in a language that Jenny couldn't quite make out. Turning to ask Chloe a question, Jenny couldn't find her either. Apparently she had disappeared with Ahmed.

With the lull of activity and her increasing intake of alcohol, Jenny began to think about Ghaith. She couldn't believe he had backed out on her, leaving her with Randy and Lin, because of another last-minute, late-night meeting. Was he working now? The alcohol was making her cynical, and an uncomfortable thought entered her mind … *Had there even been a meeting at all?*

Just then, the music changed and a hip-hop song began playing. Jenny happily put her drink down and went back out onto the dance floor. *Latin night must be over, and this is the after-party,* she thought. Then another thought went through her mind. *Fuck Ghaith and his bullshit meetings.* Within a few minutes, Chloe and Ahmed were on either side of Jenny.

"Go, Hawaii!" Chloe yelled, swinging her hips.

Everything was a blur after that—bits and pieces of Chloe smiling and dancing with her on the table. At some point Jenny had pushed Ahmed away … maybe? Fortunately, Jenny eventually ended up back in her own hotel room.

When she woke up the next morning, she had a text from Chloe: "Had the most fun last night. Move your ass to Abu. xx."

CHAPTER 14

Smoke unfurled off Ghaith's Marlboro and danced in the red interior of the sultry room. The Meat Kitchen was a trendy upscale steakhouse.

"You know, you and I could rule this city." Ghaith exhaled smoke through his nostrils and watched Jenny twirl her glass, the merlot dancing around in large swirls.

She smiled coyly at him. He could tell that she was beginning to get drunk, and he welcomed the honesty and rawness that ensued from her when she was drinking. The wine was also starting to fill him in a fuzzy way, as the room felt warmer and seemed smaller. He was focused on Jenny's red-stained lips and her toned legs.

The soft lighting and dark wooden décor of the room nestled around Ghaith with a sexiness that he couldn't resist. The Meat Kitchen was his place, where he brought his dates and got them drunk on wine, meat, and ambience. At the Meat Kitchen, he could build a strong sexual tension and leave his dates wanting more … and then having more. But this conversation, he noted, was going in a different direction. Jenny was definitely getting drunk on the wine, meat, and ambience. But Ghaith was letting himself get drunk, too, which was rare.

Also, Jenny was smart and exactly what he needed right now—a contract writer. Ghaith watched intently while Jenny crossed and uncrossed her tanned legs, and he noticed the way her inner thighs briefly touched between. He licked his lips while she talked about liaising with business owners and explained how easy it was to get information from them.

"If only you spoke Arabic, *you* would rule this city," Ghaith said. He watched her take a bite of steak, chewing slowly and efficiently, red lipstick still intact. He scooted his chair closer to hers, subconsciously licked his lips again, and looked at her seductively.

"You know, an American business owner told me to get call girls for my potential clients and keep them around while we wine and dine. Then after the clients get nice and drunk, they can pick out the girl they want for the night," Ghaith said. "What do you think of that strategy?" He wanted to gauge Jenny's ethics and see if she was truly ready for the ride on which he wanted to take her.

Jenny's jaw tightened and stopped midchew. She took a deep drink of wine and looked off into the distance. He wasn't sure if she was appalled or just thinking. As she set down her wineglass, a small burgundy splash landed on the wooden table.

"I think that's smart." She slowly reached across him and took the cigarette out of his hand. Then she took a deep drag and relaxed back in her chair with a smile on her face. "Sex is an instant way to get men hooked."

"Exactly." Ghaith nodded emphatically and lit another cigarette. "Yep, the two of us just might rule this city."

CHAPTER 15

It was yet another night on the piss, as the British say, but at the same time, Jenny was feeling very sophisticated.

Chloe grabbed Jenny's arm. "Come on, darling," she said, drawling the word *darling* so as to twist her London-cum–South African accent.

As it turned out, Chloe was an expatriate Brit raised mostly in South Africa who had moved to the UAE when she came of age. To Jenny, Chloe was like some kind of exotic zebra that had been transformed into a stunning gazelle—a gazelle with a crown of hair. As though to confirm that image, Chloe's sandy blond hair was impeccable tonight, teased high on the crown of her head. Jenny was sure she had used at least one-third of a bottle of Toni & Guy hairspray to hold the *en vogue* style in place. It was the same hairstyle that stylish Emirate women hid under their abayas, but Chloe's was exposed for all to see.

With a strained smile on her face, Jenny tried to avoid looking like Chloe was dragging her to Premiers. Chloe was wearing an extremely elegant, full-length sequined dress. In contrast, Jenny had on a sleeveless orange dress that would have come down to her mid-thighs if not for the gold belt that hitched it up a couple of inches. Her four-inch heels made her taller, but she was still shorter than Chloe—and not as thin, either. *The gazelle and the American prairie dog*, thought Jenny.

"I need a Red Bull and Vodka *immediately*," Chloe said softly, still looking straight ahead to the door of the nightclub while they got closer.

Jenny realized that Chloe wasn't so much dragging her but leaning on Jenny to support herself.

"Yes, that sounds perfect." Jenny also needed a drink immediately, but in her case it was to feel less sober. She craved the giggly, bubbly feeling. A strange feeling overcame her when she realized she didn't know this woman. In Jenny's memory, which was little more than a drunken blur, she remembered how they had held hands and giggled as if they had been best friends for years. But now that she was sober, she remembered that she didn't really know Chloe at all. Inhaling deeply, Jenny tried to familiarize herself with Chloe's scent, as if it held some secret to a relationship.

"Back again so soon?" The bouncer at the entrance to Premiers smiled at Chloe and stood a little taller, sticking out his muscular chest while sucking in his pouched stomach.

"Of course. This is home." Chloe gave him a flirty smile.

Meandering past a huddle of about twenty people, he unlatched the red stanchion and let Chloe and Jenny go directly into the nightclub. Inside, the music was louder, and Jenny knew it would be another night of half-heard conversations. Chloe was sure to introduce her to a bunch of guys whom Jenny wouldn't be able to really hear or understand. Just another night on the piss. Nothing intellectual or new, no shared conversations or interests except for enjoying shots that were *literally* on fire. Jenny remembered how the sparklers glowed on top of the shots they had had the last time they were here. The only thing missing at Premiers was a tiger in a cage.

Jenny felt the weight lift when Chloe let go of her arm and grabbed her hand instead as they walked past the low tables toward the main bar. As Jenny approached the bar, it felt surreal to be here and still be sober.

"Just a minute," Chloe said, shaking her hand free and scanning the club. At that moment, Ahmed came up behind Chloe and kissed her on the nape of the neck. Chloe didn't look surprised in the least, and a small smile crept across her face.

"My dear Chloe," Ahmed said, "come and let us have a drink." Only inches from Chloe, Jenny felt his breath across her neck.

"You remember Jenny from Hawaii?" Chloe asked, turning to draw her closer—as if that was even possible.

"Ah, let me see. The dancer, isn't it?" Ahmed scanned Jenny. He gave her a glowing smile of approval when his gaze settled momentarily on her legs, which suddenly felt too exposed. Then he leaned over and kissed Jenny on the cheek.

Smiling back, Jenny narrowed her eyes in confusion. *The dancer?* Ahmed didn't seem to notice her questioning expression, and he turned and led them to a table above the dance floor in a VVIP area. A half-dressed Russian waitress quickly came over to Ahmed's table to take their drink orders. Jenny wondered if this waitress had implants, because her perfectly C-sized breasts didn't bounce when she bounded up to the table.

Ahmed started to order, "Vodka and cran-——"

But Chloe interrupted him. "Red Bull and vodka tonight, luv."

"Make that a bottle of Grey Goose and lots of Red Bull," said Ahmed to the Russian waitress.

The waitress nodded without smiling and sashayed away. Ahmed raised his eyebrows at Chloe and smiled. "Red Bull tonight? Aw, that's right. You went to an after-party last night, didn't you?"

Chloe nodded and took out her phone.

"I'd rather be in Paris," Ahmed yelled over the music.

Jenny squinted, trying to hear him better. It must have been that time of night when the music cranked louder. No more than thirty seconds later, the waitress returned to the table with a full platter of Red Bull and a chilled bottle of Grey Goose. *Damn, VVIP is crazy fast.*

"Oh yeah?" Jenny raised her voice, too. "Do you go there often?"

Ahmed tried to tell Jenny about going to university in France, but their conversation didn't last long. More and more people were coming into the club, and the DJ seemed to crank up the music a notch each time someone else strolled in the door.

Jenny could feel Ahmed's eyes on her, but he seemed hesitant to get closer. She wondered why. The insecure part of her thought that maybe he wasn't interested, but he *seemed* interested enough. After all, he was sitting next to her and talking to her instead of Chloe. Maybe he was just insecure, especially since she had pushed him away that first night. Brushing the side of her leg against Ahmed's knee, Jenny looked up at him. He smiled at her and his dark eyes seemed hungry—until his phone lit up with a text. When he picked up his phone, he got a surprised look on his face and blushed. He bit down on his lip and pushed himself a little way from Jenny. She wondered if the text had been from a girlfriend or, quite possibly, his wife.

Jenny jumped when she felt her own phone vibrate inside her clutch, which was covering the top of her thighs. "Habibti, where are you?" It was a text from Ghaith.

Fuck. She had told him that she and Chloe were going to the Blues Lounge, because the original plan *was* to go to the Blues Lounge. But by the time they finished getting ready, it was already late and Chloe had wanted to go directly to Premiers.

On the previous night, Ghaith had picked up Jenny for a proper date—dinner and wine at the Meat Kitchen. But that had been the extent of their date. Suggestions of sex and intimacy had been floating in the smoky air, but then Ghaith had gotten a phone call. As soon as Jenny finished her last swallow of wine, he had driven her back to her hotel, where he apologized for having to run off and take care of something that couldn't wait. Irritated, Jenny had wanted to know what was so important. Although she had let it go, she also sent Chloe a text saying she would meet up with her the next night.

In Ghaith's defense, it wasn't like they had talked about being exclusive yet. *Besides I am sitting here and letting an Emirate flirt with me.* Jenny took a deep swallow of her drink, and put her phone back into her clutch, ignoring Ghaith's text. She couldn't imagine Ghaith sitting here with her, Chloe, and Ahmed. It's not like she could invite a guy to a VVIP section. Besides, she was a little annoyed with him still. If he didn't want to be exclusive, why should she be?

Jenny felt like she was living two separate lives. With Chloe, she felt alive. With Chloe, she was a single, thirty-one-year-old expatriate with a future filled with adventure. With Ghaith, in contrast, Jenny felt like she was entering into a very unclear relationship possibly filled with heartache.

By the end of the night, the club was pumping and Jenny had danced and exchanged numbers with a few very interesting men. But one man in particular caught her eye. He seemed to be watching everything in the club. He wore a simple, white, v-neck t-shirt and perfectly fitted jeans, with that beautiful ruggedness of a sexy Arab. He was obviously Emirati because the room appeared to separate around him. Jenny saw him only for a moment, and they locked eyes and curious smiles. But then the crowd filled the space between them, and by the time she had a clear view again, he was gone.

CHAPTER 16

Mohammed had designed his private room, near the DJ booth at the top floor of Premiers, to be reminiscent of an opium den. It was fully decked out with lush red couches and intricately carved teak furniture from Bali. Large gold hookahs stood next to each low-slung couch, and two attractive Russian bartenders dressed in tight-fitting Asian dresses with high slits exposing flat midriffs were always on duty. There were screens for the cameras, and from his seat on one of the low couches, Mohammed used an electronic control to search the crowd for Chloe and her new girl, the American dancer—Jenny.

He finally found the two beauties standing near the bar, hands wrapped tightly together, scanning the room. He took a deep drag off a hookah pipe, the bubbling sound popping in little whispers, and exhaled a dense cloud of smoke. The glow of his iPhone screen showed eerily through the settling of the smoke. He sent Ahmed, who was already at a table in the club, a text: "Chloe and the new girl—keep them entertained."

Mohammed smoothed out his T-shirt and snapped his fingers, his sign for a cognac. One of the bartenders swiftly moved over to the teak cupboard and poured Mohammed's drink. After watching the videos of this girl dancing from a couple of weeks ago, he had asked Chloe to bring her back to Premiers. A few of his friends had come upstairs for their weekly ritual, where they had a special round of shots and judged the best girls dancing. Jenny was currently in first place.

"Bring around another bottle of Grey Goose. And after last night, you might as well take out a bunch of Red Bulls for Chloe," he said to the bartender as she handed him his cognac.

He knew Chloe too well. Last night she had showed up with a different blond American, who was beautiful but a bit too skinny. The girl had sat around and drunk more than she had danced. Mohammed had watched Chloe become progressively drunk and then finally leave at four in the morning with the girl and Akeel, one of his cousins who was also a customer. He was sure that Chloe was hungover today.

But Mohammed was interested in seeing this Jenny again. The girl didn't seem to care who watched her and had even pushed Ahmed away. Mohammed laughed when he remembered that. There weren't too many girls who would push away a rich Emirate at their VIP table.

Taking another hit off his pipe, Mohammed watched while Ahmed led the girls to his upgraded table and they sat down, with Jenny in the middle. The conversation between Ahmed and Jenny seemed to be getting serious. Ahmed kept moving closer and closer, until he was touching her bare leg. Mohammed sent Ahmed another text: "Sitting a little close to the merchandise, aren't we?"

Ahmed picked up his phone, read the text, and scooted away a bit. Then he looked up at the camera and let out a small smile, shrugging—his innocent apology to Mohammed.

As the night progressed, Mohammed went downstairs and walked around the club to see how everyone was doing. When he got to the main bar, he locked eyes momentarily with Jenny, who smiled at him. He cocked his head to the side and returned her smile with a lazy grin just as the crowd settled between them and blocked his view. He wondered which of his cousins would like her best.

CHAPTER 17

Jenny smiled when she saw Chloe's text: "Third weekend in a row, my bitch ☺." She and Chloe had gone out dancing at Premiers again, and this time they had stayed until after closing. Jenny was still trying to get a feel for Chloe. Their snippets of conversation usually involved Chloe spewing out information about the various sheikhs (rich men or princes), and Jenny vainly trying to remember their names while guys handed her shots. She hadn't even felt guilty about flirting with those guys, since at the last minute Ghaith had canceled yet another date with some lame excuse.

"Glad we ate something last night," Jenny texted back. She was very glad that they had gone through the McDonald's drive-thru at three in the morning and ordered a couple of hamburgers each. Giggling, they had both removed the buns and eaten the meat plain, since they had already consumed plenty of carbs in various types of alcohol. Jenny also drank a ton of water when she got back to the hotel, so she wasn't feeling hungover this morning, although she was still a little drunk. She put on her purple bathing suit and then a belly chain, smiling at herself in the mirror.

Pool, Jenny thought, throwing on a sundress and her large Chanel sunglasses. She was meeting a couple of her German coworkers at the pool, and then they were giving her a lift back to Talefa. Her bag, heavy with a few of the latest trashy magazines and two liters of water, dug into her shoulders, but she didn't notice. The booze from last night pleasantly whizzed around in her veins, and she was more relaxed than she had been in several weeks. Humming to herself, she walked out into the hallway and pressed the down button. As the elevator door opened, her phone buzzed with a text from Ghaith. "Baby, I tried calling you so many times. I need to see you. X." A sigh escaped her lips as she put her phone back into her bag.

༉

Jenny did end up answering Ghaith's call after a glass of wine and a swim in the pool. Ghaith insisted on seeing her, and she realized that she really did miss him. She told him the Talefa troop was on their way out but would be stopping at Carrefour to pick up a few things. Ghaith arrived just as Jenny, Stephan, and Marcel were walking over to the car. He came up behind Jenny and whistled at her, startling her, and then got into the car with her and her two German coworkers. As Ghaith slinked into the backseat next to Jenny, he handed her a honey-mango-avocado drink, the same juice from their weekend getaway to the Emirates Golf & Yacht Resort. His breath smelled sweet as he leaned over and kissed her softly on the mouth. After such a long absence, his kiss made Jenny want long nights of lovemaking, wine, and sultry conversations in a smoke-filled room.

Ghaith pulled away, squeezing her thigh and grinning. Jenny felt herself blush when she glanced into the rearview mirror and saw Marcel's curious eyes on her. Stephan let out an embarrassed cough from the front passenger's seat.

At least this moment was finalizing the end of anything between Jenny and Stephan. The two of them had actually slept together when she first started working at Volk, before she met Ghaith. There was absolutely no foreplay, he lasted maybe five minutes, and she didn't even have an orgasm. Afterward, they acted like it never happened, but Jenny had sometimes wondered if every guy in Talefa knew about it—or if she had been the topic of any locker-room talk among the Germans.

"So," Ghaith said, "you guys need to keep an eye on my girl."

Jenny liked that he hadn't asked a question but had made a statement. She realized this was why he had insisted on meeting them at Carrefour. It wasn't only to see her for a few minutes before she left; it was also some sort of alpha male gesture to make sure her predominantly male colleagues knew she was taken. The ploy seemed to work well, and it made Jenny want Ghaith even more.

"Sure," Marcel said. Looking into the rearview mirror at Jenny and Ghaith, he smiled. "We can do that. Right, Stephan?"

Stephan turned his head and looked in Ghaith's direction, but avoided meeting his eyes. His jaw tightened and he narrowed his eyes, still looking past Ghaith. "Sure, we can do that."

"Thanks, guys. It means a lot to me to have some comrades watching my girl until she comes back to Abu Dhabi. Next time, I hope, permanently." He smiled slyly and reached over to kiss Jenny again, placing his hands over hers on the juice that was resting on top of her legs.

He winked at her. "Be careful with that. It seems to be a bit, ah, wet."

She flushed again. The more time they spent together, the more they seemed to switch roles. Her bravado was waning, especially when they were in front of people she knew. Not that she really cared what Marcel and Stephan thought, but she felt vulnerable being so free in her intimacy with this guy.

"I think I've got it this time." She smiled back at him, and looked him carefully up and down. "It seems *hard* enough."

She let the innuendo hang and bit down on her lower lip while pushing the drink between her thighs. The words and the gesture seemed to work. Ghaith rolled his eyes in pleasure and swiped his finger over her bottom lip, then brought it back to his mouth, biting it playfully. Leaning over, he whispered into her ear, "I want to fuck you."

Her breath caught in her throat.

"All right, men," Ghaith said, releasing Jenny and giving the men in the front seat a sort of salute. "I'm counting on you."

Marcel nodded. "Aye, aye, Captain."

Ghaith just laughed his deep, hearty laugh and somehow got his tall, muscular body out of the car gracefully. Shutting the door gently, he looked at Jenny through the window. The sun was starting to set, and copper and pink colors seemed to kiss his olive skin, making him appear rosy and soft. Jenny's heart stopped. He blew her a kiss, then patted the car twice. Marcel tapped the horn twice in echo and drove off.

As they exited the parking lot, Jenny risked a look back and saw Ghaith standing there and staring in their direction, but now talking on his phone. Jenny drank the sweet, fruity drink and enjoyed every swallow, because it seemed to bring her closer to Ghaith. The taste was now firmly linked to him, with honey nearly as sweet as his lips.

She lay down in the backseat and watched the passing lights on the highway, thinking about everything that had happened that weekend. The nightclub with Chloe had been fun, but being introduced to Arab men as if she was on a silver platter had felt quite peculiar. She thought back to their nods or the shakes of their heads when their eyes grazed her body in approval or disapproval. She had never felt so dehumanized, even though she realized that this culture was very superficial. Chloe had taken her around Premiers to each VIP and VVIP table and introduced her to various men. The men had all responded by looking intently at Jenny and then either looking away or offering her a drink at their table. She felt as though she had been pimped out.

And then her thoughts returned to Ghaith and the intense chemistry between them. What she had shared with Stephan was like a tiny spark, compared with the blazing forest fire between her and Ghaith. And what about him meeting her at the Carrefour *parking lot* and calling her his girl? Was this the way the exclusive talk happened with an Arab? She should be offended, but his alpha male attitude turned her on. Ghaith had a strange possessiveness that seemed to ebb and flow in little waves of amused jealousy.

Nevertheless, despite the intense chemistry they shared, he had been ditching her periodically. Jenny wondered if they could ever really be an item, in the way he had just presented them to her coworkers. She felt like she was in a play for which she hadn't auditioned. When she went out with Chloe, she didn't hook up with guys. But she was keen on meeting guys, and it meant something to have her eyes still open.

Ghaith had told her that his mother was visiting and staying with him, which is why he couldn't take Jenny to his apartment. She believed him for the most part, but if he was really interested in her, shouldn't she and his mother meet? Wouldn't that be a good thing? But that was probably just the American in her talking. After all, Ghaith and his mother were Muslim, and Jenny understood that his mom being friends with her son's lover was not the norm here. Having lived in Kuwait for two years and now the UAE for a few months, Jenny knew that.

Her thoughts turned to the next day. She was beginning to really dread going to work. Ghaith's hints of wanting a contract writer were beginning to sound appealing. She would *love* to move to Abu Dhabi, especially now that she had Chloe and a quasi-boyfriend to hang out with. Moving would also give her space from the guys with whom she worked, most of whom were married with kids back home but slept with Chinese girls whenever they went out. She frowned when she thought about that.

The sun had now set, and the streetlights whizzing by created a strobe-light effect. Marcel was easily going 100 miles per hour on the long stretch of highway. As they got farther and farther away from Abu Dhabi, the big disco ball of the city was slowly coming to a halt—the telltale sign of returning to Talefa. Marcel and Stephan were speaking to each other in German, and no one had mentioned what Ghaith had said.

CHAPTER 18

It had been almost two months since Jenny and Ghaith had met, and they were taking their second trip. This time they were going on a long, three-day weekend to Fujairah, a beautiful coastal village several hours' drive from Abu Dhabi. Jenny couldn't wait until she got into his car to have a cigarette. So she ordered an espresso and lit up at a small café in the mall while she waited for Ghaith and admired her bags of new clothes.

She went through her mental checklist to make sure she hadn't forgotten anything. Jenny binge shopped weekly to build up her wardrobe and stock up on accessories. This was the life you led when dating an Arab and hanging out with rich Arabs and wealthy expats. Girls at Premiers didn't wear the same outfit twice unless they were sure they wouldn't run into the same crowd, or be near the same place, or be seen in pictures wearing the same outfit at different events. But those things could never be guaranteed, especially with digital cameras and Facebook—so a girl had to shop. Jenny had to keep up with the Kardashians, except in Abu Dhabi it was keeping up with the Al Nahyans, who were exceptionally wealthier.

Nails filed and painted. *Check.* Hair highlighted and cut. *Check.* New sexy lingerie. *Check.* New trendy yet original accessories. *Check.* Eyebrows and upper lip threaded. *Check.* MAC makeup. *Check.* Christian Dior facial products. *Check.* Teeth whitened. *Check.* Versace perfume. *Check.*

Bikinis. *Check.* Sexy designer dresses. *Check.* Sandals, wedges, and heels. *Check.*

Puckering up into her travel-sized, handheld mirror, Jenny put on a fresh coat of lipstick. Looking up, she noticed an Emirate woman in full abaya, a long and loose black dress and head covering. The woman wore heels, Louboutin, most likely, and certainly one of those trendy large clips that contained a mound of fabric to hold up her hair underneath her hijab. It had that strong slope to it, reminiscent of the Leaning Tower of Pisa—the style of 2010. Women in the UAE were so elegant. Most people Jenny met in the States—especially those who had never traveled much—considered abayas repressive, rather than trendy and elegant. Would they change their minds if they saw women like this? That outfit probably cost more than the entire wardrobes of those same people Jenny knew in the States. The woman entered a Fendi store, followed by her Filipina maid holding the hand of a three-year-old Emirate boy. He looked up at Jenny and stuck out his tongue. She took a drag off her cigarette and looked away, exhaling slowly.

CHAPTER 19

Fujairah was indeed a beautiful town. The desert mountains surrounding it sloped into a little bay on the gulf.

Ghaith felt free and far away from everything. He had been giving Laila excuses every weekend, saying a big project was due soon and that he had to travel to find subcontractors. Actually a large contract *was* coming up with the American Oil Company, so he didn't feel bad dishing out these excuses. He'd invited Jenny this weekend not only for a romantic getaway, but also for a possible business partnership of sorts. He had already mentioned the job to her several times. But he figured a boozy, sex-filled weekend was pleasantly required to seal the deal.

As the wind blew through Jenny's straightened hair, Ghaith thought how beautiful it looked. They were having dinner on a tiled peninsula in the middle of a massive infinity pool and drinking wine Jenny had chosen. The conversation was now revolving around relationships, because she had casually asked Ghaith, "Have you ever been married?" He immediately spun it on its head—the practiced trick—and asked her the same question.

Jenny smiled tightly and told him about her ex-husband. "We were so young. I was only nineteen, and forever seemed only an intense moment. His mom planned the wedding in three weeks. *Three weeks.* I had no idea what was happening, and my head was spinning the entire time." She took a sip of her wine and continued. "I was hyperventilating just before walking down the aisle. I kept repeating to myself, *I don't want to do this.*

I don't want to do this. But everyone was there. My grandmother and my dad had driven so far to be there, all the way from southern Texas to Oklahoma City. I couldn't *not* do it. So I sucked it up and walked down the aisle." Jenny took another drink of wine, a much longer drink, as if giving Ghaith an opportunity to say something. He didn't, so she set her glass down.

"I mean, the thing is, he is a great guy. So nice, and he really loved me. But we just changed too much as we grew up. And another thing ..." Jenny looked around, and then closed her eyes for a moment, cringing as if someone was going to throw something at her. "I didn't find him attractive any longer."

She exhaled sharply. "I know that sounds really shallow, but after four years, I just couldn't do it anymore. I mean, not only was he unattractive to me, but he ... um ... was skinny and short, much smaller than me, and I felt so unfeminine." She paused again and then took a deep breath. Looking down at the table, she added, in a monotone, "I ended up having an affair with my personal trainer." Then she looked up, as though to gauge Ghaith's reaction.

Wow, did not see that one coming, he thought.

"I mean, it was like I had to have an affair so that I couldn't go back to him," she said. "I had to finalize the death of our marriage. I still feel awful that I didn't have the balls to just end it, instead of ending it with an affair."

"Well, if you had balls, we wouldn't be sitting here having this romantic dinner." Ghaith let out a deep laugh, pleased she had confessed so much to him. He lit a cigarette while Jenny chuckled.

Then, in a more serious tone, she continued, "Yes, but it really weighs heavily on me that I didn't end it properly. It took me a long time to give it over to God."

Ghaith raised an eyebrow. Even though they had both talked about their faith before, it had been more rhetorical. But now, as she said this, he realized it was very personal for her.

"What *is* your type, by the way?" Ghaith asked, in an effort to change the subject. It was one thing to talk about affairs, but quite another to extol the intimacies of faith.

Jenny grinned. "Six feet and two inches, two hundred pounds, dark hair and eyes. Successful and spontaneous." She blushed slightly, having just described Ghaith to a T.

"Well then, I guess you made the right choice being with me," Ghaith said, to unwind her nervousness. They both laughed, and Jenny's normal color reappeared. She looked the most relaxed he had even seen her, as if her honesty had removed a heavy weight from her shoulders.

"And what about you, Mr. Changing-the-Subject-After-I-Reveal-My-Innermost-Secrets?"

Ghaith paused. After hearing her secret, he hoped that maybe she would understand his. Also, he knew she felt guilty and was bothered by her past, so he was counting on her to not judge him. He really didn't want to screw up anything with Jenny. But he knew that if he didn't 'fess up now, it would be a bigger mess when she eventually found out later—and he wanted her to be around later. *Fuck it.*

"My first wife," Ghaith started, looking Jenny straight in the eyes, "was American. I met her when I was working on my undergraduate degree in Michigan, and she helped me learn English. She was from Georgia and may truly have been the love of my life."

"What happened?" Jenny picked up her wineglass and took a drink without breaking eye contact.

"Well, we just grew apart. I didn't trust her enough, and sure enough, she ended up having an affair with her ex-husband. Then we got a divorce and they remarried."

"Harsh."

"Well, yes. I also had affairs, but only because I knew she was having them, too." He lit another cigarette and breathed in deeply, then exhaled little rings of smoke, letting his words sink in while his smoke circles disappeared. He wanted Jenny to know that he wasn't completely safe husband material.

"You said first wife, so there must have been a second one?"

Ghaith let out a laugh. "You caught that, did you?" He took a drink of wine. "Well, my *second* wife, Jumana ..." He paused. "We didn't last long." The flickering candlelight reflected in Jenny's eyes, which were locked on his.

"She was much younger than me and very pretty," Ghaith continued. "I was always at her apartment, which was above her father's shop. We got married because he didn't like me coming around without being married to her." He looked around at the water and sighed. "The problem was that she was obsessed with money, and I couldn't find work at the time. It was driving her crazy. I wanted to surprise her one night, so I went out and bought her favorite designer perfume. But when I gave it to her—" Ghaith paused, caught up in the memory, and laughed.

"What happened?"

"She threw it at me and went crazy." He laughed again, remembering the look on Jumana's face. He had ducked and the perfume had shattered on the floor. The entire room had smelled like her, and he was nearly sick with the smell. He had never wanted to smell it again.

Jenny looked confused. "Why would she do that if it was her favorite perfume?"

"Because I had it in a plastic bag they give you only at the black market." He looked down at the table and shook his head. "She was mad because it wasn't in a designer bag, because I hadn't gotten it at the mall. She was hitting me and biting me."

Jenny looked at him as if in disbelief. "That's so strange." She lit a cigarette, keeping her eyes locked on his.

Enjoying her curiosity, Ghaith continued. "I left her that night, after I told her father about it. He went to beat her and try to talk some sense into her, but she refused to listen. She was just so spoiled." Ghaith took a long drink of wine and felt it surge through his veins.

"You see, there is something about me," Ghaith continued, in a louder voice and with exuberant gestures. "If you tell me I cannot have something, it just does something to me. It sets me up for a challenge—and I will *always* win." He put out his cigarette and immediately lit another one. He hadn't told this story in a long time, but the memory still made him smile. Jumana would never throw a perfume bottle at him again.

"Don't fuck with me." Ghaith noticed Jenny tense up a bit, so he let out a laugh. "Not you. You know, just in general."

"So only two wives?"

Ghaith remembered their trip to Emirates Golf & Yacht Resort, when Jenny had read his palm. He wondered if she already knew. He couldn't seem to bullshit her very well. He tried not to smile, but he knew he looked guilty and couldn't help it. "All right, there was a *third* wife—if you want to call her that."

There was no change in Jenny's soft expression, so he continued. "She was the briefest of all. After Jumana, I got a good job at Al-Narha IT and moved to Doha. I was happy—very happy—but my family thought I was lonely and that I should be married."

"Happy being single?" Jenny let out a sly smile.

"Yes, happily single with no nagging wife. I was seeing a girl from the Czech Republic and partying every night with the Americans with whom we contracted."

"Ah." Jenny's smile didn't leave her face, and he wondered how much experience at love and relationships she had. She was more understanding so far than any of his ex-girlfriends had been, although he usually didn't divulge so much information either.

"I even had a pool in the villa I was living in," he continued. "*Alhamdulillah*, I wanted to please my parents, so I went to Jordan to see them and they had arranged a marriage with a very devout Muslim girl, a Palestinian. I remember at the engagement dinner she was sitting next to me, and when she looked away, I saw this single hair on her head. It was the coarsest hair I had ever seen—all kinked up. I knew it wasn't going to last long after that. We never even had sex."

"What?! You didn't have sex with your wife because you didn't like her hair?" Jenny's mouth fell open in a soft circle.

"Well, okay, it probably wasn't just her hair. I went back to Doha where I still had my girlfriend, and I very rarely answered my phone when my wife called." He took a drag off his cigarette. "She would get so mad." He laughed again remembering the cuss words that Ehsan had come up with. She had actually said *bitch whore*, and he remembered laughing out loud because he hadn't realized that she knew any English. "The things that came out of that girl's mouth! And she was extremely religious! We ended up getting the marriage annulled, so it's kind of like we were never even married."

"So you were married only three times, or two and a half times?" Jenny let out a small laugh and put her elbows on the table, resting her chin between her cupped hands. "So did you have a girlfriend when you were with Jumana, your second wife, as well?"

"Of course. She was psychotic, and the divorce took a long time, since I complicated it to get what I wanted. The thing was that I had started a relationship with a Brazilian girl who lived across the hall from our apartment. So even after I moved out of Jumana's apartment, I still walked past her dad in his shop every day, holding hands with my Brazilian girlfriend on the way up to her apartment. He would get so mad, but he couldn't do anything." Ghaith laughed at the memory and crossed one leg on top of the other. He remembered the way that Jumana's dad had glared at him. Ghaith had initially been uncomfortable, but he quickly got over it.

"So you've slept around on every wife you've ever had?"

Ghaith took a deep drag off his cigarette, feeling like he had been caught in a trap. "I guess so." Then, "So, number *four*."

Jenny leaned forward in her seat, eyes wide. "*Four?* How many have you *had*?"

Ghaith laughed. "Only four, habibti." He winked at Jenny and saw her soften ever so slightly.

"So, wife number four?"

"Yes, she was someone with whom I worked, and she just took care of me. She would cook me dinner every night, and she would always come around. So, of course, we ended up having sex. And then she got pregnant, so we had to get married."

The candles were burning low now. Picking up the empty wine bottle, Ghaith held it over his head and snapped his fingers with his free hand. A waiter, hidden away in the shadows, nodded and ran behind the bar to retrieve another bottle. Jenny was quiet.

Ghaith looked up and saw the shock on Jenny's face. "Yes, I have two daughters."

"How old?"

"One is almost four, and the other is one and a half."

"Wow, so what happened? Why aren't you together?"

Ghaith felt the air thicken between them and wondered if he had told her too much. He set the empty bottle down on the table.

"She is a good woman, but we do not have anything in common. I married her only because it was the right thing to do. We tried to make it work, but it just didn't." He said this with seriousness and sternness. "There are things that I have had to get right with my God, too."

Jenny nodded. "So you guys just divorced because you didn't get along?"

"Yes. We were going in different directions, and I think she was having an affair."

"But you still get to see the kids?"

"Of course. They live with her for most of the week, but I get them sometimes on the weekends and when I have to go to Dubai for work, since they live in Sharjah."

Realizing the flaw in this lie as soon as he said it, Ghaith hoped Jenny wouldn't tie it together. They had spent at least one day each weekend together since they had met, and today they had actually driven through Sharjah. So it might appear that he didn't really see his daughters much at all. The truth was that Ghaith had seen both of them that morning when he kissed them goodbye at his house in Abu Dhabi. Of course, he wasn't completely lying, because they also had a house in Sharjah and stayed there sometimes.

The waiter silently arrived at their table, opened the bottle of wine, and poured a bit in Jenny's glass. Ghaith watched while Jenny swirled the wine, tasted it, and nodded. The waiter filled her glass, then Ghaith's, and walked a comfortable distance away, hiding again in the shadows.

"So when is the last time you saw them?"

As if reading her thoughts, Ghaith answered, "They are in Jordan right now visiting her family. So it's been a few weeks. They should be back soon though. Now you know everything about my *four* marriages." He shook his head with a smile on his face. "I don't think I will ever get married again."

"I bet." Jenny shook her head with a little smile and took another drink of wine. "I would love to see a picture of your daughters. I'll bet they are beautiful."

"Yes, they are," he said, and smiled. "So now you know everything about me. Would *you* ever get married again?"

Jenny paused and looked out over the water. "Yes, I suppose I would. I mean, if I met the right person."

Ghaith immediately regretted asking her that question and hoped she wouldn't read too much into it. He cleared his throat and fought for some words to reverse this possible innuendo.

"Maybe one day you will find another husband." He realized that he was just digging the hole deeper, and a redness spread to Jenny's cheeks when she looked over at him. She cocked her head to one side and smiled slyly.

"Who knows? I'm enjoying being single right now."

Ghaith felt the blood rush to his temples as he realized that she had dug him out of his hole. But now she'd made him jealous. So Jenny thought she was single. Then what were they? He didn't want her to be with anybody else, so he didn't want her to consider herself single. Fuck, he had gotten himself into a bind.

CHAPTER 20

Jenny tucked the information about Ghaith's marriages away in the back of her mind for the rest of the night. She was a bit drunk, and that was more than she could deal with right then. They enjoyed the rest of the night and spent the next day drinking, eating, having sex, and actually doing some activities. Jenny had made sure to book a snorkeling trip and a couple's massage on this getaway.

As they settled in for a room-service dinner, both of them wearing fluffy white hotel robes, they watched a movie interspersed with long conversations. During a longer commercial break, and having enjoyed more wine, their conversation turned again to relationships.

"So four is your magic number for marriages?" Jenny was curled up on the bed.

Ghaith was quiet for a moment—a silence that seemed to say *no*. He cleared his throat. "Well, the thing is, Laila, my fourth wife and the mother of my children—" Ghaith paused, and Jenny noticed his mouth twitch slightly. His eyes were on hers, and his gaze was suddenly serious.

"Yes—?" Her heart seemed to stop, and she felt her whole body tense. She wasn't sure if she even wanted the truth right now, when she was comfortable in this thick, luxurious robe and a seven-hour drive from home.

"Well, because of the children ... and in my culture ... we are actually still married by law."

Jenny looked away with a tight-lipped smile. Her first thought was, *Motherfucker, I knew it!* Her second thought was, *I need to excuse myself and take a taxi back to Talefa. Maybe when he falls asleep.* The second thought hung on a lot longer than the first. She hadn't even noticed that he had put his hand on her leg and was rubbing it softly.

"Oh, so that's how it is." She looked back at him very sharply, the smile now gone from her lips, and slapped his hand off her leg.

"We are separated and about to go through a divorce," he said. "Habibti, I'm not with her anymore. It's just complicated, so very complicated." He put his hand back on Jenny's leg, and this time she didn't move it off. "I want to be only with you. I wanted to tell you the first weekend we were together, but I didn't want to lose what I didn't even have."

"Don't bullshit me! You're still living with her."

"No, habibti, I'm not living with her. I want to spend time with my kids, and it's been hard to navigate this. But there is something so special about you. Besides, you were calling yourself single last night. So what is it? If you are single, then why do you even care?" He released his grip on her calf, pulling away.

"I was trying to see how you would respond," she spat. Her shock was replaced by anger. How many times had she asked him if he was married, and he had lied? It had to be at least a handful. "We never talked about labels. Besides, me saying I'm single and you saying you're married are not the same thing."

"I know, I know. That's not what I mean. I just want to be honest with you. Anyway, if I was still with her, why would I have told you at all? It's the truth. I was trying to feel you out too, last night." He placed his hand softly on her leg again. "Look, I really want to be with you, and I want to define us and not have you calling yourself single."

"But you're *married.*" Jenny felt her heartbeat settle a little bit even though she was still angry.

"I am only married legally, habibti, and it is only a matter of time before I am divorced. I am telling you the truth. Once my mother leaves,

I will introduce you to my kids." Ghaith smiled and sat next to her. "I think they'll like you."

Jenny felt herself lean into Ghaith when he sat next to her on the bed. She looked into his eyes and saw sincerity. She wanted to believe him, and she knew that this culture was very different from her own.

"So, to answer your question." Ghaith put his finger under her chin and lifted her face close to his. "No, four is not my magic number to be married."

Jenny felt his soft lips on hers and opened her mouth, allowing herself to believe him and letting him mark his territory on this new and official relationship.

℘

The drive back to Talefa was sobering, nothing like the festive drive on the way out to Fujairah. Ghaith noticed Jenny was acting distant today. He figured she was still reflecting on what he had told her last night, and that made him nervous. He didn't know what she was thinking, but the more he had found out about her over the weekend, the more he realized she could be an important asset to his company. She was smart, funny, business minded, beautiful, *and* she could write proposals. She would be his key to landing contracts with the American Oil Company, and he hoped she would also be his key to continual pleasure and happiness.

"I want you to accept my offer," he said.

He glanced over at Jenny. She was still staring out the window with her hands folded in her lap. Instead of the hip-hop music, she had put on a more mellow CD she had made.

"I will consider it," she said. "When would you need me to go to Abu Dhabi?" She continued looking out the window, and her soft tone echoed the music.

"In two weeks. Just for the week, to write out that proposal for the American Oil Company IT job. After that, you would move to the city permanently."

Two weeks was far enough away. He already had plans next weekend to bring the kids and Laila to his parents' house for dinner. He wanted to spend some time with them, since he had been away so much lately. Once Jenny moved to Abu Dhabi, he would be able to spend more time with Laila and his kids, *inshallah.* As refreshing as this relationship with Jenny was, he missed the familiar and comfortable atmosphere of his family.

Stretching his arm out, Ghaith put his hand on Jenny's thigh and squeezed her leg. "I had a really good time this weekend. I never knew massages were so wonderful." Then he took his hand off her leg and lit a cigarette. "This music is so sexy." He looked over at her. "Jenny."

Jenny finally turned her head toward him, searching his eyes, and smiled faintly. Then she looked back out the window. "You should see your kids next weekend. I probably won't be able to come into the city."

"Um, yeah, I probably will." He took another drag off his cigarette. She hadn't replied to any of his comments, and he was a little hurt and upset because he could tell that she was angry. There was nothing he could think to say or do that might make it better. "And I have a lot of work to get done," he said.

❦

Two weeks later Jenny did the unthinkable. She put in her resignation at Volk Engineering in Talefa and moved to Abu Dhabi to compile the American Oil Company contract offer. In return, Ghaith made her business executive director with a salary of $85,000 tax-free and a $46,000 bonus if the contract she wrote was awarded. He also started searching for a permanent flat for her, temporarily renting out a large suite at a hotel that overlooked the largest mosque in the world, an icon of Abu Dhabi.

Ghaith visited Jenny often in her hotel room, though his timing was sporadic. Sometimes he came at three in the morning, sometimes at six in the evening, and sometimes two hours late for lunch. Every day was a busy day schmoozing with subcontractors, meeting with the tech manager, and trying to crunch the numbers.

Jenny often thought about that drive from Fujairah to Talefa, when Ghaith had finally offered her some sort of commitment for the future—the job—and, simultaneously, opened up the possibility of her leaving him. She had not known which route to take. During her last two weeks in Talefa, Ghaith had called her every day. They had talked for hours on the phone, working out the details. She had liked that he was making such an effort and that he did seem committed to her. But during that time, she'd also managed to start reading her Bible again.

Now, waiting for a dinner for which Ghaith was two hours late, Jenny felt she'd gained some perspective. If it worked out between them, great. But if it didn't, that was fine, too. She could handle it either way. This job was launching her into a financially and professionally empowered position, even if she was shagging the boss.

CHAPTER 21

As Jenny sat at the desk in her hotel room, she looked at the computer screen and then at herself in the mirror above the desk. Her makeup was on evenly and looked natural. Ghaith had said he was working at his office nonstop, and that sometimes he fell asleep on the cot he kept there. That was about how Jenny felt herself. She was up past midnight most nights working on the proposal, and tonight was no exception. She reread the document once more and decided it was as complete as she could make it, with the exception of a section about the technical aspects of software. Randy would be coming tomorrow to help with that.

Jenny heard a noise outside of her hotel room and turned, just as the door opened. Ghaith walked in, looking exhausted and still talking on the phone. As he locked the door behind him, he said loudly in Arabic, "*Khalas*. Yalla, bye." Then he clicked off the phone, sat down on the bed nearest to her, and collapsed backward with his feet still on the floor. "I'm exhausted."

"I bet," she said. "I'm pretty much finished." She was hoping that would ease his stress. But before he could answer her, his phone rang again.

"'Ello? Omar. Yes … No, I don't want them as a subcontractor. *You* get the laborers. The cheaper you get them, the more money you have. Yalla, bye." He clicked off his phone again and then held it up in the air.

"I am going to throw this out the window," he said, with a tired laugh. "But first I'm going to take a shower."

Jenny couldn't help but notice that he had only glanced at her, but she was glad his second conversation was in English and that he actually *was* doing work at this hour of the night. She wondered what his cot looked like at the office and what other conversations he was having at night. *Jenny, you are being so paranoid. Everything will be much better when you move here.*

℘

When Randy and Lin arrived the next day, it was almost a relief. They were the first people Jenny had seen in a week, other than Ghaith and a bunch of strangers around the hotel. She had been working too much to even see Chloe.

"Hey, where's the phone?" Randy asked as he walked into the room. Jenny pointed over next to the bed, and he picked it up and punched in a number. "As soon as possible, send up six Coronas, six shots of Patron, and a large plate of nachos." He slammed the phone down and looked up with a grin. "Let's get this party started."

Looking back and forth between Lin and Jenny, Randy seemed to be considering a ménage á trois. Randy was one of the most obvious perverts that Jenny had met, and she was slightly sickened by him, even if he was American.

"The party can start as soon as we finish this proposal," Jenny said, motioning toward her computer. "Your part is the final touch."

"You're such a downer, Jenny. Where's the fucking Arab with the money? I need some up front. I'm putting my job on the line by helping you guys with this."

"I don't know." Jenny walked to the desk and sat down. "But I'm going to read this entire thing out loud if you don't get over here and fill in your part."

Randy sighed, then stood behind her. "Okay, get up. Let's get this done, so we can party. But he'd better get his ass here soon."

Jenny promptly stood up, and Randy took her place and began typing away in the software section. Then Jenny sat down on the bed next to Lin, who looked at with her perpetual smile exposing her crooked, yellow teeth. Jenny tried to make small talk, but—as usual—Lin just nodded or attempted to speak in English, which usually ended with her breaking down into giggling fits. Jenny was relieved when room service arrived with the booze and nachos.

"About fucking time," Randy said as the waiter came in.

"Six shots?" Jenny looked at the Patron, grinning. "I guess we get two each."

"Nah, Lin doesn't do shots. We get three each, unless that bastard Arab gets here anytime soon." Randy's grin was wider than Jenny's.

"I guess we're in preparty stage then." She picked up two shots of tequila and handed one to Randy. They clinked glasses and shot it straight. At least they had something in common.

Lin grabbed a beer. "Cheers," she said a moment too late, so Randy and Jenny had another shot. The Patron immediately began to warm Jenny's stomach, and she breathed a sigh of relief that the proposal was finished. She had taken only short breaks to exercise, sun, sleep, and have sex. Not bad, but alcohol right now was more than welcomed.

Randy walked over to Jenny's iPod at the speaker docking station and started flicking through it. "Oh, yeah." As Bob Dylan wafted through the air, he started dancing.

Jenny laughed. Randy reminded her of someone from Solid Gold in the eighties.

As if on cue, the door opened and Ghaith walked in. Jenny's brain was beginning to slow down a bit from the tequila, but she definitely noticed an energy change in the room. All of a sudden, she felt like a kid who had been caught red-handed sneaking a cookie from the cookie jar.

Randy didn't seem to mind at all, gyrating across the room toward Ghaith. "Hey, muthafucker. It's about time."

Ghaith appeared disgusted, looking from Randy to the tray of alcohol, and then to Lin and Jenny. "Guess I'm late to the party," he said, with a tight-lipped smile.

"Fuck, yeah, we are getting this shit done while you are out," Randy said as he grabbed the other shot of tequila and slammed it. "Where the fuck have *you* been?"

"Working." Ghaith picked up the remaining tequila shot and downed it. He shuddered slightly, then picked up a beer. "I've been getting quotes, and after a little deal I *know* we are going to have the best price."

Randy went back to the chair and sat down. Still singing, he resumed typing.

Jenny looked over at Ghaith. "He's finishing up the software bit."

Ghaith took a long swallow of beer and then walked over to Jenny. She was nervous because they had never had any type of PDA around people whom he knew. However, this was as unprofessional as a situation could get—an employee of the American Oil Company, in the hotel room of an American girl, working on a proposal for a local contractor, also present. This had FBI investigation and bribery written all over it. But the novelty of it was poetic, and at times Jenny felt like she was in some kind of Hollywood movie.

Ghaith brushed past Jenny, squeezed her leg, and then smiled at her as if they were two teenagers caught flirting in high school. His mood seemed to have relaxed, and he wasn't biting his smile back any longer. Maybe the tequila shot was calming him down already.

"Good, let's finish this up." He sat in another chair next to Randy— the same chair that Jenny had sat in the night before, on Ghaith's lap, facing him, as they both writhed with passion.

CHAPTER 22

As Ghaith set down his shot glass, the room seemed to vibrate. He loved the energy of the nightclubs, and he finally felt like he could relax a little. Before he left the house, Laila had told him she was pregnant, and he didn't know exactly how to feel. If Jenny found out, she would leave him for sure, but at that moment he needed her for his business.

Randy, Jenny, and Ghaith had finished writing up most of the rest of the proposal. In a week's time, Jenny was going to move to Abu Dhabi to finish the fine-tuning and editing. Now she was sitting next to him in the restaurant, in a dress and heels, swaying from side to side while she sang along with the music. Flagging down the waiter, she motioned for another round of shots.

Ghaith lit a cigarette. The place was starting to fill, and he wondered about the girl he had met here a few weeks ago. He didn't know if this was her regular hangout or not, but it was possible she would show up again tonight. *Abu Dhabi, the big, little city,* he thought with a sigh. Out of the corner of his eye, he noticed Jenny checking her phone again.

"So, if you guys want to"—Jenny paused as she finished reading her text— "we can go to Premiers. My friend can get us into the VIP section." She clicked off her phone and looked at everybody.

"Fuck, yeah," Randy said, and hit the table with his hand. "I want a bottle of champagne."

Lin nodded and smiled, and Ghaith looked away. He thought Randy was a pig with bad taste, dragging this Asian girl everywhere he went. He'd even taken Lin to their dinner with Hussain, like it was some sort of family barbecue rather than a subcontractor deal. She looked like Randy's prostitute, not his girlfriend.

Ghaith had never been into the Castle's nightclub, although when he first started freelancing, he had a small team do an IT job at the Castle. He knew that Mohammed owned the club, because he had rented out one of Mohammed's yachts some time ago. Ghaith didn't really want to go to Premiers, since it was the Emirati party grounds.

When the shots arrived, Jenny raised hers. "To getting this fucking contract and getting rich!" They all clicked glasses and drank. Several minutes later, after three more consecutive rounds, they stumbled out of the club, laughing.

Ghaith finally had agreed to go, mostly because he was drunk, but also he knew that it would appease Randy. Still in debt, Ghaith didn't have any money to give Randy until they won the contract, but that didn't stop Randy from asking for it every chance he got. Ghaith knew he was going to drive everyone to Premiers the minute he saw Randy's eyes light up when Jenny mentioned going. After all, Premiers was the so-called hippest nightclub in UAE.

"Okay, let's go!" Jenny yelled, taking such long strides in her heels that even Ghaith, with his flat shoes and six-foot-two-inch strides, was hard-pressed to keep up with her. "I want to dance!"

All four of them piled into Ghaith's car, and he drove them carefully to the Emirates, staying well under the speed limit the entire way. The last thing he needed was to get pulled over when he was this drunk. If that happened, he would lose everything. But there wasn't much traffic, and soon they arrived at the Castle. To Ghaith, it seemed to take longer driving through the labyrinth of roads and parking garages at the Castle than it did driving across the city to get there.

Ghaith started to get nervous about Jenny's plan. Her friend was getting all of them into Premiers, and he had an idea that the type of friend who could get her into Premiers probably wouldn't like him, Randy, or Lin.

"I don't know. Maybe I should just leave," he said after they'd parked, dangling this bait in front of Jenny to see how much she wanted him.

Jenny smiled at him. "Don't be silly. Come on."

"Hey, muthafucker," Randy said, "let's go inside and get wasted."

When they got to the line at the front of the club, Jenny bypassed it and went directly over to the bouncers. She was on her phone again and began waving at a tall blond girl behind the bouncers. The girl shouldered her way out and yelled into one of the guy's ears. She gave Jenny a firm once-over, smiled, and then pecked her on the cheek. She then looked over at Ghaith, Randy, and Lin.

Ghaith could tell immediately that Jenny's friend wasn't impressed with him. Then he recognized her—Chloe, Mohammed's scout. Chloe grabbed Jenny's hand and led the way to the first bar just inside the club. Ghaith, Randy, and Lin trailed closely behind.

"Chloe, this is Ghaith." Jenny gestured toward Ghaith and then toward her friend. "Ghaith, this is Chloe."

"Mmm hmm," Chloe said, without giving him a second look.

Ghaith gritted his teeth. He hated to be ignored, especially by a woman. But in this case, he was happy that Chloe didn't seem to recognize him. He was close enough to hear her yell in Jenny's ear, "I don't think I can get these people in the VIP. Where did you find the old man and the prostitute?"

This was obviously a rhetorical question, since Chloe didn't wait for an answer. Instead, she pulled Jenny to the side and they started taking selfies. Completely indifferent to this conversation, Randy went up to the bar and ordered drinks for himself and Lin, who was stuck to his side with fear on her face. *She knows everyone thinks she is a prostitute*, Ghaith realized.

Ghaith looked back at Jenny and saw her hold up an index finger in the universal "one minute" sign. Then she ran off with Chloe into a more crowded part of the club and disappeared, consumed by the throng.

Sticking closer to Ghaith than Lin was to himself, Randy nearly stepped on Ghaith's foot. Irritated, Ghaith went over to the bar and ordered a Crown Royal and Coke, lit a cigarette, and started walking in the direction Jenny had gone. *Maybe I can lose them in the crowd*, he thought. Entering the crowded dance floor, he began to look for Jenny. The room was smoky and smelled of sweat mingled with perfume, nauseatingly sweet. Luckily, he'd lost Randy and Lin, but he couldn't find Jenny anywhere.

At the VIP tables, people were drinking rounds of shots with sparklers on them. Fists were pumping in the air while people jumped around. Everywhere he looked, there were sexy blondes with little packs of Emiratis. His palms started to sweat, and he looked up to what must have been the VVIP section. Chloe and Jenny were standing up there near the edge with drinks in their hands, bumping hips while they danced next to a bunch of very interested Emiratis. *What the fuck?*

Ghaith walked over to the stage, feeling as if Chloe had stolen his property, but the bouncer shook his head. *Fuck off*, the man's look said. Not wanting to start a scene, Ghaith went around to the other side of the stage. "Jenny!" It pissed him off that she'd brought him here and then ditched him. It made him angrier to see what she really did when she went out with her so-called friends. "Jenny!" he yelled again.

She finally danced around to the side of the stage, and he was able to get up on a step and grab her arm. Jenny jumped back, surprised, and he could see disappointment settle in her eyes. She held her head down, excused herself from Chloe, and walked down the stage. The bouncer let her through without a word.

"We need to get out of here now!" Ghaith yelled in her ear.

"What?! What are you talking about?" She was noticeably drunker than when they'd arrived.

He grabbed her hand and led her across the dance floor. As if on cue, Randy and Lin reappeared, and Ghaith gritted his teeth again. He tried to move toward the door, but Jenny pulled her hand away.

"Why are we leaving?" she yelled over the music.

"I'm going. Stay if you want and have fun with that ho." Ghaith sneered at her, turned, and walked out the door. He couldn't believe that he'd been so blatantly disrespected, and he felt an overwhelming surge of embarrassment, anger, and hurt. He'd thought that Jenny had more respect for him than this, and he wasn't sure how to remedy the situation, especially if she did stay at Premiers tonight. He wished he would have been more persuasive, but he was so angry that he didn't know what else to do.

And then, as if Allah had answered his prayer, he heard Jenny's heels clicking behind him while he walked through the lobby. Ghaith sighed. He was relieved that she was following him, but irritated that she had gone up to the stage and forgotten about him in the first place.

Maybe his grip on her wasn't as strong as he'd thought.

CHAPTER 23

Exhaustion swept through Jenny's body in waves. It was her last week in Talefa, and she was mentally, emotionally, and physically exhausted. Half of her life was packed away in differently sized boxes, and the other half was scattered around her room. The last week hadn't been too bad, since she'd spent most of it in Abu Dhabi anyway. But the rest of the week had been spent with Stanley, Jenny's overweight, English boss who grumbled that she shouldn't put all her eggs in one basket. He wanted her to shop around, rather than accepting the first job offered to her, especially by her Arab boyfriend.

Jenny let out a sigh and closed her eyes. The truth was she liked Ghaith. She liked being with him. The memory of Ghaith kissing her goodbye that last day in the hotel room floated through her mind. He had been less attentive than initially, and she was sure it was because he knew he had her. The chase was over. He was getting what he wanted—a lot of sex with a Westerner *and* a new employee who was helping him win a $5 million contract. *What am I getting myself into?*

Then Jenny's thoughts drifted to Chloe. After the way Ghaith had stormed out of Premiers a couple of nights ago, she knew that she couldn't mix the two of them again. He had been so angry afterward, yelling, "That girl is a pimp!"

Ghaith didn't like having to compete with the richest Emiratis. He could usually hold his own with his flashy car, luxury resort vacations, and deep pockets. But these Emirati guys had power, money, and Western women wrapped around their fingers a little more tightly.

Jenny had thought it was funny that Ghaith called Chloe a pimp, but the more she thought about it, the more teeth it had. She remembered how she had met Chloe in the bathroom at the Blues Lounge. Chloe just happened to be putting on makeup when Jenny came out, and Chloe started the conversation. Within minutes of meeting her, Chloe introduced Jenny to Salim, and within ten minutes of meeting him, they'd gone to Premiers.

All these complicated issues were making Jenny's head hurt—not to mention that she had stopped reading her Bible after the first day at the hotel in Abu Dhabi, when she started sleeping with Ghaith. Opening her eyes, she stared at the ceiling for a while. She had painted each one of these small rooms in her apartment the color of the desert at a different time of day. Her bedroom was cozy and somewhat sultry, the color of the desert at dusk. Outside there were white Arabian-style houses across the street and beyond the compound fence, the yards lined with date trees. People actually had a bit of money here, and Talefa was certainly up and coming. In the four months she had lived here, they had put in a new boardwalk along the seaside that included sculptures and fountains and even a marker that pointed to different cities around the world.

Jenny loved her running route here that wound down windy streets, the Arabian Gulf, and through the desert. It was going to be what she missed most, besides just looking out her window, letting her mind drift while staring at the traditional houses across the street. Funny, how far away they seemed because of the barbed-wire fence, as if she was watching the Travel Channel. She knew their view wasn't quite so picturesque. Jenny sighed, and her thoughts rolled to the uncomfortable realization that if she made this move, her Bible would remain shut for quite some time.

CHAPTER 24

The Castle hotel could be deceiving, Chloe knew. Rooms ranged from $500 to more than $20,000 per night, with some rooms reserved exclusively for royalty. The after-party tonight was in a mere $750 room. And it wasn't really even an after-party, since everyone else had been kicked out as soon as Jenny and Chloe came in with Akeel.

"Yalla, out!" Akeel said when Chloe and Jenny stumbled after him into the room. Two Lebanese girls and Akeel's cousin had quickly left the room.

Chloe stared at Akeel as the three of them settled into the room. His round figure made her cringe. If he ever wanted an American girl, he was going to have to drop a few pounds.

Akeel looked over at Chloe with an irritated expression, and she knew that he wanted to be alone in the room with Jenny. But she also knew that Jenny would stay only if she stayed. Chloe had exaggerated how much fun the after-party would be, since it was the only way to get Jenny to stay. In a desperate move, Chloe turned on MTV to try to liven up the decadent gold-and-crimson room.

"Anything you would like to drink?" Akeel opened the minibar fridge and took out some Grey Goose vodka. As his shirt got caught up in his belly bulge, Chloe frowned and looked away.

"Only champagne!" Jenny slurred. "Pink Moet." She giggled, and then started moving her hips to the music.

At least she's having fun, Chloe thought. And at least *she* would get a lot of money from this job tonight.

Without hesitation, Akeel smiled, picked up the phone, and ordered the champagne. Then he looked up at Chloe and gave her a crooked grin. "Coming right up."

Chloe couldn't tell if he was miffed at spending another $400 on champagne or excited at the idea of getting Jenny even more drunk, which would increase his chances. She figured it was the latter.

Jenny stretched out in the bed. "Oh, good! Just wake me when it gets here."

Chloe crawled to one side of Jenny and nestled her head on the pillow. "Sure thing, babe." She was bone tired. Trying to keep up this façade of fun and glamour was wearing on her tonight.

Chloe had just finished a long week at her real job, working her ass off to increase her portfolio. She had her heart set on a Porsche Boxster, so she was being super focused, which meant extremely busy. She smiled to herself, remembering the flawless presentation that she had put together this week. The look on her boss's face when she had displayed her research was a celebration in itself. Over the past week, she had spent half her nights working on that presentation and the other half taking girls out to dinner with her other Arab bosses.

A knock on the door jolted Chloe out of her thoughts. Opening her eyes, she saw a half-naked Akeel walk over and grab the champagne from room service. She quickly closed her eyes before Akeel turned around.

"I guess it's lights-out time," Akeel whispered. He turned off the lights and climbed into the bed on the other side of Jenny.

Chances were Jenny wasn't actually going to have sex with the overweight Akeel. It was more likely she would just pass out drunk in the bed, but Chloe got paid either way.

Even though Chloe was exhausted, she lay there awake in the dark room, probably because of all the Red Bulls she had consumed tonight. Chloe listened to Jenny swatting Akeel's hand away for a good ten minutes before he finally fell asleep. Then Chloe fell into a deep slumber.

Chloe's phone woke her at ten in the morning—to artificial darkness and Akeel's snores. Jenny sat up in bed beside her. Using their phones as flashlights, they gathered their things. Clearly still a bit drunk, they giggled while trying not to wake Akeel. The Pink Moet bottle caught their attention in a beam of light, and Chloe contemplated opening it. Sometimes the opposite of what you thought would help actually helped. She grabbed the bottle, putting her dress over the top. *POP!*

"Shit," Jenny whispered. The two of them tried to stifle their giggles while Akeel turned on his side and resumed snoring.

Chloe held the bottle out to Jenny, who grabbed it and tilted her head back, gulping deeply. Taking the bottle back, Chloe took a deep drink and grinned. It worked. She felt better already. Jenny giggled again and held her hand out for another swig, and Chloe opened the patio door that led outside.

The gardens outside were flooded with midmorning sun. Chloe searched desperately for her Prada sunglasses and then felt the solid frame in her hand. "Yes," she whispered victoriously and then slipped them on. Jenny followed her example, but neither of them bothered to put on their heels while they walked across the Castle's perfectly manicured grounds.

"You know, there's a bunch of waterslides and a lazy river on the other side," Chloe said. Two guards on camels rode past as if they didn't see the girls clearly taking a Saturday morning walk of shame.

"Really?"

"Yeah, I went to an after-party a little while ago, and the guys bought us swimsuits in the morning from one of the stores inside. Then we sobered up at the water park, before going back to the room and getting royally hammered again."

"Nice. That would have been more fun than our little unproductive threesome last night."

"Yes, sorry about that, love. I thought more people were going to come last night. But at least we didn't have to worry about driving home or fighting for a cab with a bunch of other people."

"Very true."

As they walked past a series of water fountains, the lush grass made Chloe smile. Even though Abu Dhabi was the green city of the UAE, she didn't get a chance to walk on grass very often.

"You know, he kept grabbing me last night while I was trying to sleep," Jenny said suddenly. "I was getting so irritated."

"Yeah, he's done that to Kimberly, too."

"Really? What an ass. What's she like? We've been at Premiers together a few times, but I don't think we've really talked."

Chloe almost smiled. Jenny didn't really even know her, either, and would probably be appalled if she knew everything that happened at the Castle.

"You know, I like Kimberly, but there's something a little off about her." Chloe slowed her pace and walked quietly next to Jenny, to avoid being overheard by any other guests who might be strolling the grounds. "She was the first woman I know of who went to Premiers by herself. She just hung out by the VVIP area until she was noticed. I found that odd until I learned her age." Chloe paused. "She's almost forty. Can you imagine? She's some kind of cougar hunting for a rich Emirati, probably so she can keep up with her Botox and fillers."

Jenny let out a little laugh. "Wow, she looks great! And the balls, to go into Premiers by herself."

"Or pure desperation."

They reached the main lobby of the Castle and paused to put on their heels. As Chloe led the way down the hall, the click-clack of their shoes echoed off the marble walls. She opened the main doors and told the Indian man at the taxi stand to get them a car. Then Chloe and Jenny retreated to a couch and stared like zombies at the TV screen on the wall.

"I'm still drunk," Jenny said in a monotone, not looking away from the television screen.

"Yep, I'm taking a hot bath and detoxing all day. I think I'll call my masseuse and have her come to my house."

"That sounds like heaven. I have to meet up with Ghaith and do some work today." Jenny sighed. "He is supposed to be showing me some apartments."

"If you get a big enough apartment, I'm moving in. We could throw some great parties."

❦

Once Jenny got back to her hotel, she went for a slow run and then lay out by the pool. Stretching out on a sun lounger, she dozed briefly. The sound of traffic at street level somehow made her feel safe and protected, unlike the extreme quiet of the hotel last night. Like always, the run had made her feel better initially, but then dehydration set in and made her hangover worse.

Ghaith's driving did nothing to improve her terrible hangover. He made quick U-turns and drove speedily down side streets on route to two different flats—studios, rather. Jenny had never seen such small studios. Ghaith dropped money left and right for hotels, recreation, cars, food, and drinks, so why was he showing her such tiny places?

"I know they are small," he said eventually, as if sensing her uneasiness, "but until we get this contract, we have to work within a certain budget. I promise, this is just temporary." He paused. "So what did you and Kimberly end up doing last night?"

Jenny had told him that she and Kimberly were going out to the Blues Lounge. She couldn't tell him she was hanging out with Chloe or going to Premiers, after what he'd said and how he had acted when they had gone to Premiers together.

"Oh, we ended up just going out to dinner and then hung out back at the hotel. Had a bit to drink."

"I'm glad you had fun." Ghaith glanced at her sideways.

Although her top and jeans had looked really cute when he first picked her up, Jenny knew her cheerfulness was fading while her nausea grew. She was disappointed that he had showed her only two places, both of which were awful.

She quickly crossed off the flat in Mohammed Zin Bayed City that was close to the office. Only Indians and Pakistanis lived down there, and it was over the bridge from the mainland. Even though the second place was on the city's outskirts, at least it was on the island of Abu Dhabi and in an up-and-coming area. Jenny felt her stomach rumble and hoped she wouldn't have diarrhea. The copious amounts of alcohol were starting to leave her system, and she felt awful.

"I'll take the one with the arched window—that's on the island. But do you promise I will be out of there within six months of getting the contract?"

"Of course," Ghaith said. "I'll be spending a lot of time there anyway, so of course I will want a bigger space, too."

Jenny's stomach clenched, and she silently vowed never to get so drunk again.

CHAPTER 25

Stanley, Jenny's now ex-boss, helped her move all her belongings to the three hundred-square-foot studio the following week, even though he didn't like her leaving Talefa to work for her Arab boyfriend. Apparently the Talefa boys had told him about Ghaith making out with her in the back of their car at Carrefour, and Stanley muttered in his English accent something like "Arab stealing our white women." Jenny shrugged off the comment as old-fashioned, figuring at least she and Ghaith were dating *before* she started working for him.

Regardless of how Stanley felt, he still helped her move her Ikea furniture. Then he carried it up the stairs and clumsily reassembled it in her studio. Her queen-sized bed, wardrobe, table, and two folding chairs barely fit in the main room. The small kitchen area consisted of a sink, a couple of cabinets, and a small counter, and then a small bathroom with a decent-sized tub. At least the studio had high ceilings and a small balcony with floor-to-ceiling sliding glass doors.

But even those bright spots began to fade when Stanley looked around the room, then at Jenny, and then back at the room—and shook his head. "Don't be stupid," he said when he left. "You can do better than this, Jenny."

Stanley's words seemed like a curse later as Jenny lay on her bed and stared at the ceiling. It was the only position where she didn't feel constrained by the small size of the room.

Its location was the best thing about this tiny flat. Even though Jenny was on the outskirts, at least she was still in the city. The flat was close to a few trendy bars and hotels, and only ten blocks from the gym she wanted to join. And getting to work would take only twenty minutes. Jenny's tiny bubble of optimism began to grow, ever so slowly, as she stared at the white ceiling.

Well, she figured, she would hardly be at her new flat anyway, since she was keen on making a busy life in Abu Dhabi. Besides going out with Chloe, she had been looking into a running hash group, a running circuit group, and a wine tasting group. Also, she felt a renewal of her spiritual faith beginning to stir alongside her optimism. Jenny vowed she would not spend all her time in this tiny room waiting for Ghaith to show up whenever he wanted to. After all, they weren't married—in fact, *he* was married to someone else—so she wanted to enjoy being single in this city. Feeling renewed, she sat up and looked out her patio door. *There is even an actual church in Abu Dhabi. Maybe I should start going there.* This was going to be a new Jenny. Being single and meeting other single expats, from business people to churchgoers. *Yes! She could do it all.*

Then Stanley's remarks tumbled back into her mind uncomfortably, and the retched gut feeling she'd had while he was putting together her furniture returned. She knew she was trying to convince herself that this was going to work. As far as her and Ghaith? Stanley certainly had a point about them being so culturally different. Furthermore, Ghaith *was* married and had lied to her. Even if he was, allegedly, in the process of getting a divorce, she wasn't sure she could trust him.

Jenny felt schizophrenic: head-over-heels for Ghaith one moment and like a fool the next. The more time she spent away from him, the more she felt like a fool. Tonight, she decided, she would tell him they could work together but not have a relationship. She needed to feel some sense of control, and the more she thought about their relationship, the more she felt she'd been getting played this entire time. In this decision, at least, she could be strong and act like a professional.

ℂ

Jenny knew she wasn't following the no-repeat protocol with her light-green Roxy dress with a deep V-neck, but she had run out of options. Ghaith had seen her entire wardrobe already, but she couldn't update it until she started getting paid. So she dolled up the dress with gold accessories and heels, and turned to look at herself in the mirror. Looking good would give her the confidence she needed for this decision.

"I don't care how good he looks. I am going to end this, so that I can start a real life," Jenny said to her reflection. She smiled boldly, snatched her purse, and walked downstairs.

As usual, she felt Ghaith's eyes giving her the once-over while she approached his car. He had the passenger window down, and when she looked up at him, he let out a little whistle. *You can do this,* Jenny thought as she opened the passenger door. He was wearing a button-down shirt with funky black-and-silver designs and a pair of black jeans. The flames of facial hair on his cheeks had been freshly trimmed, and the car smelled of his cologne. Jenny took a deep breath as the cologne resurrected memories of breathing in this scent—Ghaith—only a week ago, biting his shoulder while he was inside of her. A horn beeped in the distance, bringing her out of her reverie. *He's damn sexy, but he's not my type.*

"Sorry I'm late," Ghaith said, laughing. "The traffic was awful, but it's much better than driving to Talefa." He leaned over and kissed her, then pulled back and let out a deep, contented sigh.

Concentrate on the task at hand. Jenny smiled at Ghaith and then looked out the window. Even with the good location, she was still irritated with the flat—and it hadn't helped that she had seen the bill. The rent was 40,000 AED for the year and he'd paid half already, since in Abu Dhabi yearly or semi-annual amounts up front were prevalent. This was equal to about $11,250 per year. The hotel she had stayed at while working on the proposal for *a week* had amounted to $2,800, so he was saving a lot of money.

"You okay?"

"Yes, just tired from moving all day."

She really was tired. After Stanley helped her move all of her stuff, she had unpacked boxes with overzealous ambition in an attempt to make the flat feel cozier. It hadn't worked.

"Sorry I couldn't help. It was really busy at work today. How did it go?"

"Fine. Stanley came out from Talefa and put together all my furniture for me."

When they got to Clover's, Ghaith ordered a double Crown and Coke while Jenny ordered an extra-dirty martini. The place was absolutely dead compared with the last time they had been here, the site of their first meeting. *How ironic*, Jenny thought, that this magical place of meeting would be the place where they were to break up. Only a couple of people were inside at the bar, so Ghaith and Jenny went out on the patio.

Ghaith picked up his drink: "To a long partnership." He winked at Jenny as they clinked drinks and sat down.

Jenny cringed, feeling her insides curdle. She should have felt good, since Ghaith was semi-securing her job with that toast. However, she felt like she was stepping into quicksand, and even on the wide-open patio, she felt claustrophobic. Jenny took a long swallow of her martini. When she set her glass down, it was half empty.

Ghaith lit a cigarette and offered her one.

"No, thanks. I've decided to quit again." She smiled and looking up at him, admiring his dark eyes. He was focused on her semi-exposed thighs as her crossed legs caused her dress to ride up slightly. She adjusted her dress as he licked his lips.

Jenny had decided to quit smoking this morning while she was moving her furniture. She really wanted a fresh start with this move, and her runs were getting harder and harder because of how much she'd been smoking. Her skin tone changed dramatically when she smoked, too. She had never really noticed it because it happened so gradually. But the first time she'd quit, her skin had changed from ashy white back to her natural olive tone within a couple of days.

"That's good." Ghaith smiled tightly and took a drag off his cigarette, blowing the smoke in the other direction.

"Look, we have to talk," Jenny said. She took a deep breath. "I don't think we should be in an intimate relationship when we're working together. I just think it would be too difficult to stay on track, professionally. I mean, what if it doesn't work out romantically between us? I don't want to have to look for another job because of that." Taking a deep breath, Jenny stabbed an olive from her glass and put it in her mouth—to shut herself up. She had said a whole lot in a tiny bit of time, and it had sounded more spastic than she wanted. She smoothed her hair to calm herself, as if she could smooth herself together.

Ghaith looked at her for a moment, his dark eyes finally connecting to hers. She was warmed by the intensity of his look, and her heart fluttered. Just when she began to doubt her confession, he looked away—yet she still felt that warmth resonating deep inside. Ghaith swallowed the rest of his drink in one gulp, and then put his glass down delicately and looked at the table.

"I see." He paused for a few seconds and then picked up the menu. "Do you want to order something to eat?"

Jenny stared at him, wondering what he was thinking. She couldn't read him. Was he upset, or did he just not care? She was reminded that she really didn't know Ghaith very well at all.

"How about some nachos and chicken wings?" he asked, looking at her with darkened eyes.

"Whatever you like." Jenny drank the last of her martini.

Ghaith whistled, and the young Indian waiter hurried over. Ghaith waved toward their glasses. "Another round, and some nachos and chicken wings."

"Yes, sir"

The silence was uncomfortable, so unlike any silence they had ever shared. Being alone on the patio with no distraction was almost unbearable. Ghaith picked up his phone and made an angry-sounding phone call in Arabic. Jenny tried not to stare at him while he spoke, but she couldn't help it. The flames on his cheeks seemed to light up, and his anger was oddly comforting. Jenny imagined that maybe he really did care for her. Another couple came out to the patio and sat down, and Jenny turned around to look inside the bar. People were starting to trickle in, and a little crowd was forming. *Well, that was easier than I thought ... I guess.*

The waiter set down their drinks and walked away. He glanced briefly at Ghaith and snickered, clearly understanding Arabic. The martini was heaven in Jenny's mouth. She hadn't eaten much all day and was starting to feel a little buzzed, but certainly not less nervous. She had spilled everything in one clumsy breath, and now Ghaith was ignoring her. Jenny felt a combination of mild regret and overwhelming relief, which moved in even more quickly than the alcohol she was rapidly consuming.

The waiter returned, taking in the last of Ghaith's phone conversation while he set down the food. Jenny realized that even though it had taken the skinny waiter less than five minutes to set down their drinks and return with their food, her second drink was almost gone. Ghaith's drink was gone, too. Taking a bite of the nachos, she looked over at him. He seemed perfectly normal, making comments about various people coming out onto the patio. His conversation was light, easy, and funny. It was the strangest breakup date she had ever been on. After a while, she began to think that separating the relationship from the job might actually work. She laughed at his jokes and even ordered a third martini.

৪০

Jenny was giggly and buzzed by the time they pulled up in front of her apartment. Dinner had gone well, and she was relieved that they would still have a good working relationship and possibly a friendship. Taking a deep breath, she reached for the car door. But then she felt Ghaith's hand on her thigh, and he reached around her to hold the door closed.

"Wait." He sighed heavily. "I am actually *not* okay with this."

Jenny released her grip on the door handle and looked at him.

Taking a deep breath, he looked directly into her eyes. "I don't want our relationship to end. What are we thinking? What are we saying?" His words came out jumbled and rushed.

Jenny noticed how seriously perplexed he looked. He gestured wildly with his hands while he continued to talk. "I want to be with you *and* work with you. I mean, you saw how well we got along when you were working on the proposal. Jenny, I want to build my empire with you." He paused. "It will be empty without you. I want us to officially be an 'us.'"

He then reached over and put his hand on the nape of her neck, pulling her face close to his own. Her kissed her strongly and passionately, and then pulled back. "I need you—all of you, habibti. Professionally *and* intimately."

Ghaith gazed at her, his face only inches from her own. Jenny was blown away by his apparent sincerity and flattered by his show of emotion. She couldn't help herself. She put her right hand on the back of his head and pulled him in for a second kiss, and kissing him harder than he'd kissed her. *Maybe I can try this out for a while. It might work out fine.*

"Okay," she said, "but you need to come upstairs. Now."

Ghaith smiled. "Yes, ma'am."

"But first, give me a cigarette."

CHAPTER 26

Chloe looked at her iPhone. She had sent Jenny a text more than two hours ago, asking about the hash run tonight. Chloe very much wanted two things—to feel like a normal expatriate surrounded by expatriates and to scope out some potential girls to take to Premiers. But she still hadn't heard back from Jenny.

Brushing her long blond hair, Chloe held it up in a ponytail and looked into the mirror, turning her head from side to side. She wanted to put her hair up at an angle that made her face look skinny, but she didn't want to make her forehead look longer than it was. Really, her hair looked so much better down. And her eyebrows! In this light, the tattoos looked almost purple. She picked up her brown pencil and started to fill them in.

"About fucking time," she said to herself when the ringing of her phone caught her attention. "Hi, luv," she said into the phone, with an affected lilt in her voice.

"Hey, sorry. I just got off work," Jenny said. Chloe could tell she was on speaker, because she could hear traffic in the background. "On my way now. I just got the map. Did you see it yet?"

"Yes, I did see it, and I am ready to go. You picking me up, luv?"

"I should be there in ten. I'm so happy you're coming! Shit! This fucking asshole just slammed on his brakes. What is wrong with these people?"

"Drive safe, my dear." Chloe hung up. She looked back at the mirror and saw a real smile on her face. She was actually looking forward to being around some crude expats tonight, and she was surprised to realize that she was hoping there were no beauties there. *Better to have a night off.* Chloe pulled up her shirt a little bit more and stuck out her chest, so that just a tiny bit of her midriff showed. Maybe *she* could have the attention tonight. Maybe *she* would meet someone who was actually interested in a *real* relationship.

She opted for a headband to hold her hair back from her face, to keep it nice and long.

CHAPTER 27

"All right, you cocks and muthafuckers!" Amanda yelled, declaring the start of the hash. In her forties, the woman was slightly plump and had one of the dirtiest mouths Jenny had ever heard. For some reason, however, Jenny was drawn to Amanda and knew she would be a good friend. Being around someone so real and raw, in this city of superficial perfection, made Jenny smile.

Jenny loved hashing and was glad she had found this group in Abu Dhabi. The first time she had gone hashing was in Hawaii, while writing a paper about subcultures. She had gotten a map, since they changed weekly, and met up with a big group of people, all of whom had handles like Greasy Poon or Pussy Licker. A couple of people, called the hares, would mark the hash earlier in the day using symbols made with flour. The hashers had to follow the symbols, which meant either "on-on"—on the right path—or "on-back"—dead end, circle back.

Jenny found this type of maze really fun, especially since part of their run led through the underground sections of Hawaii, which she would never have visited if not for the hash. At the end of the hash were a couple of kegs. At that gathering, called Religion, they got in a circle, started a bonfire, and sang songs with crass lyrics. Jenny didn't really care for Religion, but she liked the camaraderie, and even though people were crude, they were also very nice. So when she'd found out about the hash run in Abu Dhabi, she'd been excited to meet people who were active *and* liked to party.

Jenny and Chloe were in the front pack, so they started off at a sprint as soon as Amanda blew the whistle to start the chase. Within a few minutes, some of the more athletic guys overtook them and the two girls settled into a slower run, albeit not as slow as Jenny's usual chatting pace. Jenny looked over to see if the raunchiness of the sound-off, as well as the "assholes" and "cunt licker" comments that fellow hashers were throwing around in jest, made tiara-wearing, Castle-stomping Chloe frown. But Chloe was focused on the road ahead.

The humidity was heavy tonight, and in the evening light, the pastel blues, pinks, and browns seemed to blur into one another. The road wrapped around the sea on a peninsula opposite the coast of Abu Dhabi. Jenny and Chloe saw the pack of runners ahead of them stop, and then little groups ran off in various directions to find the trail. Jenny and Chloe slowed to a walk, waiting to see which direction was real and wouldn't lead to a dead end. The fun of a hash was always the choose-your-own-adventure type of run.

Chloe was staring off into the distance. Following her gaze, Jenny saw the humidity and the soft lighting cast a spellbinding haze over Abu Dhabi's skyscrapers and mosques.

Chloe cleared her throat. "It looks so different when you're not in it." She was looking at the Castle.

"Yeah, it's beautiful here."

"It just doesn't look the same. Out here it feels like no one is watching me, but people are really *seeing* me." Chloe reached up and pulled her long hair in a ponytail. There was an intensity in Chloe's eyes that Jenny had never seen in the pulsating lights of the clubs. She realized this was the first real conversation that she and Chloe had ever had.

"Do you have an extra elastic?" Chloe asked.

"Maybe in the car."

From the front, someone called, "On, on!"

"Oh, never mind," Chloe said. "Let's go." Her hair tumbled down her back as she broke into a run toward where the guys had called out.

Jenny took a moment to scan the skyline again. The Castle's dome glimmered and had turned a shade darker with the quickening sunset. It seemed like a beacon, calling out to her. She understood what Chloe meant about this group of people, though. She couldn't imagine Ghaith being here with her now, running around swearing and sweating. Here and now, she wasn't wearing any makeup or a push-up bra, and she didn't have to think about every move she made. Here and now, Jenny smiled unafraid.

ಎ

At Religion, Jenny began to like Chloe even more. Chloe was telling everyone jokes about her time in India and how much fun she'd had growing up in South Africa. Her long hair still hung loose, since they had both forgotten about finding an elastic in Jenny's car after the run ended. Chloe's smile was contagious, and Jenny felt like she was seeing her friend for the first time tonight.

Amanda huddled around them, and—after several beers—Chloe even invited her out for drinks. This amazed Jenny, who knew Chloe well enough to know that she surrounded herself in public exclusively with pretty, fit girls. Maybe Jenny had more in common with Chloe than she had originally thought. After all, they could both be entirely snobby at Premiers wearing a mound of makeup, running around in four-inch heels, and judging everyone else. But out here under a dark sky, they could both be down to earth. Makeup mixed with sweat, in running shoes, sucking down carb-enriched beers.

"All right, you virgins, get on up here!" Amanda roared, stepping forward and continuing to act as mascot. She handed Chloe an unopened can of beer and ushered her into the middle of the circle. A couple of other people stumbled out of the shadows, moving into the middle of the circle holding a fistful of unopened beer cans and looking around a little nervously. That was always the hesitation of a first Religion at a hash. What would the virgins—the ones to be on the hash for the first time—have to do?

The light of the fire danced around Chloe's face, now the likeness of a Van Gogh painting, colors licking her face while it changed shape effortlessly and beautifully. Looking at Jenny, she smiled widely and mouthed, "Here we go!"

CHAPTER 28

"It's a choice to fall in love," Jenny said, slurring her words and throwing her hands in the air.

Ghaith looked at her, his brow furrowed. "No, when you fall in love, you fall in love, and when you fall out of love, it just happens. No choice can change that!"

The way Ghaith held his body, straight up and down, and tightened his lips, indicated his level of adamancy. To further enhance the arrogance of his posture, he took a strong drag off his cigarette. Exhaling, he tilted his head up in a gesture of superiority. The flames on his cheeks extended, and Jenny felt herself melt. She had always had a thing for cocky men, and she would rather be taken by an overconfident guy than have to come on to a guy who was too shy. She was old-fashioned like that, and she almost never had to be the chaser.

Looking at Ghaith, Jenny shook her head side to side emphatically, as if trying to shake herself out of her feelings toward him and simultaneously command her point of view. "No, it's definitely a choice."

"So you could make the choice to love me?" Ghaith teased, and let out a small chuckle.

"Maybe I already have." She winked in an effort to make him nervous.

Jenny was feeling confident. Being out on her balcony with cigarettes and cocktails at five o'clock in the morning was becoming their normal ritual. Even though it wasn't the most traditional ritual, it was *their* ritual—and it felt alive, vivid and bold, the thing to do when in your thirties and living abroad. After all, the only grim reaper at this moment in Jenny's life seemed to be sleep itself. Even at their early morning ritual, every second in this getting-to-know-you stage trembled with life.

But the moment she said these words to Ghaith, she realized it was true—which made *her* nervous. *I'm actually falling for him. Hard. Oh, shit.* But she let her mind drift, which was easy since she was getting sleepy. There were things about Ghaith that drove her crazy, like his random disappearances.

However, he actually had many qualities that she liked, too. They could just talk, all day and all night. They could stand on her balcony at five in the morning discussing her philosophy of love. Case in point. They had insane chemistry, and she shivered to remember how he'd taken her on her office desk just a few days ago. But more than that, they had a certain type of stability. They were making a lot of money together, and Ghaith was a millionaire. Jenny was on her way to being one, too. Maybe he was the one—tall, dark, handsome, funny, rich, foreign, and into her.

She put her glass down and opened the balcony door to go back inside. Ghaith followed her, and they tumbled into bed together.

"Maybe I choose to fall in love with you," he said breathlessly, kissing her face until he reached her lips.

They fell easily into a kiss and the teasing disappeared.

"I don't know if I can stop myself from falling in love with you," Ghaith said. "But I am not sure you could fall in love with me. We are tragic."

"Then you are my Romeo." Jenny knew it was true. She breathed his scent in, and it filled her with the soft light of contentment.

I do choose to love him.

CHAPTER 29

Ghaith went over to Jenny's flat more often after they began to dive into their feelings, both drowning in that passionate sea of new commitment. At work, they won the $5 million contract, and then more contracts. They frequently drove to Dubai for meetings and to take the American Oil Company guys out for lunch. At Jenny's flat, restaurants, bars, or ritzy hotels, they were lovers who couldn't get enough of each other.

But Jenny was asking questions, more jealous in nature than before. Ghaith wasn't always at her flat, but she still hadn't seen his, and he realized that was making her more and more suspicious. The excuse that his mom was staying with him wasn't enough anymore.

"Why can't you stay over tonight?" she asked as he sat on the edge of her bed and began to put his shoes on.

"I told you, baby. I've got an early morning meeting, and I need to change my clothes."

"You could just leave some clothes here." Jenny smiled at him, playfully cocking her head to one side. "Where do you live anyway?" She stopped smiling.

"Baby, why don't we get a place together? Just find one, and we'll get it." If they moved in together, it would be easier to persuade her to marry him and he could stop living this double life. Once married, it would be easier to bring up the situation to Laila, and it would be harder for Jenny to leave him. Where would she go? Besides, he had fallen in love with her. And it wasn't a choice for him—it was an overwhelming and uncontrollable love.

Ghaith remembered how his first wife had called his love for her *infatuation*, and then after a few more weeks, *lust*. Every time he had said he loved her, she swatted him away and say he only lusted for her, especially after she found out about the affairs. But his love was true. Sometimes it might look like infatuation or lust, but Ghaith's love consumed him and colored his world. Even though he knew it could dwindle, it never completely dissipated. Ghaith's love burned so brightly that it left an eternal impression on his heart.

This was the kind of love he felt for Jenny, and it could not be reasoned with or rationed in small doses. Even though Laila was pregnant again, Ghaith still spent more and more time with Jenny. That made him feel like a prick, but he couldn't tame this love. So he was a prick who was in love, but he still had responsibilities.

Jenny smiled at him and then shook her head sadly. She looked away while he finished tying his shoes.

"We can move in together *after* you get a divorce. You know I can't live with you when you are still married."

"Habibti." He cupped her chin in his hand, turning her head toward him and looking into her the eyes. "I love you, and I am with only you. Let's just move in together."

Jenny shook her head again and freed it from his delicate grasp. "Nope, that's my deal." Her smile returned.

"But what would change? We are already basically living together. It's like we are married. I want a place with you." Ghaith put a hand on her thigh. She was still naked under the sheet, and her hair had fallen sexily around her shoulders.

"I know I don't act like a Christian," Jenny said, looking away. "But that's where I draw the line and try to live an ethical life. I just can't live with a married man who isn't married to me."

Ghaith knew there was more to it than that. He could see it in her face. Jenny was smart. She didn't want to be solely dependent on him, as she would be if they moved in together. And besides, she probably guessed there was more to this situation than met the eye.

He chuckled and tried a different angle. "Really, your Christianity thinks it's not good to live with a married man, but you can sleep with one?"

"And what does your religion say?" She looked at him intensely, her green eyes bright.

He shook his head, suddenly feeling deflated. "Why does this have to be so complicated?" He really did want to be with Jenny, but he wanted her to become his second wife. Ghaith just couldn't leave Laila yet. In fact, he wasn't sure if he would ever be able to leave her. According to Islam, he really should be married to Jenny. He wondered how much longer she would last until she agreed to marry him. It was kind of like a game of chicken, but he thought she would give in before he did.

"We really are like Romeo and Juliet," Jenny said, and sighed.

They both laughed, but their laughter seemed sad and empty. Ghaith lay back on the bed, and Jenny curled up on his chest and pulled the blanket over them. They lay like that until they both fell into a light sleep—Ghaith with his feet still on the floor, shoes on, and Jenny nestled awkwardly into the crook of his arm.

About twenty minutes later, Ghaith woke to his phone vibrating in his pocket. Carefully, he took it out. There was a message from Laila with a picture of his two daughters smiling in their pajamas. "Is your meeting over yet? Come home, habibi. We are waiting for you."

Even more cautiously, he rolled away from Jenny and readjusted the blanket over her curled-up body. He wished he could stay. Soon he would live with both Jenny and Laila, and have designated nights with each. He opened the door and turned off the light. The scented mixture of her perfume and the wine they had drunk evaporated as he walked down the stairs and to his car.

Soon it would be so much easier.

CHAPTER 30

"One, two, three, four—Go!" yelled the captain. It was sprint day with the Abu Dhabi running club, which meant running as fast as Jenny could across an empty parking lot in the tremendous Abu Dhabi heat. There were ten teams of five people. Each person took turns sprinting to the cone and back, and then tagged the next person.

Even though Jenny's mind was willing her to run fast, her lungs and legs were giving out on her. Sweat poured off her forehead, pools of sweat settled into her elbow creases, and she felt dizzy. Her body started talking to her mind. She went from thinking *I can do this, I can do this*—to thinking, *There is no way in hell I can do this.*

About three-fourths of the way back, Jenny felt her body failing. But then she looked up and saw that Alberto, the hot Portuguese guy, was next in her line. Her mind and body immediately united. *Do this well, suck in your stomach, throw your shoulders back.* She picked up her pace and sprinted to tag his hand. There. She felt him rush past her as she walked to the back of the line, catching her breath.

Turning to watch Alberto run around the cone, she noticed how toned his shoulders and biceps were, and she could make out the sculpted impression of his abs under his tank top. *Alllllbberrto,* she thought, drawing his name out. As he ran back toward the group, he looked up at her and their eyes met. He tagged the next person in line and slowed to a jog. As he reached the back of the line, he brushed about an inch past Jenny and looked down at her with a smile.

They had talked nonstop during the warm-up jog and realized they had a lot in common, even beyond being masochistic enough to belong to a running group in a desert city like Abu Dhabi. They both liked to drink wine and listen to down-tempo music. Jenny had wondered if Alberto knew more about wine than she did, since he was European. Those Europeans were just so damn sexy. She and Alberto also had similar senses of humor, joking about some of the other runners who were already sprinting during the warm-up. *Overachievers. Show-offs. Brits.*

Jenny smiled. One of the reasons she had wanted to join this running group was to meet other professional expats with similar interests, and her plan seemed to be working. At her first run, she had met Lacy, who introduced her to the hash group. Now she had met Alberto.

When Alberto caught his breath, he walked back over to Jenny. "That sucked."

"I know! And I have to go again in a minute. I'm sweating so much, I'm afraid I might slip."

Alberto laughed and shook his arms, spraying Jenny with sweat.

Jenny pretended to gag, but she'd always thought there was something primal and sexy about a man sweating. Whatever it was, she liked it.

"You'd better get ready." Alberto laughed and poked her playfully in the back, nudging her up to the now-empty spot at the front of the line.

Jenny got into position. The person ahead of her was sprinting hard and fast, and was almost back to her. "Yeah, well, you're right after me," she said, with a smile. "And when did you get in line behind me anyway?"

Alberto just laughed as the person in front of Jenny tagged her hand. She took off into a sprint. *Man, I need to quit smoking.* Her lungs were burning, and her legs were already fatigued from just one sprint. But thinking about Alberto watching her ass made her flex, push hard, and concentrate.

She rounded the cone, sucking in her stomach while she exhaled, and gathered up a huge breath of air. Alberto was watching her and grinning.

She picked up her stride, running hard all the way back to him to tag his hand. *Nothing like a sexy European to help me sprint.*

Alberto blew a kiss to her as he took off.

ℂ

Jenny and Alberto became Facebook friends and started sending each other flirty messages. Ghaith had hardly slept over that week, so it was easy for Jenny to justify what she was doing. Besides, she was fairly certain that Ghaith would never leave his wife, and sometimes she even suspected that he was actually still in a relationship with her. That week, however, Jenny did stop nagging him so much about it, which Ghaith seemed to think meant that he didn't need to stay over as much.

Whatever, Jenny thought.

She was beginning to feel indifferent about Ghaith. If he got a divorce and they ended up moving in together, she would be so committed to him that men like Alberto wouldn't even faze her. But that wasn't happening, and she felt like an idiot. It wasn't that Ghaith's philosophy about love was right, but rather that she was getting fed up and feeling like the other woman.

She only half believed him when he said he had night meetings these days, but she didn't want to become a nag. So she decided to get more active and keep her options open. After all, it wasn't as if she and Ghaith were married. In fact, he *was* married. And until he got a divorce, she was going to keep her options open—or go crazy with jealousy. Not that she was going to sleep with anyone else, but she could at least meet other people. The idea that Ghaith might be just a typical cheating Arab was playing with her mind more and more frequently. Maybe she did need to be with an expat.

Jenny sighed and turned off her computer. Once again, she was the only one in the office—or the tower, as she'd started to call it. Ghaith had asked her to be there from eight o'clock to five o'clock, six days a week. But she had started coming in late and leaving a bit early, because she was literally the only person at the office and she never took a lunch break. This was the nice office where Ghaith brought clients for meetings, but he worked primarily out of his industrial office.

Ghaith had fired both of Jenny's assistants so far, which she found strange. She actually had given one of the assistants a month's severance pay from her own pocket, because she felt terrible about how Ghaith had fired him on the spot for no reason. Both times, Jenny had seen a side of Ghaith that she had never before witnessed. She now realized he had a sinister side, which made her wonder what happened at the other office. Was it just shrewd Middle East business politics, or was it something more? She basically worked alone, with only the occasional meeting with other contractors at the tower. She and Ghaith discussed work more at Jenny's apartment or in the car than they did at this office.

She slung her purse over her shoulder and was getting up just as Ghaith came in.

"Hey, baby," he said. "Leaving early?"

"Yes, I finished up as much as I could, and I need to get out of here."

Even though they were in a relationship, he was a prude about her hours. He was very specific about work, expected everyone to work their asses off, and was very stingy with money. He did keep to his word with most payments, but she still had to fight him tooth and nail for raises and bonuses, even though she'd been instrumental in increasing their budget by millions in less than six months. She deserved compensation.

"It's not five o'clock yet," Ghaith said, looking at his watch.

"No, it's not. In fifteen minutes, it'll be five. I didn't take a lunch break, as usual, and I am going crazy being in this place all day alone. So I am leaving."

Ghaith smiled at her. "It's all right, habibti. I was just wondering where you're going in such a hurry." He walked over to her and put his arms around her, taking her purse off her arm. With his lips on hers, Jenny immediately grew warm inside, remembering the time he'd come into her office and taken her on her desk.

125

Pulling away from him, Jenny laughed. "I'm meeting Kimberly soon, baby."

She was aware that she was using Kimberly again as a lie, but it was the only alibi that he accepted. He hadn't even met Kimberly yet, but Jenny actually was starting to get to know her. She, Kimberly, and Chloe had become a little trio at Premiers on Friday nights when Ghaith had family time with his "parents."

He grabbed her again and kissed her hard on the lips. "Okay, baby." He released her and walked over to the door, holding it open for her. "Where are you guys going tonight?"

"Just to her house." Jenny smiled sweetly. In fact, she didn't even know exactly which building Kimberly lived in. Jenny had picked her up a couple times, but with Abu Dhabi parking and traffic, she'd always ended up waiting at a hotel parking lot a few blocks away.

"But I've hardly seen you this week. I came here to surprise you and take you out tonight."

"How about tomorrow night?" She nestled into his arms. "I miss you, too."

"Can't you cancel your plans?" Ghaith hardened against her as he kissed her neck.

Jenny thought about it for a moment, but she and Alberto had messaged about ten times today—quirky little text messages that made her laugh. She didn't want to detour their chemistry, plus she wanted a night out. If she went out with Ghaith, they would just have sex at her place and order takeout. Tomorrow she would be mad again, when Ghaith was not with her, and she might mess up her chances with Alberto.

"Sorry, baby, we made these plans weeks ago, and it's the only night we can meet up."

"Alllll right." Ghaith smiled. He grabbed her laptop bag off her shoulder and walked out of the office after her. "Tomorrow it is, then."

☙

Jenny and Alberto had decided to meet at the sushi place at Bliss Resort. Jenny had snuck in a quick gym workout to feel fresher, and it had made her hungry, too. She looked at the menu and picked out a couple of items. She would be doing the ordering, since Alberto had never before eaten sushi.

"Hey, beautiful." Jenny looked up and saw Alberto walking toward her, smiling.

He looked even more gorgeous in regular clothes than in workout clothes, and Jenny felt her breath catch in her throat. He was wearing jeans, a form-fitting T-shirt, and trendy shoes. Jenny loved that Europeans—and Arabs, for that matter—wore nice shoes. There was just something about it that set them a step higher than most American guys. She smiled at Alberto when he leaned down to kiss her on the cheek.

"Hi, handsome," she said, echoing his greeting while he sat down. "You are going to love this! Do you want chardonnay or pinot grigio?"

He grinned. "You pick."

"We will have a bottle of pinot grigio to start, as well as the dragon roll, sashimi, and seaweed salad," Jenny said to the waiter who'd come up to the table.

"I'm starving." Alberto licked his bottom lip and kept staring at Jenny. *Man, he is hot.* "Well, then you are going to love this."

She tilted her head to the side and moved her hands off the table as the waiter opened the bottle of wine and poured a sample. She gestured for Alberto to try it. He smelled it and sighed, then took a little sip, swishing it around in his mouth.

"Perfect." He smiled at her and winked.

She couldn't stop grinning. "So how long have you been in Abu Dhabi?"

"About a year. How about you?"

"I've been in the Emirates for a while, but I've just moved to Abu Dhabi recently."

"Where else have you been? Dubai?"

"Not even close. Talefa." Jenny smiled ruefully. "It's a tiny fishing village near the Saudi border."

"Wow, that sounds interesting." Alberto let out a high-pitched laugh that made Jenny wince. "So tell me, what is the most interesting thing that happened to you there?"

Jenny thought about it for a moment. "Well, when I first moved there, I had to go through all the bureaucratic bullshit to get my driver's license. I had to drive from the field site office into the main town in Talefa to get water and coffee for the office with no license. I was the office bitch." Jenny rolled her eyes.

"I bet you were." Alberto laughed loudly.

Jenny furrowed her eyebrows at his clumsiness, which was so different from Ghaith's smooth ways. "My boss knew I didn't have a license and he didn't care, as long as I was just going to 'downtown' Talefa. But he made me use drivers to Abu Dhabi." Jenny crossed and uncrossed her legs, easily taking over the conversation.

"Okay, so what happened?" Alberto had sat back in his chair and extended his long legs, so that his foot touched her heel.

"Well, I sort of reversed into a van in a parking lot on the main street." Jenny cringed.

"Oh, shit."

"And of course a cop just happened to be sitting at the intersection, practically right next to me."

Alberto's eyebrows went up as the waiter set down their food.

"Yeah. Exactly. So I called the wife of one of the guys with whom I worked, who worked at a school in town and actually had a local driver's license. The school she was working at was just around the block, so she walked over in her abaya and passed me her driver's license while the cop was checking out the damage." Jenny picked up her chopsticks and took a bite of the sushi roll.

Alberto grinned, and she could see his neat white teeth. "You used someone else's driver's license?" He picked up his fork and took a bite of the sashimi. "Mmm ... Wow, this is great. Sorry. Please continue."

"That was the plan." Jenny smiled and went on. "So I had to go to the police station for the paperwork, and they asked for my driver's license, of course. I knew that if I didn't have one, I would be in big trouble. So I handed it to him, but he kept looking back and forth from the driver's license to me. Finally, he finished the paperwork and charged me a small fee. I was so relieved that I almost passed out. But when I got up to leave, he started laughing at me and said, 'Not same face, not same face.' You see, this lady has a very narrow face and I have a round face. So the only thing I could think of saying was, 'I've gained a lot of weight.'"

Alberto busted out with his high-pitched laugh again. But this time, instead of annoying Jenny, it filled the room and made her giddy. "So he bought the story and just let you go?"

"Oh, he didn't buy my story, but he did want to buy me something else. He asked me out for a coffee, so I gave him a wrong number."

"Wow, girls in this country have it so easy." Alberto chuckled and tapped her heel again with his foot as he finished his glass of wine.

Jenny reached for the bottle and refilled both of their glasses. "So now that you've heard about my illegal actions here in this country, what do you do here in Abu Dhabi? Please don't tell me you are a cop."

"I'm an engineer." He picked up his wineglass and saluted her in thanks. "And what about you? What do you do, besides lie to the police and smash up cars?"

Jenny laughed. "Business development."

"Of course. I was going to guess that or teaching. Half of the expats I meet here are in business or education." Alberto took another bite of the sushi. The plate was nearly empty now. "This really is amazing. I am so surprised that I've never tried it before!"

"I'm glad you like it." She grinned at him, feeling prickles up her spine when he began circling the bottom of her heel with his shoe. The tablecloth ran all the way to the floor, and the motion seemed like a sexy private joke that they were pleasantly enjoying.

"We might need to get some more food," he said, motioning to the empty plates. "So your boyfriend won't mind if you are out with another guy?" He looked at her speculatively.

Jenny felt her cheeks redden. She picked up the empty wine bottle and quickly changed the subject. Did dating an Arab to whose home she had never been invited qualify as being in a relationship? Of course, whenever she was with Ghaith, it felt like they were on the cusp of an engagement. But when they were apart, the feeling dissipated and she felt single. It was almost as if Ghaith wanted her to feel that numbing separation.

"Well, I was thinking more about your girlfriend. She must not get jealous much." Jenny was finally able to put a sentence together and deliver it with confidence.

"Oh, I am a very single man." Alberto licked his lips, reminding Jenny of something Ghaith would do.

Wanting to quickly change the topic, Jenny blurted out, "Why don't we go upstairs to a club and get a drink?"

"Sounds good." Alberto raised his hand for the waiter, and they both got out their wallets to split the bill.

Downside to Europeans, Jenny thought, pulling out a few bills. She stood up, and he grabbed her hand and led her to the second floor. Looking at the row of clubs, Jenny opted to go into a bar she had never before visited, the door of which was manned by a couple of bouncers.

"Um, I don't think we can get in there," Alberto said, peering at the bouncers. "Isn't that a private club?"

But the wine had made Jenny confident, and she silently concocted a simple plan. A line was already forming at the door, which made her want to go in even more. When they got closer to the bouncers, she let go of Alberto's hand.

"Excuse me," she said to the bouncers, warmly but without smiling. "Is Mohammed inside?"

The two bouncers looked at each other and then back at her. The bigger of the two looked at her intently. "Ah, yes, did you want to go in and see him?"

"Yes." She motioned back at Alberto and continued, "Mohammed invited us to have a little business discussion." Mohammed was one of the most common Emirate names, so there was roughly a 75 percent chance that a Mohammed owned the club or was a regular VIP at the club.

The bouncer unfastened the red gate, and Jenny and Alberto walked by the bouncers and into the club. When they were out of view, Alberto grabbed Jenny's hand and spun her around. "That was amazing!"

"I know!" Jenny let out a giggle. "You owe me a shot!" *Screw buying my own drinks.*

"Absolutely! Of course, that will be after your glass of champagne, because we are celebrating that sneaky entrance."

Thank God, he has some manners after all. Jenny smiled at him.

As the long queue had suggested, the club was absolutely packed and hard-core hip-hop bounced around in the heavy air. The club was very dark, with flashing lights and four stages at different levels, creating a multidimensional dance floor. On the main floor, Jenny realized a startling fact—Alberto couldn't dance. At first she thought he was just drunk, or maybe he couldn't dance to hip-hop, which wasn't unusual among Europeans. But she soon figured out that he simply couldn't dance.

They raised their champagne glasses in a toast, and Jenny continued to dance while Alberto bounced around next to her. As the alcohol in her system intensified, she found Alberto's flapping around funny and free. She had been around too many suave men since she met Chloe, and now she was having fun crashing a club with this tall, dark man. He sure as hell couldn't dance, but he was definitely handsome. As they downed shot after shot, they screamed into each other's ears, trying to have a conversation despite the noise. Alberto's words came out in little accented bites that sweetly warmed Jenny, as if they were rolled as artfully and precisely as the sushi they had eaten hours earlier.

At one-thirty in the morning, they stumbled out into the parking lot. Jenny couldn't feel her cheeks and knew she was very drunk, but she couldn't stop giggling during the entire stumble to her car. Neither, she noticed vaguely, could Albert.

"Jenny, just share a cab with me," he said for the fifth time. "We can't be driving like this."

"No, no, no. I am fine. I live like literally five minutes from here. It would take an hour for a cab to get here, and then I would have to figure out how to retrieve my car at seven in the morning." Cabs were notoriously and bitterly battled for in Abu Dhabi, especially at this time of night.

"Oh, no! We have to work tomorrow," Alberto croaked in a slurred voice, as if realizing that they had to work on a Thursday was an epiphany. "Text me as soon as you get home. And drive, like, ten kilometers per hour. The whole way. Okay?"

Jenny laughed. "Okay, but you need to do the same for me. You live a lot farther away than I do."

Alberto was suddenly quiet, and Jenny sobered slightly, noticing the change in the atmosphere. She looked up just in time, as he awkwardly stumbled forward and kissed her. Pulling back sheepishly, he smiled. But then his eyes hardened and he kissed her again, this time deeper, and his long tongue stroked the inside of her mouth with passion and confidence.

Jenny wasn't able to enjoy the intimacy, however. Even drunk, she couldn't numb the thought of Ghaith. If he saw her kissing another man, he would have a fit.

They pulled apart naturally, and Jenny knew that Alberto could stay over at her house. That would be a smart move for both of them, safety-wise, but she wasn't about to sleep with him. The kiss and the date had actually made her realize she wanted to be only with Ghaith. Maybe moving in with Ghaith wasn't such a bad idea after all. *I must be drunk to be having these thoughts.*

"Be sure to text me." Her statement immediately snubbed out the flame of passion in Alberto's eyes. He had obviously thought that they would be hooking up tonight.

"Uh, okay." He looked away, and she knew it would be awkward to see him at the running group again. Maybe she would just stick to the hashes from now on, since he didn't go to those.

"Good night." Hurriedly Jenny got into her car, shutting the car door too soon and catching her dress in the door. *Fuck it.*

"All right, good night." Alberto waved goodbye to her, turned, and began walking toward his car.

She hadn't even offered to drive him to his car. She was a twat, but she needed to get home. She felt like she had been caught red-handed, even though no one else was in the parking lot. Tomorrow night with Ghaith was going to be painful. The guilt of kissing another guy was going to be worse than the hangover she was sure to have. Jenny moaned, knowing that she couldn't rewind time to straighten this out.

ℂ

Luckily the hangover took precedence the next morning. With each pounding of her head, Jenny beat back the fuzzy memory of the kiss, burying it deeper and deeper in her memory. Then her luck improved even further, because Ghaith was pulled away to some emergency meeting and had to bail on dinner. Usually this would have upset her, but this time it was a prayer answered.

Then she got a text from Ghaith: "Sorry for missing tonight. Pack your bags and be ready tomorrow morning. Weekend trip. X."

Maybe she was being rewarded for feeling guilty and for not going any farther with Alberto. Maybe Ghaith could somehow sense the intensity of her regret and her new commitment to him. Maybe the kiss had been a good thing, a gift of enlightenment that helped to seal her future with Ghaith. Maybe, just maybe, he would feel Jenny's strong commitment this weekend—and divorce his wife first thing next week.

CHAPTER 31

A week later, Jenny woke up to Ghaith's regular Friday morning phone call and realized she was in a relationship with an asshole. Not just any asshole, but a married one. An asshole who had two kids, was "separated" from his wife, and supposedly lived with his parents—his Arab, Palestinian-Jordanian, *very* Muslim parents.

"My mom found your shirt. You know, the see-through one that goes over your bathing suit?" His voice was sharp. "I mean, this isn't what I needed after today, and now I have to talk to her. She asked me, 'Is this the American's?' You know how women always want more information."

There was a distinct pause in the conversation—signifying something, although Jenny wasn't sure what. A flurry of thoughts ran through her head as she waited for him to speak again.

Then Jenny's sleepiness lifted, and she clearly saw Ghaith for what he was. *He is hiding me! I am his bloody mistress! How did my shirt end up in his suitcase? Why was his mother unpacking his suitcase? Oh, he's too tired to deal with me, but I've never met his mom?* And finally, *I don't even know where he lives!*

Ghaith let out a pitiful, tired sigh and drawled into the phone, "I don't have time to deal with this right now."

Jenny realized that Ghaith was *actually* upset—as if his mother had never noticed that he stayed somewhere else half the week and was gone for long weekends.

"Did you leave your shirt in my suitcase on *purpose?*"

Between one breath and the next, Jenny experienced an instance of complete clarity. At that moment, she actually wished that she *had* intentionally left the light pink linen shirt folded carefully like a swirly-handwritten letter depicting, in romance-novel fashion, the sultry details of their weekend lovemaking. If only she *had* intentionally left something that Ghaith's Arab, very Muslim mother would not want to read. By now, however, the woman had probably washed and ironed Jenny's light pink shirt, imagining what Jenny looked like. *At least she has a better blueprint than I do,* Jenny thought.

"Yeah, that's what I did. I put my shirt in your suitcase on purpose, because I know your mother does your laundry. I wanted her to find out about me, just so you would have such a fucking shitty day." Jenny hung up with a satisfactory stab at the "end call" button. She tried to turn her phone off, but it immediately began vibrating again and Ghaith's picture came up on the caller ID.

"Fucker!" Jenny yelled, and then switched her phone off.

She was sick and tired of being a secret. Obviously Ghaith was lying to his parents about where he was going. *Why aren't we using condoms? Regularly?! And, for that matter, why are we even having sex? Lies, lies, lies.*

"Jenny, what are you doing?" she whispered in the quiet of her flat, putting her hands over her eyes to stop a tear from rolling down her cheek.

CHAPTER 32

The hotel surpassed Ghaith's expectations. The room was one of the nicest he and Jenny had shared so far, and it was perfect for her birthday. The thing he liked about it most was the bathroom, which was huge. There was a large footbath in the center, a large double-sink area, and a large enclosed rain shower, and the room opened into the living and dining room area.

The hotel room itself overlooked a polo ground complete with horse stables, yet it wasn't far from Dubai's downtown clubs. After they checked out the room thoroughly, oohing and aahing like little kids, Jenny took out the Keurig espresso machine and grabbed some Irish whiskey from the minibar.

"To freshen us up." She smiled as the soft whirring of the machine started up.

Lighting a cigarette, Ghaith put his feet up on the coffee table next to the window and looked out at the horses. This place was magnificent. He smiled. He hadn't really wanted to come down to Dubai, since he knew it meant he would be away from Michelle, his new American girlfriend, but Jenny had pouted. Now that they were here, however, he was a little relieved. The past couple of weeks had been stressful at work. And with Ramadan coming up soon, it would be harder to be away from home, so he had to take off the precious time while he could.

Jenny walked over and handed Ghaith his mug.

Ghaith looked up. "Thank you."

Jenny looked amazing, her hair ruffled and her makeup a little faded. She looked so comfortable with herself, so confident in their relationship. It made him want to get a little more comfortable with her. He took a short sip of his drink, savoring the mix of liquor and strong coffee. Then, setting it aside, he reached for Jenny's mug and set it down next to his. Grabbing her hands, he pulled her down onto his lap and felt her strong thighs tighten over his.

"It's good," he said, "but you taste better." He kissed her and then led her hands to his shirt, which she dutifully began unbuttoning.

CHAPTER 33

Hakeem, Ghaith's friend, came to the hotel later that night. He was Jordanian and seemed nice enough, but Hakeem and Ghaith spoke Arabish, a combination of Arabic and English, and Jenny couldn't follow along with what they were saying. Moreover, it was her birthday, and she didn't want to entertain someone she had just met—in their hotel room. She sighed heavily and finished off her glass of wine. *The nerve!* She could hardly believe that Ghaith and Hakeem wanted to stay in and talk, or that she'd had to persuade Ghaith to go dancing with her.

Jenny went into the other room and looked at her reflection in the high-tech bathroom mirror. She looked frustrated and tired, so she washed her face. Glancing into the main room, she noticed how the men looked comfortable, sitting there nibbling leftovers from the feast, drinking wine, and smoking cigarettes. Ghaith was still in his bathrobe, and the way he was leaning back on the daybed made him look like a king. He was propped up on one elbow with the top of his bathrobe open and his curly black chest hair tumbling out. He was chewing on a toothpick and talking to Hakeem, who sat upright in a chair, fully clothed, grinning and nodding emphatically. That arrogance that enveloped Ghaith— sometimes it disgusted her.

Jenny shut the door and changed clothes. Since she had gained weight, she had bought a new black dress. Definitely black. The alcohol always painted a better picture, though, and Jenny felt confident in the way the dress exposed the length of her back. Her hair swung back.

There was something. Something ... She couldn't quite put her finger on it. It was that feeling that she got after dating a guy for a while, when she started sensing that maybe it wasn't working out. She pushed the thought away and began brushing her hair. *I want this.* Jenny looked around and remembered how childlike she and Ghaith had been when they first got to the hotel. Maybe she was just tired.

Ready to go out to the club, Jenny walked back into the room.

"You should work for me," Ghaith said to Hakeem, and gestured toward the ceiling.

"That would be great," Jenny said. And she did think it would be good. Having someone at work who was a friend of Ghaith's and who knew about their relationship was good. Also, Hakeem seemed to be slightly starstruck by her.

As if confirming her hunch, Hakeem looked sheepishly at her and smiled.

"All right, boys," Jenny said. "Let's get up and get going."

When Ghaith looked up at Jenny, his mouth fell open. Apparently the new black dress was a hit, and she had brushed her hair so much that it was shining. She knew she looked on point.

"*Mashallah*, habibti," he said. "You look amazing!"

However, it took Ghaith so long to get ready that by the time they reached the club in Jumeirah, the doors were about to close. All the clubs Jenny knew about in Dubai shut down at two o'clock in the morning, so they just went back to the hotel.

Jenny lay on her back in bed, freshly showered and staring at the ceiling. Ghaith had told her to go up to the room while he walked Hakeem to his car. Now it was almost three in the morning. What was taking him so long?

ഇ

When Jenny woke up, she had an overwhelming need to pee. The room was still dark and the clock read *five o'clock.* She reached across the bed, but the sheets were cold. Still no Ghaith. She got up, used the bathroom, and then called him. His phone was off. Worry began to overtake Jenny, even though she was used to his disappearances at random hours of the night. Ghaith needed only a few hours of sleep and still had energy all day. She had no idea how he did it. He escaped the grim reaper more easily than she did. But she wasn't always sure what he was doing when he disappeared. Mostly, he said, he went on walks. To where? She had no clue.

Jenny drank some water and then lay in bed, unable to fall back to sleep. Then she heard the door open, and Ghaith stumbled in. "Ouch," he said. She heard a crash and then giggling.

Jenny lay on the bed and felt anger replacing her worry.

"Oh, you're up," he slurred.

"Where were you?" Jenny snapped.

"Just sitting with Hakeem. We started talking and neither of us could sleep, so we sat downstairs and played cards."

"Are you serious? On my birthday, you'd rather be downstairs playing cards with some guy? I was *worried.* I tried calling you, but your phone was off."

"My battery died," Ghaith said eventually, his face lighting up. It was obviously a lie.

"The fuck it did," Jenny said softly while Ghaith walked into the bathroom. She turned off the light.

After brushing his teeth, Ghaith climbed into bed and spooned her, then began stroking her shoulder. Brushing off his hand, Jenny turned onto her stomach and fell asleep.

CHAPTER 34

It was so hot that sweat was dripping between her shoulder blades. *Whoever said the desert is not humid was wrong,* Jenny thought. Even with her car's air-conditioning cranked all the way up, she was still sweating. It didn't help that the American Oil Company parking lot had absolutely no shade. Ghaith *still* hadn't finished processing the paperwork for her work visa. If she had a work visa, she could get a gate pass and wouldn't have to wait around in this hellishly hot parking lot all the time.

She should really take off her blazer, but it pulled her whole outfit together and covered the weight she had gained. She was up to 145 pounds, the heaviest she had ever been. She was running upward of thirty miles a week, but the weight was still creeping up. All the heavy drinking was catching up with her—that and the takeout she got from the gym every night. She always ordered a healthful meal, but they automatically gave her four fresh bread rolls with any meal. And despite promising herself she would eat only one, all four rolls would be gone before she got home. No matter what. Obviously her carb monster out of control. The only way to stop eating the bread was to stop taking it.

Jenny watched a truck drive out of the gate and pull up next to her. Jim waved at her through the window. He was extremely handsome, and they flirted whenever she came by to drop off invoices or pick up a payment. There was something about Jim's crooked smile that made Jenny smile back. Despite his perfect handsomeness of white-boy America, Jim had something original that wasn't perfect—and *that* made him interesting and even more attractive. Originally from rural Virginia, he still lived a simple lifestyle, based on what he told Jenny in their short but enjoyable conversations. He was very different from the other people she met here. If she had met Jim back in the States, he probably would have bored her, even though he was cute. But here, he was familiar and comfortable.

As Jenny opened the door and got out of her car, Jim jumped down from his truck, landing right next to her. "Hey," he said, smiling that infectious crooked smile.

"Hey, how are you?"

"Yeah, good." Jim scanned her body with his eyes, and gave her a wide, Cheshire cat grin, his crooked mouth straightening out. "What have you got for me today?"

As Jenny leaned into her car for the documents, she could feel his eyes on her ass. At least one thing looked better with the extra weight.

"Payment request for the initial IT work," she said, handing the folder over to him.

Jim opened the folder, still looking at her out of the corner of his eye. "You know, we are going to have to go out there and see some samples of the databases running other programs." He looked down at the paperwork and then smiled at her again. "Do you think you can plan a day for us? Soon? It would be nice to hang out somewhere other than this parking lot."

"Sure." Jenny shuffled through her purse and took out her iPhone. "I'll confirm with Ghaith and the subcontractor, but we can tentatively plan for later this week." She entered the date in her calendar and reached for the signed documents.

"These prices look fine, as long as the products are in good working order," Jim said. "So what have you got going on next weekend?" Even though Jim couldn't leave the compound unless it was for work, he was genuinely interested in her life in Abu Dhabi—or at least he seemed to be.

"Well, I'm going to stay at the Atlantis with some friends." It was only

Sunday, the first working day of the week in Abu Dhabi, and it was going to be a long week. "Ramadan begins tomorrow, so we got a great deal."

"That's awesome! Man, I wish I could get off this compound and come with you. But I will see you at Iftar next week, right?"

"Yeah, I've got the ballroom booked at the Bliss Resort." Iftar was the breaking of the sunup-to-sundown fast, and hotels like the Bliss Resort were notorious for having the most decadent buffets the entire month of Ramadan. Jenny had scored a great deal, and she was excited about organizing this event for the multitude of American men who would be there.

Jenny wiped the sweat away from her forehead. She hadn't eaten at all today, and she was starting to feel a little light-headed from the heat.

Jim nodded, as if reading her mind. "All right, Jenny, let's get out of this heat. I'll see you next week for sure, but let me know if I can see you later this week as well."

That crooked smile made her want to kiss him. Looking at Jim, Jenny couldn't help but wish things were a little different. She smiled at him. "Will do."

Sliding back into the car, Jenny felt relieved to escape men for the time being. She could feel sweat gathering in her high heels. Jim gave her a small wave and jumped back up into his truck. In the driver's seat, he turned and smiled one last time, and then gestured for her to go. Sweat dripped off his forearm when he waved, and Jenny felt a desire to wrap her hands around those sexy forearms. *Such a gentleman,* she thought. Even though Jim probably couldn't leave until she did, the gesture still seemed chivalrous. Jenny promptly kicked off her heels and yanked her skirt up, easing the gas pedal down.

Ramadan. She took in a deep breath. She was starting her own Ramadan a day early and with a fast. A ten-day fast. Nothing but lemon, maple syrup, and cayenne pepper mixed into water. This was going to be good! And she quit smoking—again.

ॐ

Back at the office, Jenny filled a glass with her lemon, maple syrup, and cayenne pepper mixture and looked at Ghaith's new iPhone. Since it had a camera, he couldn't take it on the compound with him today, so he had left it with her. This was the first time Jenny had had access to his phone without him, and she looked at it suspiciously. As if reading her mind, the phone began to ring.

"Hello?"

"Uh, who is this?" The woman on the line spoke with a slight Arabic accent, and she was obviously very irritated that Jenny had answered the phone.

"This is Ghaith's, um, secretary. He's on the American Oil Company compound right now and had to leave his mobile. Can I take a message?"

"I'll call back." The woman hung up.

What the fuck? Jenny held the phone out and looked at it as though she had been slapped. Hmm … *Angry woman on the other line, completely not expecting me to answer.* Her thoughts immediately went to Ghaith's wife. Not separated after all?

Jenny couldn't help herself. She began to scroll through Ghaith's text messages. There were some from Jenny, but her name wasn't saved, just her number. *What the fuck?* Ghaith had a picture and his own ringtone on her phone, but she was a random number on his?

Not far down, she found the number that had just called. "Hey, baby, I am here at the airport. Come and get me."

Farther down, "Hey, baby, I need three thousand for the flight." And Ghaith's response, "Done."

Further down, from Michelle, "I'm coming." And from Ghaith, "I'm downstairs."

Then an even earlier text from Ghaith. "I know a great place for a stake dinner and wine, and I want it to be with you." Jenny's heart was racing, but it skipped a beat when she read this text. Ghaith had sent her this exact same text. She remembered it because he had misspelled the word *steak.*

Jenny kept scrolling through Ghaith's texts and reading them. There were more texts to and from more girls, and more calls to and from their numbers. Jenny felt sick.

As if on cue, Ghaith walked in and saw her looking at his phone. He turned pale. "What are you doing?"

Jenny looked up. For a split second, the only thought in her head was how adorable he looked wearing that baseball cap. Then she hurled the phone across the room, but failed at hitting him in the face.

"Whoa!" Ghaith successfully dodged the phone.

"You motherfucker!" She stood and backed up against the wall, continuing to scream at him. "You lying, stinking motherfucker! How many girls are there? For how long!?"

Running over to Jenny, Ghaith grabbed her by the shoulders and kissed her on the head. "No, darling. Only you, sweetheart, only you!"

Jenny shoved him away as hard as she could. She kept screaming at him, but her words had stopped making sense. "I'm so stupid!" she finally said, groaning, and then the tears came. Ghaith tried to comfort her, but she shoved him away again.

"Fuck off! You can't touch me anymore. You aren't allowed to even come *near* me!" She grabbed her purse and stormed out, with Ghaith running after her.

Jenny made it into the elevator without him and let out another little groan when the doors shut. She had always suspected Ghaith was still with his wife—but not with other women. When the elevator opened, she was still shaking from anger and shock. The stairwell door slammed open opposite her, and Ghaith sprinted out, panting. He really needed to quit smoking.

"Jenny!"

She just kept walking toward her car. Then she fumbled for her keys, beeped to unlock the door, and slid into the driver's seat.

Ghaith was next to her by then, and he caught her door so it wouldn't close. "Jenny," he gasped. "You can't just leave. Where are you going? I love you, habibti."

"I'm sure you say that to the other girls I saw on your phone," she said evenly, refusing to look at him.

"No, sweetheart. Look, I can explain everything. Just let me explain. Don't leave like this."

"Let go of the door."

"Please, I am begging you. Let's just go back upstairs and talk."

Jenny finally looked at him. He was sweating and had a desperate look on his face. She could either slam his hand in the door, or she could get out and meet with him. Sitting there and looking at him, she realized she couldn't bring herself to leave. That was how much she loved him. That was how much it would hurt. *Fuck, I'm in deep.*

"We aren't going back upstairs." If she agreed to that, he would just wear her down with flattery and kisses, doing everything he could to make love to her and distract her from his flaws. And she would probably fall for it, just like she had every time before. "We can go in there." She nodded toward a small Lebanese restaurant a few doors down.

"Okay," Ghaith said, smiling a little, relief washing over his face.

Jenny felt defeated. She needed space to process this, away from his bullshit—but she wanted answers, too.

It was still early afternoon, and they were the only customers at the restaurant. An overweight Lebanese man, with a cigarette in hand, sat watching an Arabic sitcom on TV. He seemed annoyed when they walked in. Jenny winced at the smell, because she was really wanting a cigarette. The withdrawals were hitting her at an exponential rate as the shock started to wear off.

"Two coffees," Ghaith said to the guy, who was probably the owner. He didn't take his eyes off Jenny.

"Just water for me, actually." Jenny looked away from Ghaith's eyes.

The owner grunted, got up out of his chair, and walked over to the kitchen. He yelled in Arabic at a young Indian boy in the kitchen, who flinched and then began banging around some dishes.

"So what the fuck, Ghaith?" Jenny swung her head around and looked him directly in the eyes. "What the fuck?" Jenny repeated, surprised at her own calm voice. "Who the fuck was calling you today? And why the fuck did you text her that you had sent her three thousand dirham?"

He looked a bit taken aback. Were there so many girls that he wasn't even sure who she was talking about? As he took a breath, Jenny couldn't tell if he was contemplating telling the truth or devising another lie.

"The girl who called when you answered the phone."

"Your wife, you mean?" Jenny couldn't help sneering.

"No, no. I told you, we are getting a divorce. The girl who called is from Tunisia. I, uh, met her when I traveled there a long time ago, and I got her a ticket here so that I can completely end it with her."

Jenny's jaw dropped. The most bizarre part of this blatant lie was that she knew how racist Ghaith was about other Arabs. "She's Tunisian, and *you* gave her money?"

"Well, she doesn't have a lot of money herself, and she wanted to see her grandmother who lives here. So she is here and I was going to end it. Then she can have a nice visit with her grandma."

Jenny almost laughed. This was so ridiculous. "And what about *Michelle?*"

"She's just a girl I met one night when you wouldn't go out with me. Nothing has happened. We just talked."

"Really? Then why did you pick her up and take her to The Meat Kitchen? You sent her the exact same text that you sent me when we went."

"What? No, I didn't."

"You spell *steak* wrong, Ghaith. I remembered the text you sent me, and it was the same one you sent her. Do you take all your dates there?"

Ghaith let out his hearty laugh, which uncontrollably lit Jenny up. "Oh shit, I spell steak wrong?"

Jenny leaned back in her chair and crossed her arms. Were there no limits to his arrogance?

"Okay, okay," he said. "I asked her there, but we never went."

"I saw the text, Ghaith. You picked her up."

"No, she never came downstairs. I sat in the car waiting for half an hour, and then I left. She stood me up."

Jenny shook her head.

The owner walked out of the kitchen and turned up the television to cover the noise of their conversation.

"Look, I've got to go." Jenny pushed her chair back and stood up.

"Wait, we haven't even gotten our coffee yet." Ghaith reached out toward her.

"You ordered coffee. I didn't."

The best thing was that he couldn't follow her out, because he wouldn't leave a bill unpaid. At least he was devoted to some kind of good, Jenny thought, listening to him call her name.

She slid into her car, reversed without putting on her seat belt, and then threw the car into drive, causing the tires to squeal as she peeled away from the curb. *Fuck him,* she thought, and stepped harder on the gas. The car accelerated to one hundred miles per hour and then started to shake slightly. *Fucking Toyotas.* The shaking began to even out when she hit 120. Her exhilaration and fear at the speed soothed her, as the wheels finally matched the rhythm of her rapidly beating heart.

At home, Jenny threw on some workout clothes and her running shoes. Grabbing her iPod, she got back into her car and drove down to the Corniche, the boardwalk that bordered the city and the sea. If she didn't go running right now, she would call Chloe, drink way too much, and smoke an entire pack of cigarettes. Or she would stay home and eat an entire pizza. She needed to process everything, and getting her endorphins going was the best way to do that.

As soon as her feet hit the pavement and the music poured into her ears, Jenny began to think. She and Ghaith had never had the exclusive talk, but it had been highly insinuated. They were a team. He had said he wanted to build his empire with her, and he hadn't meant just professionally. They were an item, even though they hid the fact at work and in front of the American guys, to remain professional.

When Jenny had gone out with Alberto that one time, and even when she was out with Chloe, in the back of her mind she had always known that she was with Ghaith. To be honest, she had figured he was still living with his wife. The perpetual weekly arguments drove her crazy.

She would leave church group on Saturday evenings thinking she should end it with Ghaith anyway. But when she went back to work on Sunday mornings and saw him, she knew that it wasn't going to end that easily. On Sunday and Monday evenings, she would go hashing or out for drinks with the girls, and that was when she started thinking about him being with his wife. But apparently, it wasn't even his wife she should be worrying about. It was random women—Tunisian women and girls named Michelle. *Paying for her ticket to break up with her?* What bullshit.

And Ghaith was giving her zero security in anything. He was still married! *Fuck him.* Then the reality hit. *Shit.* They didn't always use protection. If he didn't consistently use protection with her, he probably didn't with the other girls either. Jenny's pace picked up. *Oh, shit.* She needed to schedule a pap/STD test as soon as possible.

ॐ

That thought was still bothering Jenny the next morning. All of a sudden, she started itching in places she had never before itched. She swore she felt a burning sensation and was emaciated, although that was probably from the liquid diet and run, rather than from a sudden advanced case of HIV.

Jenny had taken into account her own actions, and she felt guilty about the kiss with Alberto. Maybe a little tinge of guilt for flirting, too? But it wasn't like she and Ghaith were engaged or married—and she had never seen the commitment *from* him that she had given *to* him. Hooking up with all those girls *and* being married. Jenny shook her head. Man, she was vulnerable. And here it was—the reason she had never before been with an Arab in her four years in the Middle East.

All her friends in Kuwait who had dated Arabs or were still dating them—same thing. Their charismatic lovers were married, which was one reason they had never been home to meet the family. In Abu Dhabi, it was the same thing. Another friend of Chloe's, Zooey, a beautiful blond

American, had echoed these issues just a couple of weeks ago. She was fed up with catching Ali, her wealthy Emirati boyfriend, in strange lies. But Zooey knew she was going to give in and go back to Ali because maybe, just maybe, he was telling the truth. The only thing Zooey could do to get back some self-esteem was go out with Chloe and the girls and get approached by other guys.

The problem was that these other guys were just like Ali—and Ghaith. Smooth liars.

Jenny sighed and dragged herself out of bed, wanting to drink her maple syrup recipe and go for a run before going to the clinic. That was the only thing she could control right now. She turned on her phone, saw that she had fourteen missed calls and three messages from Ghaith, and immediately turned it back off. She needed space right now. Finishing her drink, she threw on her running clothes. But when she opened the door, she nearly tripped over a large bouquet of flowers.

An involuntary smile appeared on her face as she stared down at the beautiful roses. The only time Ghaith had given her flowers was when they first met and went out with Veronica. On the drive back to the hotel, he'd stopped at a gas station and grabbed a bouquet that had seen better days. Her smile increased as she thought of how he'd looked that night, on one knee outside the passenger door, singing in Arabic and offering her the wilted flowers.

She picked up the humongous arrangement of multicolored roses and baby's breath. Carrying the vase back inside her studio, she set them on her little corner table, and the overpowering smell of roses immediately filled the small room. Written on an envelope placed in the midst of the flowers were the words "I'm sorry." Jenny hesitated and looked away. Her fire to go for a run returned, but her lack of self-control burned more intensely as she ripped open the envelope.

Ghaith had written her a four-page letter in a tiny, flowing script. "Jenny, you are my star … You are my only one … You are the one I love … I want to marry you … I want to build my empire with you and only you … I want to have children with you … Possibly losing you has made me realize how much I need you and can never lose you ... You are the love of my life ... I screwed up, but have you never screwed up? I want us to commit to each other."

She knew he was full of shit. Nevertheless, she could see them together in her mind's eye. They had this amazing relationship where they could talk for hours and hours every night, and they were a dynamic duo at work during the day. She had never known of any other relationship with such an intense synergy, and she'd certainly never before experienced it herself.

When she put down the letter, she couldn't hold back a small smile.

⁖

When the Egyptian doctor came into the room at the clinic and asked what was going on, Jenny finally broke down and began to sob. She poured out the entire story to the doctor, who looked a little bored. But it was impossible for Jenny to not say everything once she got started.

When she finished, the doctor just nodded and looked at her with a sad smile. "Yes, dear, I am sorry about your affair. But are you pregnant?"

Jenny's eyes widened. She hadn't even thought about that. She'd been more concerned about having STDs. "I don't know," she said, and then began sobbing again.

The doctor raised her glasses to glance at Jenny's chart, and then patted Jenny's thigh lightly. "There, there, this happens all the time. Don't worry, we will find out. But let's do a pregnancy test, too."

An excruciating couple of hours later, Jenny got her test results. Chlamydia—positive. Pregnancy—negative. HIV/AIDS—negative. She cried in both relief and anger. *Fuck.* She had chlamydia, but at least she wasn't pregnant and didn't have AIDS.

Jenny went to work afterward, since she still had payments that needed to be made at the American Oil Company, and she wasn't going to be unprofessional just because Ghaith was a cheating bastard. She was angry as hell about the chlamydia and was going to tell him, for sure. He was so selfish. Now all these women had chlamydia, probably including his wife.

Ghaith's car was parked outside the office tower when she got there. No doubt, he was waiting to see if she was coming in today. Jenny slammed the car door hard and went inside. *Clack-clack* went her heels.

CHAPTER 35

Ghaith had thought the messages and flowers would have eased Jenny's fury a few notches. But when he heard her stomping down the corridor toward the office, he knew otherwise. She looked even angrier than she had the previous day. He stood aside when she came in, but she pushed passed him anyway, her elbow catching him in the ribs, along with a whiff of her perfume.

As soon as he closed the door, she started screaming. "Did you even think about diseases? Do you know I just came from the doctor? Do you have any idea what disease you have?"

Ghaith's face completely dropped. This was unexpected. What diseases did he have? He cringed, thinking about his wife—his *pregnant* wife—and began to panic. "What are you talking about?"

"So your other girlfriends have it, too." Jenny grabbed some paperwork off her desk. "Go to the doctor and find out for yourself." She tried to walk past him again to get to the door, but Ghaith blocked her this time.

"What is it, Jenny?" he demanded. "What's wrong?"

"Like I said, find out for yourself."

But Ghaith wasn't going to let her pass. "Either you're lying or the test is wrong. I told you, I don't have anything."

"Think again. Look, I've got to get these to the compound. Get out of my way."

"What is it, Jenny?" He could feel himself starting to sweat.

"Chlamydia. You need to let your girlfriends know—and your *wife*."

Ghaith backed up and felt his shoulders thud against the door. He let his weight sink backward, surrendering to the knowledge that he probably did have something. But what was chlamydia? He'd never even heard of chlamydia. "What is that?"

"It's an STD. What do you think?" She furrowed her brow at him.

For a minute, Ghaith thought she was going to spit at him. It wouldn't have been the first time a woman did that. "How do you spell it?" he asked, with a deflated sigh.

"Seriously?" Jenny pushed him to the side, opened the door, and walked out to the hallway. He had been leaning against the door, so he stumbled to keep his balance. She charged past him and left without looking back, murmuring under her breath, "Thanks a lot, asshole."

Ghaith stared as Jenny stormed down the hallway and into the elevator, and then just hung his head.

∓

"Well, I could have gotten chlamydia from you." Ghaith knew immediately that he shouldn't have said that, even if it was true.

Jenny snarled at him.

"Baby," he said, "I'm just saying. I swear it's only you I love." He'd persuaded her to let him talk to her after the meeting with the subcontractors, but she agreed only to let him sit in her car.

Ghaith had been to the doctor the previous day and had already started giving his pregnant wife the pills. He told her they were a special multivitamin that she needed to take because there was a flu going around. Laila had been so sweet. She'd been pleased that Ghaith was thinking of her and the baby, even though he was hardly ever home. Ghaith had held her for several minutes, then kissed the crown of her head and left to meet Deema.

He really couldn't lose Jenny, though. She was too important to him—too important to the company. He would have a very hard time replacing her. The oil company guys loved her, and she was great with them. Finding a blond American with whom he could build his empire was amazing, and besides, he wanted to marry this girl. Of course, she would be his second wife, but she would get used to it after a while. They always did, especially if they had a child together.

Ghaith really wanted to get Jenny pregnant and have a son with her. He already had three girls—well, two and one on the way. This chlamydia was probably from his scandalous love life, but it really *could* have been from Jenny, who must be screwing around. She had hung out with Chloe at Premiers, and she went out with different friends all the time. Or maybe she'd had unprotected sex with someone in the past. After all, she was American.

"Are you fucking serious?" Jenny glared at him, and he could feel the intensity of her anger. "I gave it to you, when you are sleeping with— remind me, how many girls? Three? Four? *Five?* The number keeps getting higher and higher."

Ghaith laughed and gazed tenderly at her. "Baby, baby, baby, it wasn't like that at all! I am just stating a fact. Did you have a check the last time you had unprotected sex?"

Jenny looked away.

Ghaith knew he could not push too much further, because she was getting increasingly agitated. Man, she could be a hard person to soothe. Laila would have calmed down as soon as she got flowers, but Jenny hadn't even mentioned them.

"It was you," Jenny said. "And even if, by some *miracle*, it wasn't, that doesn't change the fact that you are fucking around left and right."

She wouldn't let him change the subject, Ghaith realized, and he began to get angry. *Fine.* He slapped the dashboard with his open palm and then raised it into the air, facing her. "I swear on the Holy Quran that I have slept only with you since I met you!" Then he looked at her with all the intensity he could muster. He could see her eyes soften ever so slightly as she held his gaze.

"You promise?" Jenny whispered.

Ghaith could tell she actually wanted to believe him, so he nursed it for all it was worth. "Yes, habibti, my dear. Mashallah, you are beautiful. I love you. I swear to you." He took her hands in his, leaned over, and kissed them. "I swear."

"So what happened with the Tunisian girl who flew in?"

"I met her last night and ended it with her, just like I told you I was going to."

"You actually met up with her?!" Jenny recoiled, pulling her hand from his as if she had been stung.

"Habibti, I told you I was going to end it with her! I had to do it in person."

"Where?"

"That coffee shop, ah, the Coffee Bean. She cried, and then she left. That was it."

The reality was that he and Deema had met at the Coffee Bean and then made out in the car, but he knew he couldn't sleep with her. After Googling *chlamydia* and learning about it, Ghaith didn't want to pass it on to someone else. So he had just told her that he had a job in Doha for the next seven days. Deema was upset, of course, but he had given her a gold bracelet. He knew he had to do something if he wasn't going to sleep with her, so he had gone to the gold souk between seeing the doctor and meeting with Deema.

Jenny looked out the window. "I still don't see why you paid for her ticket."

"Sweetheart, I told you. She is poor."

Jenny asked, "What about Michelle?"

"She's nothing, sweetheart. I am just not going to return any of her calls."

"And your wife?" Jenny rolled her eyes.

"What about her?" Ghaith began to get upset. "I've told you a million times, we aren't together anymore. We are just waiting for when we can get a divorce."

"Well, when will that be?" She looked at him with disgust.

"I've told you, it's complicated." Looking at her, he softened. "It's the kids. Every time I tell my family I am going to get a divorce, they take us to counseling. My father gets all upset and smacks his cane on the ground. Then, all of a sudden, we are in a counseling room and the Imam is telling us to stay together because of the kids."

"And so you are just never going to get a divorce?"

"I am going to, but I have to calculate the right time. Soon, soon." Ghaith took Jenny's hand, and this time she let him have it, although it fell limp in his hand.

"When?"

"I am looking at the spring."

The thing was, Ghaith really did want to be with Jenny. He wasn't going to divorce his wife, but if it came down to it, he might set the paperwork into motion. Maybe then Jenny would marry him. But he would never divorce his pregnant wife. Laila was a good woman and she put up with everything. She took care of his girls, still cooked for him, and got mad at him less and less.

Sometimes, though, he imagined living with Jenny and their children in America. He did love Michigan and still owned a house there. Sometimes he thought he might like to move them there. But then reality would hit and he would think about Laila. Besides that, it was a good thing to have more than one wife. Or, if he was sleeping around, it was good to actually *marry* the girl. Men like Ghaith could afford multiple families, and his friends and competitors would be jealous of him for having both Arab and American wives.

"That's like seven months away. Why wait so long?"

"It will give me several months to work out some financial issues."

It was already August, and Ghaith knew that if he began to pressure Jenny, she might marry him well before the spring. At least, that was his plan.

His thoughts swung back to the present when Jenny put the car in gear and drove toward the industrial office.

"Well, you better take your medicine," Jenny said, with each word becoming harder and sharper.

Ghaith could tell she was getting angry all over again. "Habibti …" He let the word hang in the air, as if to magnify it. "Will I see you tonight?"

Jenny let out a long sigh. "I don't know."

She was in her business clothes, and Ghaith was suddenly glad that in all this time, she'd never left a job uncompleted and she'd never quit. She had been so professional at the meeting today—icy toward him, but he knew it wasn't noticeable to the other men.

Of course, she really *couldn't* quit yet. He was still processing the paperwork for her work visa.

CHAPTER 36

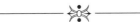

That night Jenny met Ghaith at an Italian restaurant. They sat on the patio, where she drank a glass of water and he ate a plate of pasta and drank a few beers, clearly his Iftar being unconventional. She had agreed to meet him because she knew they needed to figure out how to work together—or whether she was going to leave. She had been too pissed off to start looking for other work, but the problem was that her work visa was still tied up with Ghaith's lawyers.

Jenny noticed, not for the first time, that Ghaith was cockier when he was drinking. He went on and on about things happening at work or in his family—siblings and parents, never wife or children. He apparently didn't notice Jenny getting more and more annoyed, or maybe he was so self-centered that he actually didn't notice or care.

Finally, Ghaith walked Jenny back to her car. She quickly got inside and shut the door, glad to be away from him. By now, she was even more frustrated than when she had arrived at the restaurant. She had just sat there and listened to his arrogance for nearly an hour. Of course, nothing had been resolved about them.

Ghaith tapped on the window. "Habibti, look. If we are going to continue, I need you to forgive me and we need to move forward and be truly committed to each other." He was serious now, and the lightheartedness of his dialogue had worn off.

"I am still angry with you."

"You can be as angry as you want, but I need forgiveness so that I can move forward with you."

Jenny let out a sigh as he walked around to the passenger side of the car and sat next to her. She rolled up her window and turned on the air-conditioning, feeling the cool air prickle her skin.

"Jenny, I love you."

Ghaith didn't say those words often, and somehow they sounded even more foreign than his Arabic endearments. It made her want to believe him. It made her hope, even if the emotion was so fleeting that it seemed to flutter in her chest only for a moment, before her quickening heartbeat chased it away.

"We need to move in together," he went on, with his eyes misting over. "I've been looking at this nice apartment. Please, habibti, I want to live with you and come home to you every night. I never want to lose you again. I couldn't bear it."

Jenny felt her hope sprout into a lovely blossom. But it was a delicate blossom that required much nurturing, and she knew it could wither in a second. "You know I'll move in with you only when you finalize your divorce," she said, with downcast eyes and in a voice so low, it was almost a whisper. When she looked up, Ghaith was smiling.

"I love you," he mouthed silently. For once, he didn't argue with her and try to justify his allegedly broken marriage.

CHAPTER 37

The East Coast sea breeze felt like freedom. Toward the water's edge, the sand firmed up and Jenny was able to regain a good running pace. She was back in the States only for Eid, the short holiday that fell after Ramadan, but it was refreshing to get out of the Middle East and back to North Carolina. This was her family's first reunion in a neutral location and everyone was having fun, for the most part, until they started asking questions about Ghaith.

He had actually talked about joining her and meeting her family, but that was before the affairs. Besides, she'd known that her extremely conservative brother's family didn't create the best environment for her married, Palestinian boyfriend. And she couldn't even begin to think about the sleeping arrangements. Now Ghaith's excuses about his conservative Muslim family seemed almost reasonable—and, more shockingly, believable.

This morning, Jenny's brother had asked her to join him on the veranda, and they had sat there sipping coffee and watching the sunrise together. Paul had eight children and a full-time job, which didn't leave him much time for one-on-one conversations with people, so this morning had felt like a treat to Jenny.

But she'd also been nervous, especially when Paul started asked questions—hard questions—about the kind of life she was living in Abu Dhabi. When he asked where she stood in God's eyes, all her prayers for truth came back to her as a weight in her stomach, and the coffee began to taste like ash.

"Well, I feel kind of far from God right now." She had answered honestly, tears creeping into her eyes. "But I've really been searching for truth. You know, I'm really praying for God to reveal Himself to me. Islam can be such a peaceful and devout religion, and being around it all the time has made me really question my own faith."

"I'm sure that is true, but it's not God's truth," Paul said, quickly getting to the real point of his conversation.

That word *truth* struck Jenny hard, as if he had been reading her mind.

"What are you doing over there besides partying? I mean, look at the guy you are seeing. Married? Come on, Jenny."

Obviously Paul had talked to their sister and knew the story, but he wasn't condemning her. When he looked Jenny in the eyes, she felt love and caring flow out of him, and tears began to pour down her cheeks. Jenny had always been very sensitive, especially with her brother, and this morning had been no different.

"They are Muslims over there, Jenny. 'Do not be unequally yoked,'" Paul quoted from scripture. "It'll never work out. You'll just end up with a broken heart."

At that moment, Jenny felt that Paul was right. It was easier to see things clearly when she had distance. And talking with her family, none of whom were familiar with Middle Eastern culture, she saw her situation more for what it actually was—or what they thought it was. At the same time, however, Jenny knew that people in the States, including her brother, just didn't know what it was like in the Middle East. Being a Christian in America was easy, but isn't our true faith revealed only when we test it?

"It's okay, Paul. I am seeking the truth, believe me, much more than you think."

"Are you, Jenny? Or does evil get into your life so easily because you're surrounded by it over there?"

"Don't worry, okay? I've got this." Jenny smiled at her brother as her tears began to dry in the wind. Paul had looked away, and she looked at his light shadow of facial hair and wondered where the other guys like him were—guys who cared.

Settling into the rhythm of the waves, her feet pounding against the sand, Jenny knew leaving Ghaith was the best thing to do. She was even looking for a new job. His empire had become her dream too, and she knew that they could do extremely well together professionally—but only if they were together intimately. Their professional success was driven by their unique symbiotic relationship—or maybe it was not unique at all. Jenny thought about Beyoncé and Jay-Z, Brad Pitt and Angelina, and other great couples working together. Maybe she and Ghaith had that same rare and amazing chemistry.

CHAPTER 38

The white dress Jenny wore when she walked into the office reminded Ghaith of the one she'd worn on their first vacation together—pure white, showing off her gorgeous tanned legs, but not as short. She had lost a little more weight and seemed to have put on some muscle, too.

When Jenny caught him eyeing her, Ghaith felt himself blush. He was nervous again, just as when they'd first started dating. It had been only ten days since he'd seen her, but he realized at this moment that she was *the one*. He knew he loved her before, but now he knew he couldn't live without her. If she made him feel like this after only ten days apart, how could he be apart from her for a lifetime? He couldn't fathom the thought of ever losing her.

"Mashallah," he said, looking her up and down. He might have been nervous, but he was not shy. She had never responded to him when he poured out his heart to her just before she left, but he could tell that she was happy to see him. Her family had probably tried to convince her that relationships with Arabs were wrong and that leaving him would be the smartest thing she ever did. This wasn't his first relationship with an American woman, so he knew how things worked. Ghaith had been heartbroken when Jenny left, though. He really was in love with her. When he said those words to her in the car, he had felt them in his heart.

"How was your trip?"

"Very refreshing."

"You look amazing." He headed around to her office as she went inside, and said to her, in a quieter voice, "I, on the hand, am miserable without you. I can't sleep. I can't eat. Nothing has any flavor or interest for me any longer."

Ghaith gave his best pout and knew that she had missed him, too, as she looked up with a smile in her eyes. When she rested her gaze hungrily on his lips, he couldn't help himself. "Habibti, please let me just hold you for a moment. I am so sad without you."

Wrapping his arms around her, he felt her tense slightly. But then, in the smallest flicker of time, she surrendered her body to him and melted into his embrace. He noticed how they fit together perfectly, her head against his chest as though his body was made just for her. No gaps. No second thoughts. Just them. He then began kissing her head, slowly moving down to her neck and ear. Jenny softly moaned, and then he felt her tense up again as she pushed away from him.

"Okay, so here's how this is going to work." She looked around to make sure the guys in the conference room couldn't see them. She still had a grip on his hips—an arm's length away, as if she didn't trust herself to be too close to him but couldn't completely let go of him. "While I was gone, I really reevaluated my faith and my life."

Ghaith swallowed. He really did not want to have a religious debate right now.

"If you really love me and you really want to be with me ... No sex."

Ghaith let out a laugh. "What?"

"No sex," Jenny repeated.

"For how long?"

"Until we get married. That's the direction this is headed, right? Either marriage or not being together?"

Ghaith smiled coyly at her and bit his lip. All of a sudden, he wanted her. Desperately. This girl never ceased to surprise him. *This could be a fun game.* "Yes, marriage is where this is headed. I can do abstinence. Even if *you* want it, I am not going to give it to you."

He felt his heart suddenly begin to soar. They were back together and she was considering marrying him. He was clearly being rewarded for not being with Michelle and Deema. And the abstinence? What a fun twist. Oh, yes, this would be a game, because he was sure she would be begging for it long before he was. Jenny was one of the most sensual people he had ever met, which was something he loved about her. She enjoyed sex completely and unabashedly. And anyway, he still had Laila to meet his sexual needs. He wouldn't feel guilty about sleeping with his wife, but he wasn't going to sleep around with any other girlfriends any longer. That was a big commitment for him.

Jenny smiled and nestled back into his arms. "I think you'll be pleading first." She pressed herself against him and slid her hand down to his backside, squeezing before she pushed herself away. Winking at him, her green eyes darkened against the bright white of her dress.

Oh, yes, this is going to be fun.

CHAPTER 39

For the last twelve weeks, Jenny's training had been complicated by massive hangovers, a cheating boyfriend, and an STD. So it did not surprise her that the run was much harder than she had originally anticipated. The intense heat and the crappy route were fundamental factors in the difficulty of the race, she was sure. They had to do a double back—not once, but twice. The Abu Dhabi Half-Marathon from hell. She saw some people walking in front of her and knew they were suffering the same negative self-talk she was going through. She slowed down even further and walked for about a quarter mile, falling into the predicament of the mind being stronger than the body.

She was thinking about Ghaith. Where had he been last night? At the same time, she hadn't minded that he wasn't around, because she had wanted to eat a good dinner and go to sleep early. He had asked her if she wanted him at the finish line today, but she had said no because this training had been such a private matter for her. Also, she needed to rush off to the annual desert hash right after the race ended.

Now she regretted telling Ghaith not to come. It would have been nice to know that he was waiting at the end of this, that someone she knew was there for her.

Around the next bend, Jenny picked up her pace and cranked up her music. It was on. The final three miles. The last double back of her first half marathon.

CHAPTER 40

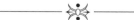

The typical hash raunchiness was refreshing, and Chloe wouldn't have hesitated to say she was having the time of her life. The theme this year was music, with a matching themed alcohol to go along with each genre. Chloe, Karen, and Jenny were manning the Rasta stop. They were already completely bombed on rum, since they'd been both making and sampling it for the past hour.

Chloe pulled her hair into a ponytail and climbed the sand dune to see where the other stops were. Apparently there was a band at the rock-n-roll stop, and she wanted to have a look.

"Hey bi*a*tch, nice ass!" Jenny yelled at Chloe.

Chloe turned around and saw Jenny dancing on top of the jeep and yelling, "Let's get this party started!"

Laughing, Chloe stumbled to the bottom of the hill and took a bite of the rum-soaked fruit, then climbed onto the jeep with Jenny. Karen threw on a Rasta wig and cranked up the music.

"I shot the sheriff, but I did not kill no deputy!" They all sang together as Karen climbed on top of the jeep. Soon, all three of them were swaying and bumping hips. Just then the hasher in the lead ran up between the dunes and stopped dead in his tracks.

"Holy shit!" he said, laughing. "From the other side of this dune, it just looks like you guys are dancing on top of the sand dune. I didn't realize you were on top of a jeep!"

His Australian drawl was melodic and danced around playfully in Chloe's mind. She recognized this guy as Short-Long from other hashes, but his hash name was all she knew. He had a sprinkling of freckles across his nose, and his strawberry-blond hair fluttered in the breeze. The fact that she noticed these details, in spite of him being bare chested, surprised her. When she let her gaze fall to his torso, he noticed and flexed his muscles. She had an animalistic sensation, and the image of herself straddling him and licking him wafted quickly through her mind. *I must be drunk.*

"Grab a drink," Chloe said, gesturing toward the table.

"Hmm." Short-Long studied the various drinks and grabbed a rum with watermelon.

"While you're down there, can you hand me one, too?" Jenny asked.

"*Three* watermelon rums!" Chloe called.

"Well, for fuck's sake. All the other stops are *serving* people!" Short-Long laughed, filling three more cups with watermelon rum and handing them up one by one. As Chloe leaned over to grab the drinks, she noticed him looking up her shirt. So she pushed out her chest a little farther.

"Mind if I come up?"

"Not at all." Chloe winked at him.

He crawled up on the hood and started dancing as close to Chloe as he could. With four adults on top of a jeep, they were so close that she could smell the clean scent of his sweat.

"You know, you're our virgin." Chloe smiled, teasing him. "You might want to keep it that way." She pointed across the horizon where there were more hashers running toward them.

"Oh, shit. Yeah. All right, ladies. I think you are the last stop, but definitely not the least." He winked at Chloe. "See you at Religion tonight." He crawled down from the jeep and gulped another drink, chewing on a bit of the watermelon. "See you all!" He gave a little salute, and then started running.

"Overachiever!" Karen yelled at him.

"Wannabe American!" Jenny shouted.

Chloe couldn't see the hashers any longer since they were now climbing up the other side of the dune. She sang along with the lyrics as loudly as she could and then ate the rest of her watermelon. She idly wondered if Mohammed would like Jenny's drunken jeep dancing moves—and then laughed aloud. He probably had a satellite up in the sky right now, recording their every move. Singing a little louder, she flipped off the sky.

⳹

As the evening wore on, packs of hashers reached the Rasta stop, each one more exorbitantly drunk than the last. Chloe was completely inebriated. She kept having laughing fits with tears running down her face unabashedly, and she knew it was one of those ugly laughs that probably looked more like she was crying. But the rum drinks seemed to be playing a clever trick on her, and she just couldn't help herself. She felt so free, and she knew Jenny did too. Her friend's phone had been ringing earlier, but when Chloe pointed it out, Jenny insisted it wasn't working and avoided meeting Chloe's eyes.

Chloe effortlessly read that signal. Jenny was avoiding Ghaith and trying to pretend that part of her life didn't exist, same as herself. *Fuck Abu Dhabi right now*, Chloe thought. For that matter, fuck Dubai. Right now, that part of her life seemed completely surreal. None of these girls were wearing makeup or too-tall heels—and none of them were trying to hook up with rich Arabs. Eventually, Chloe would have to go back to the real world, but not tonight.

Jenny, on the other hand, had stopped drinking at sunset when they packed their Rasta table into the jeep. They drove back to the main sand pit, already set up for Religion, and sat around the bonfire and chatted. Eventually Jenny leaned toward Chloe.

"Hey, chick," she said, sounding sober. "I've gotta go."

Chloe smiled sadly. "Why are you running off? Stay. Sleep out under the stars with me."

"I've got to go to work in the morning."

"Nobody works six days anymore. Just tell him you can't go in. That's bullshit!"

"I know, it sucks. But I'm also tired from the half-marathon I ran *this morning* and from drinking in the sun all day."

"You crazy bastard." Chloe sighed. "All right, I'll let you go—but only if you agree to come to the F1 with me. I scored some tickets." She couldn't help but smile. She'd never been able to keep a secret for long, and the Formula One was all anyone was talking about this month. Abu Dhabi was the final city for the F1, which was being held at the new Yas Marina Circuit on the outskirts of Abu Dhabi. The F1 wasn't just race cars zipping around the Yas, though. Kanye West was playing, the infamous Sky Tent would be there, and all the rich Emiratis would be docking their boats in the marina where the real parties would be. Of course, Mohammed had given her some tickets, and she would be inviting only a select few girls.

"You did?" Jenny laughed, punching the air.

Clearly still a little drunk, Chloe thought fondly.

"Yes! I will *so* be there."

Jenny put her cheek against Chloe's and kissed the air, the typical hello and goodbye greeting. Then she got up and walked away.

Chloe watched Jenny's silhouette drift away from the bonfire, and then she saw Jenny's phone light up. Obviously Jenny was finally checking her texts and missed calls.

Then Chloe looked across to where Jenny had been sitting and saw the Canadian guy she'd been talking to staring at her.

CHAPTER 41

Ghaith was pissed off. Jenny had told him the area of the desert where she would be, but she had not given him specific directions. Apparently those were hard to come by pre-hash. Ghaith had never before been to a hash. The only hash he had known about before meeting Jenny was the kind he liked to smoke with his brothers from time to time.

He hadn't even planned on going to the hash, but after calling Jenny's phone several times and getting no answer, he got curious. He had first tried to call her from Abu Dhabi to let her know he could not make it, but she didn't answer. Then he texted her. No reply. He called again. Still no answer. So Ghaith knew something was up. Jenny was always good at getting back to him unless she was mad or drunk or—with Chloe. She had run the half marathon this morning, and he figured she was pretty drunk right now and possibly hanging around with Chloe. So he got into his car and drove out to the desert, but in vain.

Jenny finally returned his phone call around one in the morning, when Ghaith was already home in bed. When he noticed his phone light up with Jenny's phone number, he had to get out of the bed, careful not to wake Laila, and walk outside to talk to Jenny.

"What the hell?"

"Hey you," Jenny slurred.

"Are you driving?"

"Yep, but I am almost back to the city. Where are you? Sorry I missed your call. I just got reception on my phone."

"Well, that would have been nice to know a few hours ago," Ghaith said, with frustration in his voice. "I drove out to the desert twice trying to find you, and I wasn't having any issues with reception on my phone."

"Hmm. Well, I don't know. I didn't think you were really going to come."

"Well, I did." Ghaith hadn't meant to snap at her, but he was pissed and jealous.

"Why don't you come over to my place in about thirty minutes?"

"No, I am already in bed." From the yard, he noticed the light turn on in his bedroom. Laila must've heard the door close when he went outside. "You've had a long day anyway and should get some sleep." He sighed and asked, in a gentler tone, "How was your race?"

Jenny laughed. "Oh, my gosh! It was horrible. It took me two hours, and it was so hot."

"Good. Good. Well, I wish you would not have driven tonight." A genuine worry crept into his voice. "Look, you've been drinking, and I need you to drive carefully, so I am going to get off the phone. Text me when you get home safely. I'll see you tomorrow, baby."

"Ohhhkay."

He could hear irritation set into her voice as if she knew the reason he mellowed out so quickly and was trying to get off the phone with her. He clicked the phone shut just as Laila stepped outside.

"Ghaith?" she asked sleepily into the night.

"Yes, habibti."

"What are you doing outside?" She tightened her robe around her in an automatic fashion, although it didn't quite fit around her protruding belly.

"I just forgot something in my car." Ghaith walked over to Laila and wrapped his arms around her, placing a kiss on her head. "Come on, sweetheart. Let's go inside and go to sleep."

CHAPTER 42

"Oh, you have to come!" Jenny said, adjusting her *jillayeh*. It was loose and ankle length, as tradition demanded, but Ghaith could see the crevice between her calves as she crossed her legs to adjust one of her four-inch heels.

Ghaith licked his lips meaningfully, stirring sugar into his espresso. Looking away he pursed his lips—his thinking face. The café they'd chosen was in the atrium of the Castle, their table directly beneath one of the largest domes in the world. It was decorated in a splendor of colored marble and twenty-two-carat gold leaves, a reflection of the wealth of the current generation of Arabs. Rich. Rich enough to build new dreams. Their cakes were drizzled with real gold too, bringing the old saying "You are what you eat" to mind.

Ghaith picked up one of the cakes, said the words aloud, and let out a little chuckle. "That is how the saying goes, no?" he asked Jenny in his almost perfect English, and then took a bite. He wasn't sure how he felt about eating gold, though. If his enemies knew he'd eaten it, they would kill him just to cut it out of him as soon as he and Jenny left the film festival.

All of a sudden, Ghaith became uncomfortable underneath all this gold, surrounded by gold, eating gold, looking at gold. Jenny's golden hair. Golden shoes. Suddenly there was too much attention on him, like a golden spotlight. People could be watching him.

"Yeah, that's how the saying goes. So let's embrace this richness and decadence." Jenny lifted a piece of cake and fed it to Ghaith, then licked the fork clean. "So strange. But you didn't answer my question," she said, pointing the fork at him. "We're going over to Karen's for dinner tomorrow night. Please tell me you can go."

"Okay, just let me know what time. I have something else I need to sort out beforehand." He mimicked her actions, picking up a piece of cake and feeding it to her. Reminded of the custom from American weddings, Ghaith grinned. He and Jenny were feeding each other like the stereotypical groom and bride.

Now that people were starting to fill the atrium, Ghaith felt more comfortable. The piano player ran his fingers across the keys, and music comfortably covered Ghaith as if it was a blanket. The golden air began to lose its frightening allure, and he reveled in the softness. He wanted Jenny now, and he didn't want anything else.

"We are like a family." He pulled her close to him and continued, in a whisper, "One day, we will have everything we desire, even a child." He swept back a lock of hair that had fallen across her forehead. "Mashallah, they will be beautiful."

He wanted so much for Jenny to be his wife and show him more of the world. At first, he hadn't wanted to come to this film festival. He was too nervous that some Emirati would recognize him or that his sister would be there to show off her latest fashions. Mainly, though, he remembered the night Jenny had taken him to the nightclub Premiers and how that slut Chloe had ignored him. He remembered seeing Chloe at Mohammed's yacht party several months before Ghaith met Jenny. Chloe had taken shots off another girl's stomach—body shots. And she hadn't been with anyone in particular, but took girls to Mohammed all night, including two girls for Ghaith.

In this dark theater, though, he saw nobody and enjoyed the film immensely. The film was about the Iraqi war through the eyes of war correspondents from Washington, D.C. Ghaith appreciated being exposed to Western culture without having to leave the comfort of the Middle

East. It was not at all like when he had lived in Michigan, where he had been focused on perfecting his English and adapting to culture shock. This learning was comfortable, and Jenny was a wonderful teacher.

℞

Mohammed adjusted his cuff links as he came out of the theater and cleared his throat as he rode up the escalator. Just behind him, his brother Abdul whistled softly and nodded across the atrium toward the café.

"Look," Abdul said, and Mohammed followed his gaze.

Jenny, Chloe's latest protégé, was sitting at a small table beneath the dome, looking very Arab in a black jillayeh. And was that Ghaith at the table with her? The last time Mohammed had seen him, they'd been fucking some Bulgarian girls on his yacht. Well, actually Ghaith had ordered them, but Mohammed had gone along for the ride. It was his yacht, after all.

He watched as Jenny giggled, feeding Ghaith some sweets, and then their conversation seemed to turn serious.

"Looks like that dancer has been hired," chuckled Abdul as the brothers stepped off the escalator into the atrium.

Mohammed was interested in Jenny, but not if she was out for hire. No, but his cousin Farhad would appreciate her.

"I've got the perfect job for her then," Mohammed said. He took out his phone and texted Chloe: "Bring Jenny to the F1 for Farhad. Cheers." He did not bother to put his phone away as he and Abdul walked across the atrium. Snapping a quick picture of Jenny, he then immediately forwarded it to Farhad. "My gift to you," he typed. They continued across the floor, moving away from Jenny and Ghaith.

Before they got across the atrium, Mohammed received a text from Chloe: "Sure, babe. A very suitable match. BTW I invited her last week, since I anticipated you asking. Do I get a bonus? X."

CHAPTER 43

"There will be traffic!" Ghaith dismissed Jenny's text as he walked up the stairs to her flat. He was late, but only by about forty-five minutes. Considering how long it took Jenny to get ready, he was really only about ten minutes late. When Ghaith knocked on her door, Jenny answered it almost immediately.

"Yay! You're here. Let's go."

Ghaith pushed her back into the studio, shutting the door behind him, and kissed her deeply, passionately.

"Let's just stay in." He slid his hand down her back and felt her soft skin exposed by the deep V-neck opening of the back of her dress.

Jenny pushed him away playfully. "Now, now. You promised me that we would go to Karen's for dinner and actually hang out with some of my friends."

"Okay, okay." With a crooked grin on his face, Ghaith looked her up and down. The tight, backless black dress she wore made his toes curl. It had been too long since he'd made love to her. He couldn't believe they were actually playing this abstinence game.

At the moment, however, his mind was still with Laila. Ghaith had felt his child move in her stomach that night. He had been reading the Quran, and the baby girl had kicked him. Looking up at Laila, he had laughed out loud, and she had beamed down at him with pride.

Telling her that he had to leave was hard, and he imagined what his life might be like when he married Jenny—divided and always trying to please everyone, including the children.

Ghaith looked at Jenny again. His desire stirred, shutting down any further thoughts of his Arab family. It had been so long, and seeing her in this black dress awakened his drive—the drive he had committed only to Laila and Jenny. He certainly was a changed man, holding true to his commitment to be with only his wife and the woman he would one day call his wife. But with Jenny wearing this little black dress, that day better be soon.

"Come on, I'm starving. You must be hungry too. You've been working all day. Why the late meeting anyway?" Jenny asked.

"I don't even need any food when I'm around you. You are my food." He grabbed her again and nibbled her neck.

She laughed tightly and, taking Ghaith by the hand, led him downstairs. "Yalla."

"How long will you make me wait?" He panted, but she didn't turn around, so he gazed at her naked back. Her shoulder blades moved rhythmically as she walked down the stairs, and he felt himself harden.

"You know our deal. And you thought I would be begging you first?" Jenny teased.

As they got into the car, Ghaith found the darkness comforting.

"Oh, hey, Chloe invited me to the FI next weekend," Jenny said. "I am so excited. Kanye West is going to be there!"

Immediately Ghaith's blood curdled. *Mohammed!* If Chloe had tickets, that meant she was taking Jenny to Mohammed's yacht. "How did she get tickets?" Even he could hear the bite in his words.

"I don't know. Through work, I guess. She always gets a bunch of perks from the company." Jenny looked out the window. They were both silent for a while, just listening to the Porsche changing gears.

Short of revealing previous affairs, Ghaith couldn't tell Jenny what he knew. He felt stuck. "Work? She gets a lot of really good perks, Jenny," he said with a sneer. "You know, she's a madam and she's just hooking you up with some guy. That's how you are getting that ticket."

"What?! Ghaith, Chloe's my friend. We said we wanted to go a while ago, and now we're going. It's a flipping concert!" Jenny's voice rose to a hiss. "Besides, I asked you to take me a couple of times, but you never wanted to go. Anyway, where the hell were you tonight? Not hungry because you just ate with your wife? Work meeting, my ass."

Oh, here we go, Ghaith thought. "Yes, work. We had a meeting. You know I am working on a bid for the bridge project." The gears shifted again and they both fell silent. Ghaith could feel the air in the car intensify as Jenny's words settled uncomfortably, making him sweat.

"When are you divorcing her, Ghaith?" she whispered.

Ghaith gripped the steering wheel a little harder. His wife thought he was going to Dubai tonight, working on a cost for an upcoming project. There really was a bidding project for an IT project. Jenny would be working on the actual proposal, but he was going to have to figure out costs.

This was why Ghaith was such a good liar—he took 90 percent of the truth and twisted it all into a lie. Of course, Laila didn't know he was working on this project with a woman with whom he was having an affair. But soon Jenny wouldn't be an affair—not that Laila would be much happier about there being another wife in the picture.

"Soon." He parked in front of Karen's apartment building, a tall complex glistening in the darkness against the Abu Dhabi skyline. He was happy to pause the argument, since Jenny always seemed to win when she pulled the marriage card. If only she knew what he had been doing.

ଚ୦

Jenny was a bit drunk. An hour after the revolving argument that she and Ghaith had in the car, she walked into Karen's apartment and immediately began slamming drinks. The alcohol helped her shake off the argument, or at least ignore it.

Ghaith sat on Karen's couch, quiet and uncomfortable.

Jenny was surprised to see he wasn't drinking. *Fuck him,* she thought.

He can go anywhere and do anything he wants to. But the minute I want to go out and do something fun—something I've been asking him to do with me—he gets all mad, just because it's with Chloe.

She'd known he wouldn't like it when she mentioned she was going with Chloe, but she was sick of lying to him. Since she'd taken sex off the table, their relationship had begun to feel real, and she didn't want to taint it with any more lies. Jenny wanted commitment, the real deal. She wanted what Ghaith had said to her so passionately in the parking lot that day so long ago, when he'd confessed his undying love for her.

Jenny couldn't help but wonder if he had been with his wife earlier tonight. She suffered through this insane jealousy at least once a week. When he spent the night at Jenny's house, she felt secure and knew he couldn't be with his wife. But the nights he didn't sleep over and she didn't see him, she felt certain that he was with Laila. This constant ebb and flow of emotions was exhausting.

And even if Jenny didn't want Ghaith to see Laila ever again, the fact that he never saw his daughters clearly demonstrated what a shitty dad he was. Sometimes he admitted to Jenny that he had not seen them in weeks, and she wondered why. Even when they went to Sharjah for meetings, he never stayed longer to see them.

Nor had she seen his condo in the city, a fact that she brought up as ammunition nearly every time they got into a fight. *I don't even know where you live!* Of course, he would play the culture card and say that because his mom was staying there, he could not take Jenny home with him. Palestinian men did not have female friends. He would properly introduce Jenny to his mother after they got married, but until then, it was just too disrespectful.

Most of the time, Jenny thought Ghaith was full of shit. *Fuck him! I can go out and have a good time with my girls and meet whomever I want to.*

"I had so much fun at the desert hash!" Karen said in her slurred British accent.

"Oh, I know. Me too! We're just destined to have a good time together, us three."

"I can't believe how drunk everyone was by the time they got to our Rasta station." Karen let out a long laugh. "Or should I say, how drunk *we* were? Seriously, making everyone dance on the jeep while they had a drink? Ours was definitely the best station. I'm still so sad we didn't win."

Jenny began to laugh, too. "Yes, that rum-soaked fruit was the best *and* the worst. I wish I could have camped out with you and Chloe, though. I was having the best conversation with that guy from Canada. What's his name, Rich? I know for sure only that his hash name is Wide Angle, and I'm a little curious to know what that means."

"Good ol' Wide Angle. He was asking where you went, you know." Karen sighed. "But you and your six-day workweek. I still can't believe you ran a half marathon in the morning, got completely blitzed in the afternoon, drove home that night, and had to wake up for work the next morning."

Suddenly Jenny became aware that Ghaith had walked into the kitchen to fill up his water glass, and she wondered how much of the conversation he had caught. Quite a bit, apparently, since he shook his head in disappointment and walked back into the living room where a few other people were talking.

Karen looked at Jenny. "Oh, shit."

Jenny just shrugged and slammed back her drink. "Whatever. Fill me up, bi*a*tch." She held out her glass.

Karen laughed. "Sure thing, ho."

CHAPTER 44

Things had been tense between Jenny and Ghaith the entire week, right up to the day of F1. Twice, already, they had repeated the same argument that had started in the car. Needing to release some tension, Jenny ran sixteen miles that morning. Surprisingly it went more smoothly than her thirteen-mile half marathon. Her feet beat against the Corniche, as if she was slapping Ghaith with each step for eight miles one way. During the eight-mile return, she mentally slapped herself. She kept playing the argument over and over again in her head as if she might find a secret solution.

The marathon was in a couple of months, and Jenny was training well and taking long runs weekly. While she ran, her interior monologue also ran, usually at full speed. *Stupid Jenny, he must be seeing other girls and/ or his wife ... I wonder if I should go out with guy X ... I am so in love with Ghaith ... What will my wedding dress look like?*

Sweaty and tired when she got back to her car, Jenny stretched and tried to focus on what she would wear today. She would need to take two outfits. The crappy thing was that she would have to either go home tonight or go directly from the F1 to work. She couldn't call in sick to work tomorrow, since Ghaith clearly knew where she would be. Having her boss as her boyfriend really sucked sometimes.

CHAPTER 45

The pre-F1 opening was an absolute riot in the Sky Tent on the previous night. Chloe couldn't wait to get back there and out of her apartment, where she had gone to meet up with Jenny and Aliya so they could take a cab to the F1. Chloe waited with Aliya, her rich Lebanese friend, who was Muslim in a way that meant she didn't drink—but she did just about anything else.

"When will she get here?" Aliya asked.

Chloe knew Aliya was talking about Jenny, who was keeping them waiting.

Aliya twirled a dark curl around her finger and then let it go. It bounced back into place as though she had never pulled it.

"Any time now," Chloe said, taking another sip of her drink. "She needs to yalla!" As she began to drift back into drunkenness, her hangover slipped away and she let out a sigh of contentment. Music wafted into the apartment as a car squealed to a stop in the driveway. Chloe grinned. The music stopped as the engine turned off, and then she heard a bunch of jingling as Jenny ran up to the door.

Chloe smiled even wider as she heard Jenny's heels. She was always so happy when her friends knew not to wear flip-flops to yacht parties. Some Western girls were beautiful but clueless about image. Not Jenny. She always knew how to dress, and that made Chloe confident of her selection.

Chloe walked over and opened the door. She kissed her breathless friend on the cheek. "Oh, babe, you look great!"

Jenny was wearing an Armani sundress, open low in the front to reveal a tiger print bikini, with simple gold bracelets and nude-colored heels that elongated her legs. Super classy with some trendy pieces. Perfect. And those legs! Farhad was going to love Jenny—and he was going to love Chloe for bringing her.

"Come on in, so I can fix a roadie. Then we're going to par-tay," Chloe said, ushering Jenny into the house.

CHAPTER 46

Yet another race car zipped across Yas Circuit and past Mohammed's yacht. *Zzzzzzzzt!* Slipping on his aviator sunglasses, Mohammed walked up the stairs to the top deck to prep for the yacht's barbecue. Even though he had three servants on the yacht, he liked to do this himself. In some small way, the laying of coal, the lighting of the fire, and the tender arrangement of the kebabs and chicken skewers made him feel more appreciated.

He often thought the modeling world might have been a better pastime, but this yacht and the popular parties it hosted generated a nice little side income. One of four yachts that he owned, it also served as a perfect brothel.

As another race car zipped by, Mohammed looked over the marina. Several yachts were larger and more expensive, but his was still on the higher end of the lot. People were starting to stir in the cabins, and he could hear girls' laughter between the whipping noise of the race cars intermittently speeding by.

His cousin Farhad had his yacht docked next to Mohammed's. He looked over to see if Farhad was awake from his late afternoon nap. Mohammed had gotten a couple of grams of ecstasy, this weekend's drug of choice, from Farhad on the previous day, and he couldn't wait to see the effects on his guests. Many a man would be thanking Farhad the next day. Mohammed was not the only yacht owner who had bought some.

When Mohammed lit the barbecue, a distinctive smell rose into the air—the smell of an impending party. As he waited for the coals to heat, he poured himself a drink of Johnny Walker Black, and then turned to watch a golf cart bumping over the grass toward his boat. There were three girls on it. His own girl had arrived the previous night and was still passed out in the cabin below. He was very excited for the real party tonight with these three women.

As the golf cart came closer, Mohammed could see their faces. Chloe looked striking in a colorful sarong, Aliya wore a strapless sundress, and Jenny was fresh and tan in an Armani dress. Farhad was really going to eat her up.

Mohammed watched as Chloe looked around, first taking in Farhad's yacht and then looking up at Mohammed's yacht. When she saw him, she gave him a playful salute, and he lifted his glass to her. All three of the beauties got out of the golf cart and teetered out on their heels. *Quite a little orgy we will have tonight*, he thought, laying the lamb and chicken on the grill. Almost immediately, he smelled singed flesh.

CHAPTER 47

Jenny wasn't entirely sure *why* she was kissing Farhad, but it felt amazing. Turning her head into the sweaty, pulsating crowd, she looked up at Kanye West and tried to gather her thoughts. She was several rows from the stage. Jenny knew she was missing her chance to go backstage as she saw Aliya and Chloe push forward, but she couldn't tear herself from Farhad's arms. His hands felt like they were melting into her skin and touching her very core.

The music was loud, and it was really hot outside, making Jenny feel dizzily enveloped in a dark red haze. Farhad turned her head back to face him and began kissing her again. His tongue was soft and thick, and she started to imagine what else would be.

What the hell, Jenny? Why was she making out with this guy she'd just met, when she was still thinking about Ghaith? She'd had only a few drinks and was oddly aware of her surroundings, but she wasn't drunk. She felt like every one of her senses had been amplified, and somehow that had made her powerless against Farhad.

Since they met that afternoon, Farhad hadn't left her side. Attractive, athletic, and slender with mahogany-brown eyes that had been focused on her during the entire evening. Jenny was flattered by his interest. Chloe had been yapping about him all week, and the whole thing felt oddly like a blind date. She'd probably been talking Jenny up to Farhad, too.

It was Jenny's own fault, though. She hadn't told Chloe the extent of her relationship with Ghaith. She hadn't wanted Chloe to look her in the eye and ask the two questions that she knew only Chloe would be wise enough to ask: Had she been to his house? And had she met his parents?

Jenny knew that Chloe had many expat friends who were in tragic, Arab-Western relationships. But she also knew that Chloe was fucking an Emirati, a man—as she'd told Jenny point-blank—with whom she would not let herself fall in love. That was Chloe's rule, and she hadn't broken it yet.

Jenny wasn't sure how Chloe kept her distance, but again, maybe that was just Chloe's choice. When Jenny had initially tried to share with Chloe some of her feelings about Ghaith, her friend had cut her off and spouted, "Never let them have your heart. We aren't Arab, and because of that, we will never really be part of their lives. You will never be an exception."

As if to prove her point, Chloe had introduced Jenny to Urma, a Swedish woman who'd given Jenny the number of a private investigator. Urma told Jenny about Abdul, her very wealthy Emirati boyfriend whom she had been dating for two years without ever meeting his family. Fed up with catching Abdul in strange lies, Urma had hired a private investigator, who had given her proof of Abdul's affairs.

Urma swallowed another drink and admitted to Jenny and Chloe that she was going to give in to Abdul's calls and go back to him. Why? Because maybe—just *maybe*—he was telling the truth when he said he loved her more than all the others. That's how much she wanted to believe him, despite his atrocious lies. Nevertheless, Urma carried around her broken heart like a bird with a broken wing. Only going out with Chloe and the girls, and being approached by other guys, gave her some level of self-esteem.

The problem was that these other guys were just like Abdul—and for that matter, just like Ghaith. Jenny sighed. She felt sorry for Urma and knew that this story wouldn't have a happy ending. But she understood Urma and obviously saw herself in Urma. Of course, Jenny heard what Chloe was saying and listened to Urma's experience. But when it came down to it, she retained a glimmer of hope that she was in a real relationship with Ghaith, despite his affairs and time away.

Jenny's thoughts returned to the present, where Farhad's lips were now kissing her neck. She automatically arched her back to meet his warm lips, finding it difficult to believe what was happening. She had not been this intimate with a guy since meeting Ghaith. Sure, there was that one-off kiss with the Portuguese runner, but they had not pawed each other like animals.

Farhad came up for air and looked at her hungrily. His eyes were even darker now, and his breath was coming fast as though he'd just been running. Seeing this hunger in his eyes, Jenny knew he probably saw the same in hers. She wanted him like she had never wanted anyone—with primal lust. Her desire for him was so strong that it made her panic, and she spun on her heels and marched away.

"Let's go, yalla!" she said. The other couple, Mohammed and Laura, followed her.

"In a hurry to get to the after-party at the Sky Tent?" Farhad asked. He let out a little laugh and ran up to walk right behind her, saying in a low voice, "I want that ass."

Jenny was somewhat taken aback by how blunt he was, and his intrusion into her space suddenly made her feel claustrophobic. As she walked farther away from the crowd, Kanye West screamed out, "Thank you, Abu Dhabi!"

Then her phone rang. Opening her clutch, she took out her buzzing phone. It was Ghaith. *Oh, shit.*

"Hi, babe," she said, trying to sound nonchalant, even though she was still trying to catch her breath from the kiss.

"Hey! Just calling to see how it's going."

She could hear the sting in his voice. For a moment, she thought maybe he was there and had seen her, and she looked around and swallowed. "Yeah, the show just finished, and we're leaving."

The words just tumbled out of her mouth. She couldn't believe that after only three drinks—*three drinks*—she was having a hard time forming words. She slowed down to let Mohammed and Laura pass her. Eventually Farhad walked past her, although he turned back and motioned for her to follow them. She couldn't figure out how to get anywhere from the concert hall on her own, so she followed Farhad.

"How's that bitch, Chloe?" Ghaith asked, his voice full of venom.

"I don't know. She went backstage. I'm with some other friends." The words left her mouth too quickly, and she mentally kicked herself for being so open with him.

"What other *friends*? What do you mean? She fucking left you?"

"Um, yeah. It was so crowded here and we got separated, so I am hanging out with this Canadian girl and her boyfriend and a couple of other people."

"What other people?"

"Just some people."

"I can't believe that bitch left you! You're going home now, right?"

Jenny looked up and somehow, as though she had levitated, was back at the marina in front of Mohammed's yacht. Crowds of people were running around in every direction, screaming and laughing, DJs played on every other yacht, and girls were dancing half nude. Jenny had to crush the phone against one ear and put her hand over the other, just to hear Ghaith on the other end of the line.

Up ahead, Farhad looked back at her, grinned, and held a finger up as if to say "Wait one minute." Then he walked onto his yacht.

"I don't know. Um, I don't see any taxis, since I am in the marina. I don't know where the taxis are."

"You didn't take your car?"

Even though he sounded far away, she could tell Ghaith was getting angrier by the second.

Suddenly Jenny felt something grab her leg, and she jumped and let out a little shriek. A white guy was on his hands and knees, ogling her legs.

"Those are the best calves I have ever seen. Can I touch them again?" he asked, with a British accent.

As Jenny walked away quickly, he crawled after her.

"What's wrong?" Ghaith asked. "Are you okay? What's going on there?"

"This guy is chasing me on his hands and knees. I don't know. This is so weird. I've got to go."

Before she could hang up the phone, Ghaith said, "Meet me at the front. I'm coming to get you."

Fuck.

At that moment, Mohammed walked off his yacht, four passes for the Sky Tent in hand. "Yalla," he said, and smiled at her.

Jenny promptly threw her marina pass toward Laura, Mohammed's girl. She still felt confused and claustrophobic from the music pounding all around her. She ran onto the yacht and was packing her things when Laura came in behind her.

"What's going on, Jenny?" Laura asked.

"I've got to go!" she screamed into Laura's ear. "It's work. I've got to be there in the morning and—fuck! The truth is that my Arab boyfriend is coming." Jenny glanced over at Mohammed, who was outside laughing with his arm around Farhad.

Laura gave her an understanding look. "Why can't you just stay for the Sky Bar party and then go straight to work?"

But Jenny was looking at her phone, not really listening. "Shit, he's almost here. Look, just tell them I got pulled into an emergency meeting. It's IT shit gone awry."

Jenny didn't even look back at Laura, too busy texting as she walked off toward the circuit to try to catch a golf cart back to the main hotel. But the first one she took drove her only in circles, and she realized she wouldn't be able to get back through the hotel without a marina pass—the one she had thrown back to Laura. She was dizzy again, and her paranoia was intensifying even though she was outside. Her heart was beating so fast, it scared her. Everything around her spun—the colors, the noise, and the lights from the yachts.

Finally, she broke down. "I've got to get out of here and to the main entrance!" she yelled at the cart driver. He looked at her with amusement, but finally found a way past the hotel and to a party bus that was going to the front of the hotel.

An hour and a half later, Jenny finally made it to the entrance. Ghaith sat waiting in his Porsche, frowning deeply. She could tell he was angry, angrier than she had ever seen him before. She was still so dizzy that she could hardly look at him. She tried to tell him what had happened with the golf carts, but he didn't seem to be listening.

In no time at all, they were swept back up into the same old argument about his wife, and how he still wasn't divorced, and how much he hated Chloe. Their screaming was so high-pitched that Jenny felt like she was swimming in it.

Then, quite suddenly, they were parked outside a building downtown with a bright neon sign that read "Florida Laundry." "This is where I live." Ghaith stabbed a finger toward the building, nearly poking her in the face.

Jenny looked around and tried to remember the landmarks, but she didn't know where they were at all. In fact, she hadn't even been aware that Ghaith was driving. They had been dating for more than six months and this was the first time he'd ever told her where he lived. Ironically, she was so bombed that she couldn't even read the street signs, except the glimmering "Florida Laundry."

Before Jenny could manage to remember—or for that matter, even look at—other landmarks, Ghaith shifted into gear and drove her home.

That was the first night he took her home without going up to her flat.

CHAPTER 48

It had been a week since Ghaith had picked Jenny up from the F1, a week since she had fallen into the passenger seat of his car, crying and saying she'd had only three drinks. She had definitely consumed something other than alcohol, and he wanted to find out which one of Mohammed's guys wanted Jenny. She had finally broken down and said that someone had kissed her, but she couldn't remember the guy's name.

Ghaith suspected she wasn't telling the entire story, but he'd won the argument. He knew she wouldn't be going out with Chloe again. He was definitely going to use the F1 night as a comeback whenever Jenny mentioned his wife from now on.

Another positive result of that awful night was that Jenny had invited Ghaith over that week, still apologizing for her behavior, and they had made love for the first time in two months.

What still bothered Ghaith, however, was that something *had* happened that night at F1. He had sent his cousin Latif to the Sky Bar Tent the following night, knowing that Mohammed would be there all weekend. And sure enough, Latif found him. The way Latif told it, when he showed Mohammed a picture of Jenny on his phone and asked if the girl was still available, Mohammed had started laughing.

"Let me ask my cousin," he said, gesturing to Farhad.

"Are you fucking kidding me?" Farhad said when his eyes landed on the picture. "That bitch split on me last night."

"I've never seen anything like it," Mohammed added. "She has a big dose of E, right, and my boy is all over her at the show. You should have seen her—clay in his hands. Then she gets this phone call and marches off, even though she has no idea where she's going. As soon as she gets back to the yacht, she packs her shit and just splits. I mean, who has a conscience on E? I had to find another chic for Farhad last night, and Chloe had to pay for it. Fucking bitch. I've never had a girl run off my yacht and not want to hang out at the party of the year." He shook his head, grinning.

"But you know what, Latif?" Mohammed continued, in a more serious manner. "Now I'm more interested in her than I was before. I mean, it's sexy to be so devoted, even when someone is dangling all of this before you." He waved an arm around the room.

When Latif told him what Mohammed said, Ghaith was relieved Jenny hadn't slept with anyone. Sure, he was pissed off that Farhad had been all over her and that they had dropped E in her drink. Mostly, however, he was flattered she'd left the party for him. Now he knew for sure that he had her wrapped around his finger.

CHAPTER 49

Chloe held Jenny's Chanel sunglasses on her lap and punched Jenny's phone number in her iPhone.

"Hello," Jenny answered.

"Finally. I've been calling you for weeks. What happened?" Chloe had been shocked that Jenny left the F1, until Laura told her about Ghaith.

"Sorry, I've just been really busy."

"I have your sunglasses that you left on Mohammed's yacht. Farhad was mightily disappointed you left."

Pause. "Yeah, I still don't understand why I was so bombed that night. It's not like we drank a lot, yet there I was making out with him."

Chloe cleared her throat and changed the subject. "So Laura said that Ghaith picked you up. I didn't realize you were so committed that you would miss the party of the year to go home with him." She put on Jenny's sunglasses and looked at her reflection in a mirror.

"Yeah, well, it just happened. And yes, he is married. And no, I haven't met his parents—but we really are in love."

Chloe's face dropped and she took off Jenny's sunglasses. "Jenny, you can't be serious," she spat. "That's a death sentence. Look, Ghaith isn't exactly who he says he is."

"What do you mean?"

"Let's just say that when you introduced him to me at Premiers, it wasn't the first time I had met him."

"What? How do you know him?"

"I've seen him on Mohammed's yacht. He buys girls, Jenny. He's not innocent, and you are not an exception." Chloe knew she was being harsh, but she wanted to save her friend from a lifetime mistake.

"How do you know he buys girls? I mean, I know he used to fuck around, but he's changed. Maybe these girls were for someone else?" Jenny sounded desperate.

Chloe sucked in her breath. "I found the girls and hooked him up with them. Jenny, he paid me."

CHAPTER 50

Jenny had to be imagining this. She squinted and tilted her head.

"Hmm," she sighed, putting her free hand down on the rim of her bathroom sink. "There is *no* way."

She squinted again, and then tilted the pregnancy test. The vertical line faded into white. Then she slowly tilted it back and watched it reappear, ever so faintly. This line either said "You're pregnant!" or "I am always here, and your pee just made me a bit more visible." She stood there, shifting her weight from side to side for a few minutes, like a monk in deep meditation.

"No, I can't be," she said firmly, putting the pregnancy test down on the flat sink. Then she immediately looked at it again. Her hands gripped the porcelain in defiance, but also for support. As she squinted again at the "hardly there, but there, nonetheless" blue cross, it seemed to be blushing slightly, like a metaphor for her own feelings.

Abstinence had led to pregnancy—not in the Virgin Mary way, but in the "I want what I can't have" way. They'd had unprotected sex for months and nothing happened. Then they didn't have any sex for two months, slept together once, and now she was pregnant. Jenny couldn't believe the irony.

She thought of Ghaith, who was, despite his assurances, still very much married. The phone conversation with Chloe, her friend the pimp, went through her mind. Ghaith had bought girls for sex. Somehow, when

Chloe had told her this, it hadn't made her angrier at Ghaith, because it actually proved his honesty. For months, he had been telling her that Chloe was a madam, and now it all made sense. And anyway, based on the timeline Chloe gave her, he bought the girls before Jenny met him. Maybe he bought the girls for other clients, just as he had mentioned to her at the Meat Kitchen so long ago.

Jenny's hands gripped the cold sink as she glared at the dim cross— blue, white, cross, line, pregnant, not pregnant.

Jenny yanked her hand away. *"Really?"* A rush of emotions fused together and overwhelmed her—joy, fear, and shock. She closed her eyes and shook her head, as if to clear and refocus her eyes. She wasn't just imagining this sacred cross of pregnancy—the cross she was about to bear.

ೞ

Three days and five pregnancy tests later, with each cross getting darker and darker, Jenny knew she had to tell Ghaith. They were planning to go out to dinner at a Thai restaurant that night, but she didn't want to blurt it out while they were munching on pad Thai. Pregnancy was the only thing she could think about, and she knew it was just a matter of time before it popped out of her mouth.

Ghaith's distinct padded steps echoed as he walked up the stairs to her flat. She sat on her bed with one slightly shaking hand on her stomach, staring aimlessly at the white wall. When he knocked, she winced and stood up quickly, smoothing out her long black shirt.

He kissed her passionately, and her arms naturally wrapped around his neck. "Habibti, I missed you," he whispered into her hair. He sat down on her bed, since there was nowhere else to sit in her small studio.

She sat next to him and quickly curled up in his arms. With her mouth less than an inch away from his neck and slightly brushing his ear, Jenny whispered, "I'm pregnant."

Ghaith's hands, which had been gently pressed around her waist, quickly grabbed her shoulders and jerked her back so that he was looking at her, his eyes widening.

"W-what?"

"I've taken five tests, and they're all positive."

Ghaith took his index finger and lightly rested it on her cheek as his thumb slid under her chin. He gently lifted her face toward his and smiled. "I am so happy." He kissed her, delicately at first and then with increasing force.

Jenny shuddered, and all of her nervousness washed away in a flood of elation. "I guess this is what abstinence will do to you," she said. They both let out small, nervous laughs.

Ghaith shook his head in disbelief. "No kidding."

"Well, we don't have to worry about that any longer." She straddled him in one smooth motion and began unbuttoning his shirt, feeling his chest, the soft hair a contrast to his hard muscles. Their mouths met, hard and wet, and she moaned into him. This time it felt different. He was in her, on her, around her, absorbing her.

CHAPTER 51

"Well, what are we going to do?" Jenny's question broke Ghaith out of his reverie. She leaned her elbows on the table and the V-neck of her black shirt deepened.

"I don't know," he said. "I don't know." He had grown unintentionally distant during the drive to the Thai restaurant. Now they just sat there, neither of them looking at the menu. He could tell she was getting desperate to talk, but he was frozen at the thought that both Jenny and Laila were pregnant at the same time.

Ghaith really wanted to start a family with Jenny, but finding out she was pregnant was finally sinking in. He wanted her to be pregnant. Of course he did. But now she *was,* and they still weren't married. The whole issue was so complex and tangled that it paralyzed him to try to think about it in concrete terms. He gripped the place mat and stared intensely at his empty plate.

"So, what's next?" Jenny asked, looking up at him.

"What do you mean?" His knuckles turned white.

"When are we going to get married?" she asked softly, and then narrowed her eyes. "You don't seem happy."

"I can't do anything at this moment!" He slammed his hand on the table, and his plate jumped. He knew his mouth had twisted into a snarl. Jenny's head jerked back, and he felt a momentary spasm of guilt, but the reality of the situation was suddenly too much for him.

"I told you that I am happy, and I meant it." And he did. But even he could tell there was no happiness in his voice.

଼

Later that night, Ghaith lay on his back and stared at what he could make out of Jenny's ceiling in the dark room. She quietly snored next to him, facing the opposite direction, her Christian Dior perfume hanging softly in the air. He usually breathed in these sensations deeply, feeling like a conqueror and sometimes—involuntarily—getting hard again. But not tonight.

Pregnant? He had fantasized about this—Jenny's blond beauty and his genes eternally entwined together. But now that it had happened, he could not help but think of the other reality.

Laila would be wondering where he was right now. He had planned to take Jenny out to dinner and be back home by eleven o'clock. He had told Laila that he had a quick dinner meeting, and she had already called him twice. Usually she would have grown tired and gone to bed, figuring he was asleep at the office. But since she was getting further along in her pregnancy, she was becoming increasingly stubborn about getting in touch with him.

Soon he would have to tell Jenny about his wife and his other unborn child. *She must agree to marry me now, as my second wife, and then I will tell her. Eventually she will forgive me and be happy that I can be a father to all my children.* Yes, he decided, that was the way to do this. He would have to wait to tell his family and be sure the marriage date was before the obvious conception period. If they knew the child had been conceived out of wedlock, they would never accept it.

Laila will get everything she deserves, but I will give Jenny my heart, he thought. He turned on his side toward Jenny and thought about the child she was carrying. *Allah, a boy, make it a boy,* he prayed, and then rolled onto his back. *She will have to agree to be my second wife.*

Ghaith breathed deeply, inhaling Jenny's scent. As he fell asleep, his phone began to blink on and off again, flashing Laila's phone number on the dark ceiling.

201

CHAPTER 52

"Something's wrong," Jenny said, turning toward Ghaith immediately after his alarm went off.

He rubbed the sleep out of his eyes. "Um, what?" Then he shut his eyes again.

She placed a hand on her lower right abdomen and grimaced in pain.

"I'm sure you are fine." Ghaith got out of bed, went to the washroom, and started humming as he turned on the shower.

Jenny stayed in bed, pressing her abdomen, searching for the exact place it hurt. There. Midstomach, left side. *Something is definitely wrong.* Grabbing her laptop, she started searching the Internet for a hospital— one that would treat an unmarried pregnant woman. A quick Google search resulted in 63,400 hits for "unmarried and pregnant hospitals in United Arab Emirates." Jenny sighed as she saw a lot of sites about women being imprisoned for being unmarried and pregnant, or others just saying explicitly that "It is forbidden to be pregnant out of wedlock in the Middle East."

Ghaith walked out of the bathroom with a towel still wrapped around his waist and a smaller one in his hand. "Still hurting?"

Jenny narrowed her eyes and glared at Ghaith. He looked so pompous, standing there in his towel with his hair dripping slightly, tight ringlets springing up as if in surprise. She wondered if their child would have his hair—and panicked for a moment, thinking she had no idea what to do with hair like his.

"Okay, don't come to the meeting today. Just go to the hospital," he said.

"We're not married. I can't just waltz into any old place. One of the first questions will be 'Are you married?' And that will be followed quickly by 'There's a doctor who can help you in jail.'" Jenny tapped the computer screen as if it was agreeing with her.

Ghaith didn't respond. He seemed so smug and happy. Didn't he realize this could be serious? She was pregnant and having stomach pains!

Ghaith put the hand towel on the floor and faced the same direction as the little black arrow on her ceiling—toward Mecca. He kneeled on the ground and began his prostrations. When he had finished, he quickly got dressed and combed his hair in her mirror, whistling the whole time.

Jenny gritted her teeth and tried not to glare at him, and then went back to trying to find a hospital.

"The Holistic Hospital in Dubai." She looked up at Ghaith. "They don't ask for a marriage certificate or insurance while you're pregnant. But if you give birth, the authorities will come in and ask for the documents."

"Okay, well, I'll be down in Sharjah for the meeting. So just take your car to Dubai, and I will come by right afterward." Ghaith finished getting dressed and winked at himself in the mirror. "There. How do I look?"

"Conceited."

"Ahh, come on. I need to look good. We're going to have a baby." He leaned down and pressed a kiss into her hair.

Jenny smiled tightly at him. "Okay, you look gorgeous."

"Better." He paused. "Okay, baby. I'll go to the hospital when the meeting is over."

"Just come as soon as you can, okay? I really am worried." She pressed her hand against her aching abdomen and whispered a small prayer. "Help me, Jesus."

CHAPTER 53

Where is he? It was nearly three o'clock in the afternoon, and Jenny knew the meeting should have been over by noon at the latest. Sharjah was just a twenty-minute drive from Dubai. Jenny lay on the hospital bed and waited for the final results. So far, she had had a urine test, which ruled out any infection that might be causing the pain. Next, she had blood work done and an ultrasound. There wasn't anything apparent in the ultrasound, not even pregnancy, but the technician said it was probably too early to see anything. She was still waiting on the blood tests.

Finally, Ghaith walked in and sat in the chair next to her bed, with a quick "Hey."

Before Jenny could even respond, his phone rang. He answered it in Arabic. Not more than three minutes into the phone call, he put his sunglasses back on and yelled into the phone for the next fifteen minutes. Jenny stared at him, his sunglasses, his foot propped up on his knee. *Why can't he just be a normal guy right now? Turn off his fucking phone, and stop sitting like some smug gangster with his stupid feet crossed and his sunglasses on indoors?*

When the British doctor came in, he looked a little baffled to see Ghaith sitting there and yelling into his phone. Ghaith looked up at the doctor and mumbled, without preamble, "Yalla, bye." He took off his sunglasses, but neither put them away nor uncrossed his legs.

"Uh," the doctor said, still looking at Ghaith.

"It's okay," Jenny said. "He can be here."

The doctor eventually sat down, but he spoke directly to Jenny.

"Well, you *are* pregnant," he said. "Your HCI levels are high and your uterine wall is thickening. You're a negative blood type, so we'll need to give you a specific shot when you give birth. As far as the pain you're feeling, I think you might just be adjusting to the hormones and to being pregnant."

"So everything's okay?"

The doctor nodded, and Jenny breathed out a deep sigh of relief.

Ghaith twisted the end of his sunglasses in his mouth, looking between the doctor and Jenny as if they were in a play and something funny was about to happen.

"Be sure to get some rest and make an appointment to follow up in two weeks, so we can keep an eye on you," the doctor said. Then he nodded curtly and left the room.

Jenny sat up and looked at Ghaith. "I even packed a suitcase, just in case." She hoped that would be a hint for them to get a room in Dubai, because she wanted some down time with him to discuss things. "What took you so long?" Relief had softened her anger toward him, and her words weren't as harsh as they would have been before the doctor came in.

"I had to go out to lunch with Randy and Hussain. I've been blowing them off a lot lately. Now I've got to go back to Sharjah to discuss a few more items."

And just like that, all her anger came rushing back. Her stress levels had been completely out of control all morning and well into the afternoon, and he'd been having lunch while she sat alone in the emergency room for hours. A wave of nausea passed over her, and she gripped the hospital bed.

Ghaith helped her up and led her out of the room, but he barely looked at her. He clearly hadn't noticed how upset she was or how ill she felt. "Why don't you grab some lunch, and I'll meet you at that little café in the Crowne Plaza in an hour or so," he said.

She didn't have the strength to argue, so she agreed. Maybe food would help with the nausea and anger. As she waited in line at the reception desk to set up a follow-up appointment, she watched Ghaith walk jauntily out the main doors. He slid his sunglasses on as he stepped into the parking lot.

He had said he was happy to have a baby, but the cold tone between them at dinner the previous night wasn't going away. Something had changed. What had seemed like magic now felt like static, a barrier. Jenny didn't understand his attitude, and every touch seemed to cause her pain.

CHAPTER 54

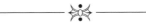

Ghaith shifted into third gear and turned up the music. *What am I to do?* The music did not help him think, but he turned it up louder anyway as he sped past Dubai's skyscrapers and onto a highway heading to Sharjah. The landscape changed as the tall skyscrapers became shorter buildings and date trees dotted the median. He slowed near an upscale condo area and pulled into his parking space.

Aminah, his five-year-old daughter, opened the door before he even stepped out of the car. *"Baba!"*

"Mashallah, my prettiest daughter." Locking his Porsche, Ghaith ran to the house and scooped her up in a hug. She removed his sunglasses and put them on her own head.

"I am Daddy now." Aminah had lost another tooth, Ghaith saw—a left, front tooth that had been loose for days. It must have finally come out that morning, or last night when he was with Jenny.

As Ghaith walked into the house, Sada, his younger daughter, ran up and grabbed his pants. *"Baba, Baba,"* she said.

He leaned over and grabbed his pants out of her small hands. "Sada, don't pull Daddy's pants." He smiled at her, thinking how much she had grown. Ghaith remembered how he had been late to Sada's second birthday party because he had been out with Jenny. How was he going to balance this new chapter in his life, with children from different wives?

Laila waddled out from the kitchen, sighing heavily. Pressing her hands against her lower back, she stretched slightly. She looked further along than she was, but apparently that was normal for women who'd had more than one child. She was trying to frown, but her eyes were smiling.

"Did your meeting run all night?" Her voice was small but stern.

"Oh, my beautiful, pregnant wife." Ghaith let Aminah down, then rushed over to Laila and got on his knees, kissing her belly until she giggled. "No meeting will last all night, silly. I just didn't want to drive home so late. I was exhausted, and I might have crashed."

Laila sobered up when he stopped kissing her. "Well, I called you three times. You could've just answered."

Ghaith started kissing her again. "Girls, go in the other room."

Aminah and Sada ran off together, giggling and holding hands. Ghaith then slid his hands up Laila's legs, kissing more vigorously. She let out a soft moan as he lifted her dress.

CHAPTER 55

Jenny had already moved to three different tables, trying to find somewhere comfortable *and* private. She settled in at yet another table closest to the floor-to-ceiling windows that opened up to the main street in Dubai. She had been to a popular nightclub at the Crowne Plaza, but she'd never hung out in this café or been inside the hotel during the day. It was a nice hotel with a clean, modern look accented by various blood-red fabrics and drapes, but her enjoyment of the beautiful surroundings was diminished by the fact that Ghaith was late.

In fact, he was already an hour late. Growing more and more annoyed, Jenny wondered why they hadn't just booked a room in Dubai. Now, after her very long day, they would have to drive in separate cars back to Abu Dhabi late at night. The stress of the day, compounded by her early pregnancy fatigue, was settling in fast.

"Hey." Ghaith's sudden appearance broke her out of her thoughts. He sat down opposite Jenny and picked up the menu.

"What took you so long?" she snapped.

"I just couldn't leave." He took off his sunglasses and set them down on the table. "Ah, cappuccino, please," he said to the pretty Filipino waitress who had practically run over as soon as he sat down.

"Yes, sir," the waitress replied, and glanced over at Jenny. Sipping on her second cup of tea already, Jenny shook her head.

"What are we going to do?" Jenny asked, resisting the urge to pick up his sunglasses and throw them at him.

"I don't know." Ghaith looked down at the table. The smugness disappeared from his face, and he actually looked a little desperate.

"Well, when will your divorce be final?"

"Soon. Soon." He rubbed his hands together, a nervous gesture she'd never before noticed. "It's just complicated."

Jenny gestured toward her belly. "And this isn't?"

"Let's just get married," he said. "The paperwork for your residency should be complete within three days. Then we can just go to the court, get married, and then sort out everything else."

"My residency should have finished months ago. You promised it was going to be. Why has it taken so long?"

"I've already told you."

But he hadn't. He always had some long explanation, which he didn't want to go into because of something or other having to do with legalities. Then after Eid, when she returned from the States, he had to start the process all over again. Jenny had become so frustrated with asking him about it that she'd just dropped the topic entirely.

"But even when it *is* ready, I can't complete the process." She looked at him evenly.

The waitress brought over Ghaith's cappuccino and set it down in front of him. Smiling, she bent over farther than she needed to, clearly wanting Ghaith to have a look at her cleavage. Jenny noticed his eyes light up as he took advantage of that opportunity.

"Why not?" Face calm, he looked back at Jenny when the waitress walked away—as though he didn't expect her to have noticed what he'd just done.

"Because," she spat out with disgust, "you have to get an X-ray done to get residency, and I am *not* exposing this baby to radiation. The first question they ask is 'Are you married?' But what they're really asking is 'Are you pregnant?' And, of course, you can be pregnant in this country only if you're married. If I admit to being pregnant, and they ask to see a marriage license, what then? *Jail.* Because here, it's actually illegal to have a kid out of wedlock."

"Okay, okay," Ghaith said.

Jenny could tell that her frustration was starting to affect him, so she looked out the window and tried to calm down. All she could think about was how he had just lustily looked at the waitress. But that seemed like a petty distraction compared with what they were facing, so she let it go. It would only lend a further squabble to this mess, and Jenny didn't have the energy for that. *Is this why women just let their men have affairs? Are they just too tired for more arguing?*

"Get your divorce *now*, and then we can just go to the American Embassy and get married straight away," Jenny said. They won't ask us for any unnecessary paperwork. That's the clearest solution."

"I can't."

"Why not? You were going to get a divorce anyway, and this is the perfect time to do it." Jenny had really thought that her pregnancy was going to expedite his divorce. Now, sitting across from him, she felt like she'd hit a wall.

"Because my *wife* is waiting to take her examination for a medical job in January. If she doesn't pass it, then she has to wait until March. And then it will take her about a month to get the job going. I have to sponsor her in this country until she can get the job. Then her employer can sponsor her, and I can divorce her. But if she doesn't have a sponsor, she has to go back to Jordan—and she'll take my daughters with her. I will not have my daughters in that country. I cannot do that to them."

Ghaith slammed his hand on the table and a little cloud of froth from his cappuccino puffed up into the air and settled down onto the table.

Jenny stared at it as it slowly settled. She could not believe what she was hearing. "Why can't you just sponsor her as an employee under your business license until she gets the job? You don't have to sponsor her as your wife. I mean, you guys aren't even living together anymore."

"No, that's impossible. There are different employers, and it is all very complicated. Look into it if you want, but I'm sure you won't learn anything. It is different for Jordanian passport holders."

"So you aren't divorcing her until January or maybe April?! What am I supposed to do?"

"I don't know. I thought, with the residency, we could just get married here." Ghaith paused, and then went on in an oddly flat voice, as if reciting something he'd memorized. "Or better yet, we can just go to Doha and get married. I know the minister of foreign affairs, and he owes my father some favors. I will check into that."

"But I would still have to get the X-ray for my residence permit. Why the hell are you bringing up Doha?"

"Well, let me talk to him. I have to go to Doha in a couple of weeks, so I will find out. But you should have the baby in the States anyway, because the paperwork here is terrible. You can stay in Michigan. I have a condo there."

"Michigan? Why would I stay in Michigan? So you want to send me away—halfway around the world, no less—but I'll have a condo." *Condo* came out in a strongly sarcastic tone.

Pregnancy should be a happy thing, but Jenny felt like she was watching her entire life spin out of control. She was going to have a baby, but she would also have to move, change jobs, and possibly lose the guy with whom she was in love—the father of her unborn child.

CHAPTER 56

"I'm pregnant." Jenny's voice cracked on the word *pregnant.*

"Oh, dear," blurted out Jenny's mom, Ellen.

After the complete disaster of a conversation with Ghaith, Jenny had come home a mess and immediately did the only thing that made sense. She called her mom and let out the entire story in little hiccups of sob-interrupted words.

She would have called sooner, but she had been waiting to tell her mom she was pregnant *and* getting married. She had really thought that Ghaith would've divorced his wife immediately when he found out Jenny was pregnant. Oh, she had been so naïve. Now Chloe's words seemed like an oracle of sorts.

"Well, I think you should come to Guam. Just come here until Ghaith has time to figure everything out."

Ellen had lived on Guam, a small island in the Pacific Ocean, off and on for years. When Jenny was only sixteen years old, she had traveled to Guam with her mother for the first time. Ellen hadn't been able to find a teaching job in the States, so she had moved out during Guam's economic boom. Over the years, she kept returning to Guam, drawn to the people and culture. Now she was focused on her research and finishing her doctoral dissertation.

Jenny had always wondered what hold the island held over her mother, but she knew it was probably the simple lifestyle. Guam was more advanced than many parts of the States, partly because of its proximity to Japan's edgy trends, but the culture retained the sentiment of island living.

A true hippie in many ways, Ellen had lived in many different countries, which was probably why Jenny felt so comfortable bouncing around the world on her own. In fact, Ellen was actually the reason Jenny first went to the Middle East. Living in Kuwait at the time, Ellen had gotten Jenny her first international job. So Ellen was the only member of Jenny's family who understood Middle Eastern culture—which was why they were viewed as the black sheep of the family.

"But he should be marrying me legally." Jenny sobbed again. "I thought he loved me."

"Oh, honey, he does love you, but he is in such a complicated situation."

"*He* is?" Jenny's tone turned venomous.

"I know you don't want to hear this right now, but we both know that Middle Eastern culture is just different. Come to Guam and let things work out in time. It's too dangerous to be there and not be married."

Jenny hung up the phone and realized she was no longer crying. Inhaling deeply, she finally felt calm.

CHAPTER 57

Taking a deep drag off his cigarette, Ghaith looked at Jenny sound asleep next to him. She'd had this idea that they could go to Guam and get married, but he couldn't bring himself to tell her why he couldn't do that. It was probably for the best that she left, even if it was by herself, now that she was fixated on going to be with her mother. She wouldn't listen to him about going to Doha. He wished he could just tell her the truth, but she broke down upon hearing the little bit he had already told her.

They had gone to a remote desert island with a beautiful, Arabic-style hotel on a private nature reserve. It was lavish and lush, and he loved it. Jenny had persuaded him to go dirt-bike riding and they had played tennis. He had had such a good time—until their last night there, when he told her he'd slept with Laila.

That was supposed to be his segue into telling her that Laila was pregnant, which was the real reason why he couldn't get a divorce—and why Jenny needed to go to Doha to marry him. When they were married, she wouldn't have to leave him and run away to Guam with their unborn child.

But he never got beyond introducing the topic. Jenny had leaped up and immediately started packing, screaming at him the whole time. It was worse than Laila's meltdowns. Watching her throw clothes into her suitcase, Ghaith realized that she had believed him, all this time, about not living with his wife. Her confidence in him made him nervous, and he wished he could have been honest with her from the beginning. On the other hand, if he had been honest from the start, there never would have been a *them*. Luckily, Jenny didn't leave that night, and she had finally settled down enough to fall asleep, although she didn't talk to him again until they left.

The drive back to Abu Dhabi had been horrendous. Jenny had yelled at him for the entire three hours. She even asked if Laila was pregnant, but he didn't tell her the truth. That definitely would have caused an even bigger meltdown than the previous night, and he worried about the effect that an emotional outburst might have on their unborn child.

Later, back in Abu Dhabi, Ghaith had tried a different angle. As they sat on her bed in her studio, surrounded by all of her boxes and packed luggage, he had felt such remorse. She looked so beautiful sitting on her bed, just starting to show a little.

"Look, you don't have to leave." Before he could stop himself, he was telling her the plan he had been devising since the night at the Thai restaurant when he had found out she was pregnant. "I can spend three days with you, three days with Laila, and one day with my mom."

Jenny slapped him across the face just as he said the word *mom*. The pain had been stinging and immediate. Then she snatched her hand back, screaming, "Are you fucking kidding me?" In tears, she had collapsed back onto the bed.

She had never before hit Ghaith, and he had a hard time composing himself. Hit by a woman! And she didn't even chase after him when he left, the way Laila had done time and time again.

As he lay there in their Dubai hotel during Jenny's last night in the UAE, he felt her move in her sleep, and then she began to snore quietly. He took another drag off his cigarette.

She was leaving. Of course, they both said it was just until they could figure things out. But Jenny was also leaving him professionally, and it would be hard to find someone to take her place at work.

Ghaith stubbed out his cigarette and wrapped the fluffy white hotel robe around himself as he got out of the bed. He took a bottle of Crown

Royal out of the minibar, poured some into a glass, and opened the curtains to look out at Dubai's glittering night skyline. Planes were taking off in a constant cycle of deep rumbling. And in fewer than twelve hours, Jenny would be leaving on one of those planes.

Sitting on the daybed next to the window, Ghaith sipped his drink and considered his options. He could go to Guam and marry Jenny the way she wanted, since Guam was a U.S. territory. But that could get him into a lot of trouble, because he had sponsored his wife and children as U.S. citizens. If the feds found out, Ghaith and his family might lose their citizenship.

If only Jenny would marry him in the Arab world, where he could legally have more than one wife. Jenny would falter and have sex with him and drink, and he would do the same. But when it came down to it, they were bound by separate laws. Islam and Christianity are just about as far apart as you can get.

Lighting another cigarette, Ghaith sighed. It would be so much easier to get married in Doha, but Jenny refused to do that as long as he was still married. And yet—*and yet*—she was carrying his child.

The only people he had told were Hakeem, who had been pleased, and his father, who had been angry for several hours and then switched into solution mode. "Marry her or let her go."

Ghaith knew those were really his only two choices. The former was proving difficult, but the latter would happen in fewer than twelve hours. Looking at Jenny sleeping, Ghaith felt a deep pain erupt within him. He did love her, but maybe it was good she was leaving. This way he could focus on Laila. On the previous night, he had sat up and watched Laila sleep, in the same way and feeling the same pain.

Noticing that his glass was empty, Ghaith opened the Crown Royal and took a deep gulp—directly from the bottle.

CHAPTER 58

Jenny was already sweating. She hated flying, but Xanax was off the table since she was pregnant. And the way Ghaith left her at the airport did nothing to lessen her anxiety. He had just grabbed her, kissed her hard on the lips, and said, "Yalla, bye"—like he was getting off the phone. Then he turned and stormed away without giving Jenny a second glance. Was that the only way he could deal with her leaving? Or could he just not deal with her leaving at all?

He certainly hadn't made this easy. She had to leave the country because he wouldn't finalize the divorce paperwork, and he wasn't even offering her severance pay. It was bad enough that she would have to figure out a birthing place without insurance, which she had angrily pointed out to him. She would have a hard time finding another job, too, since she would start showing soon.

And as if that wasn't enough, she was pissed at him for another reason. As they were eating dinner on the previous evening, he had asked about her brother's adopted kids and what their last names were now. When she told him that they had taken her brother's last name, he said, "Well, you know you have to tell our child that their cousins are adopted."

Jenny's jaw dropped. Why was that necessary? "No, they are cousins. I am not going to refer to them as *adopted* cousins—they're just cousins. I'm not going to hide the fact that they're adopted, but neither will I use that label every time we talk about them."

"But you need to. We do not let adopted kids take new last names. You need to always show truth." By *we*, of course, he meant Muslims.

Jenny was still fuming about that when the plane began to accelerate for takeoff. She had to close her eyes and think of something else. What did Ghaith know about the truth? He had been lying to her this entire time. After he told her that he had slept with his wife, Jenny had started to feel like a statistic. She was a wallflower, not exceptional in any way, simply part of the background of Ghaith's life.

PART III

CHAPTER 59

When the plane landed at Guam's A.B. Won Pat International Airport, Jenny breathed a sigh of relief—and then immediately began to worry again. Of all the places she could have gone, why had she come here? Jenny hadn't been to Guam for fifteen years, and she remembered it as being hot and isolated. A tiny Pacific island, just thirty miles long and twelve miles wide, Guam is closer to Asia than to Hawaii.

Jenny was not looking forward to being pregnant here, but she *was* looking forward to seeing her mom. Ellen had raved about a birthing center in Guam, and she said that Jenny could take long walks on the beach, watch the sunset, and just enjoy being pregnant.

Looking out the window, Jenny saw tin roofs flooding the crowded villages and wild dogs darting between cars on the roads. She could already smell the heavy fragrance of plumeria trees and feel the thick humidity. Both had once seemed exotic to her, but now they just seemed stifling and an embarrassing contradiction to Abu Dhabi.

Ellen was waiting for her daughter outside the baggage claim. The moment Jenny's hands were free, her mother grasped her in a tight hug. Hugging Ellen back, Jenny wiped away the sweat already forming on her forehead.

"How are you feeling?" Ellen asked with a worried frown.

"Okay, considering everything that's going on."

"Let's talk in the car, hmm?" In the parking lot, her mom put Jenny's luggage in a mini SUV.

Jenny raised an eyebrow when she noticed that the SUV was a standard. "A stick shift, Mom?" She knew her mom could drive an automatic, but driving a standard was a little disconcerting.

"Don't look like that. I think I've mastered it." A proud smile lit up Ellen's face. She lowered her voice and let out a small laugh. "It did scare me a little at first, though."

Jenny put the seat belt on and held her breath as her mom backed out and began to drive. Ellen did seem to be handling the driving well, and they were moving forward as though floating along on some strange river. But the farther they drove, the more nauseated Jenny felt. The settled pollution, combined with the thick fragrance of flowers and the relentless rattle of the potholes, was making her queasy.

"So, um—" Ellen hit another pothole, and Jenny gritted her teeth. "There's something you need to know about the apartment. It's a bit older. And it used to be a shop, so the front door is actually one of those metal gates that rolls down."

Jenny took a deep breath to prepare herself for the worst. She looked away from the traffic and toward her mother. Ellen had a way of glamorizing the worst parts and playing down the best parts. That still confused Jenny, who looked at reality the way she thought most everyone else did. She wasn't sure if it was her mother's hippie mentality or what, but it was not encouraging.

She sighed. "What do you mean by *older?*"

"Well, it's a really good price." Ellen nodded emphatically, and Jenny could tell she'd said that often, probably to herself. "Ah, here we are."

They turned onto a dirt road and drove through a small shanty neighborhood. People sat outside on their porches or in their yards. At the end of the road was a little place that had indeed once been a shop of some kind, with the metal gate pulled down. A pair of hens pecked at the ground in front of the entrance.

Ellen got out of the car and called softly to the hens. "Out of the way, ladies." As the hens strutted off, Ellen squatted down, unlocked the metal gate, and rolled up the entire front wall.

Inside, the front room was very modest, with just a small desk and chair, plus a couple of overcrowded bookshelves. There was nowhere to sit except for some cushions on the tiled floor.

"Oh, and because we leave the door open to get air and light inside, there's—um—frogs that come inside." Ellen twisted her hands together, obviously nervous. "The hens sometimes come in, too, and I really wish they would get the frogs out of the house. They piss and shit everywhere. The frogs, I mean."

Jenny stared at her mother. All she could think was, *Get me out of here!* She'd been willing to give living with her mom a chance, but frogs pissing and shitting on everything? She felt sick, and she knew she would not be comfortable here at all. What if the frogs peed on her baby after it was born? *Oh my gosh,* she thought, *I am going to die.*

Ellen held out her arm. "Okay, let me give you a tour of the house." They walked down a hallway to a bedroom with a simple bed and dresser. "This is my room. I would have you sleep in here, but there is a lot of mold." Indeed, the ceiling was almost completely black. Jenny quickly backed out of the room.

They went back into the hallway, and Ellen pointed out the bathroom with its toilet and small tiled shower. She then led Jenny to the end of the hallway, to a decent-sized and fairly clean kitchen, with open windows lining the back of the room.

Ellen pointed at the windows. "If you have any trash, you can just throw it out here."

Jenny walked over, very carefully, and peered out. The back of the house was on a steep hill, and there were piles of rubbish in a ditch on the backside.

"Really?" The air left Jenny's lungs, and she felt like she was suffocating.

"Well, not plastics and that sort of thing, but coffee grounds and rinds from fruit." Ellen smiled, as if this quasi-compost was really environmental. But it wasn't just coffee grounds and rinds out there.

Jenny could see broken toilets, too, and cardboard, and various kinds of plastic, despite what Ellen had said. Apparently this was the dump for the local village—and it *smelled*.

"Okay." Jenny blew out the word in exasperation, as oxygen seeped back into her body.

Ellen looked down nervously at the floor. "All right, now to show you your room!" she said, with forced cheerfulness. "It's on the outside of the house."

Jenny nodded mutely.

They walked back down the hallway, out the *door*, and around the corner. On the side of the house were two small rooms and a bathroom. Ellen told Jenny that a local surfer stayed in one room, but that he was currently at his cousin's house. A wardrobe stood in the second room, along with a bed and a standing fan. Mosquito netting and fabric curtains were nailed across the windows.

Her mom smiled and pointed to the netting. "I just put up your screens last night."

"Thanks," Jenny mumbled. She sat down on her bed, the only piece of furniture in the whole place on which she could sit. It was already very hot and humid.

"I'll just get your luggage," her mom said, and left the room.

Even though this place was going to make Jenny cry, she held in her tears for now. She didn't want her mom to feel bad when she was trying so hard, putting up curtains and giving her privacy. But yesterday Jenny had been in a city with golden streets, and today she was in a village with a garbage dump behind her house. She closed her eyes, willing it all to disappear. How could a tiny thing, not even the size of a walnut, change her world so much?

CHAPTER 60

Two days later Veronica arrived in Guam, and she was a refreshing breath of fresh air for Jenny. The bubbly Veronica always made her feel like it was the first day of spring after a long winter. Originally, she was supposed to meet up with Jenny in Abu Dhabi for Christmas, but after finding out that Jenny was pregnant and moving to Guam, in a heartbeat Veronica changed her flight.

Jenny was glad Veronica was there, mostly because Veronica could help talk some sense into Ellen about their current living situation. After all, the last time they had been together was at Veronica's dad's posh hotel suite in Abu Dhabi.

"If it's okay, Ellen, I can even help you and Jenny find another place while I'm here," Veronica said, when she saw the house. She let out a hearty laugh. "It'll be fun."

The three of them were in Ellen's living room. Veronica sat in the only chair, Ellen was curled up on a cushion on the floor, and Jenny lay on the tiled floor, since it was the coolest place in the house. A fake Christmas tree already sat in the corner, but even the twinkling lights irritated Jenny. She rolled over and looked out the window—really the entire front of the house, since the shop door was open.

"Oh, Jenny," Veronica said as she looked down at Jenny in a fetal position on the floor. "You doing okay down there?" She let out another chuckle.

"Yep, just trying not to throw up." Jenny gazed out onto the street, where the skinniest cow she had ever seen stood grazing. One of the hens—named Henrietta, Ellen had told her—wandered past, clucking and pecking at the ground.

"Just let us know when you start to feel better and we can leave," her mom said, as though that was the most encouraging remark anyone had ever made.

Jenny felt another wave of nausea settle over her. She wanted to get out of this place, but she couldn't face standing up and walking anywhere, not even to the car. Right now she could not even sit up, although she knew the pissing-shitting frogs probably made a daily route right through where she was lying.

"Veronica, how did Donna get through all of this?" Jenny croaked. Veronica and Jenny knew another American teacher in Kuwait with a son who was half Palestinian. "I don't know the whole story. I know you and Donna both taught third grade. What happened to the father of her kid?"

Veronica cleared her throat. "She told me that when she was like eighteen years old, she actually went to Israel to be a nun." Jenny almost sat up, her nausea instantly forgotten. This was going to be an interesting story.

"A nun?" Jenny asked, and let out a little laugh. Donna wasn't exactly the type of woman you could easily imagine as a nun.

"Yep, a nun," Veronica echoed Jenny's laugh and then continued the story. "But instead, she met this Palestinian guy who charmed the pants off her—quite literally—and she got pregnant."

"Wow, from becoming a nun to being knocked up with an Arab's baby." Ellen snickered.

"Right? So he ended up proposing, since he allegedly wanted to do the right thing."

"Sounds familiar."

"Well, the thing is, he wasn't a Christian Arab. He was a Muslim, so she had to convert in order to marry him. You know how you have to say something in Arabic to convert? Like some confession?"

"Oh, yes. I know what you are talking about. Ghaith made me repeat after him one day something beautiful in Arabic, and then he told me I had converted. I found it ironic that I could be converted after saying something I didn't even understand."

"Really? That guy never ceases to amaze me." Veronica let out a sigh.

"Come to think of it, you can become a Christian by just saying a confession. But at least you are supposed to know what you are saying and fully believe it."

"Well, Donna said the words in Arabic, knowing that it meant she was converting. She told me that she was just praying, 'God, you know I'm not really converting. I'm just doing this to get married.' She said after they got married, it was really good for a while. But then they went to the States to have their baby and so that her husband, Bader, could get a green card. As soon as they got to the States, Bader became a different person, disappearing a lot and not answering calls. After the birth, Bader disappeared with the baby for a few months."

"A *few months*?" Jenny felt her mouth fall open.

"Oh, my gosh! Didn't she go crazy? What did she do? How did she find him?" Ellen asked.

"I know, right? That must have been insane for Donna. She said that she called the police and FBI. But, I mean, this was back in the seventies, so there wasn't a lot they could do. And then, one day, she got a phone call from some American girl with whom she'd spent time in Israel. The girl told her Bader was at her house with a baby."

"What do you mean? Where did he go?" Jenny was completely absorbed, and almost turned around to look at Veronica, but the nausea welled up again.

"Well, apparently he had charmed a lot of American women in Jerusalem. So he was visiting them in the States, one by one, with the baby." Veronica laughed. "Can you imagine? Those women must have been so confused. But he married Donna only to get a green card—and then, since the baby was a boy, he wanted him."

"Was the baby okay?"

"Yeah, the baby was surprisingly fine."

"Has she ever let him see his dad again?"

"I think so. The kid's a teenager now, and Donna's always joking that if Bader wants to kidnap him now, that would be fine with her." All three of them laughed. "But as it is, Bader hardly ever visits the kid. Donna says she is conflicted. Part of her wants Bader to be part of her kid's life, but the other part of her can never really trust him—for obvious reasons." Veronica paused. "I mean, I kind of see her point. Even with my dad and his hot new wife … Well, if I was my mom, I'm not sure I would have let him see me all the years that they have been separated."

Veronica's last remark and the story of Donna settled uncomfortably around Jenny, making her think about Ghaith and the baby inside of her.

"Well, that's how I feel about Ghaith a lot of the time," Jenny said. "You know he hasn't even called me to see if I made it here okay? It's out of sight, out of mind—and now I'm starting to remember what an asshole he is. It's like, on one hand, I want him to come here tomorrow so we can get married. And I *would* recite a conversion like Donna did, with my mouth although not with my heart, just so we could raise this child properly. But on the other hand, Ghaith has screwed up so much already. Now I'm really seeing that our core values are very different. Maybe it's better if he's not around."

The room was quiet for a minute, until Ellen spoke. "Well, you have time. There's no rush to make any decisions right now."

"Plus," Veronica rushed to add, "you have a lot going for you. You have an education, you're employable, and you're actually in a good place to raise a kid if Ghaith doesn't step up."

"I guess," Jenny said in a small voice. A tear ran down her cheek, seen by nobody except the skinny cow. "I just don't *want* to be a single mom." She quickly wiped her face, then turned over and looked at Veronica and Ellen, her emotions overtaking the nausea.

Ellen smiled at her. "You know, if you do marry him, it could work out. But you would have to accept that it wouldn't be the type of marriage that you want. You would have to be fine with him taking another wife and raising the baby as a Muslim."

"I know." Jenny paused, then looked up again. "Do you think it really could work out?" She wanted someone to tell her to go back to Abu Dhabi and marry Ghaith. She wanted ease and comfort, but she also knew that going back would probably be a different form of hell. Ghaith would never be able to give her the comfort she needed, since he was going to stay with his wife—to split the week between her, his wife, and his mother. And anyway, he let her leave Abu Dhabi without making any plans to be together again. Just like that. *Poof.* A quick kiss and yalla. Jenny had replayed that departure in her mind again and again.

"Well, it might," Veronica said as she and Ellen exchanged a grimace. "But I have one more story for you. Remember Diana?"

Jenny nodded. Another American teacher at the school in Kuwait, Diana was married to a Kuwaiti. Jenny knew that she had married the Kuwaiti many years ago when they met at college in America.

"Well, everything seemed fine for nearly *two decades.*" Veronica paused for full effect, and Jenny felt an involuntary smile spread over her face as she thought about being happily married to Ghaith for the next twenty years. Then the bubble popped as Veronica continued. "But when they were building their house last year, Diana found out that he had married a Lebanese woman *and* has a baby with her."

"No!" The fantasy smile fell from Jenny's face.

"Yep. And not only that, but the third bedroom they were building—directly above their bedroom—was intended for the Lebanese wife and baby."

"Motherfucker!" Jenny said.

"Yep."

"So what is she going to do?" Ellen asked with a groan.

"Well, their kids still have a couple of years before they go to college, so really there's nothing she can do. You know, kids can't leave the Middle East without permission from the father. They are literally his property until they are eighteen years old. Of course, she is not happy about it, and she forbids the wife and baby to move into the house. So now he spends half of the week with her and the other half with the other wife."

"Wow, just like Ghaith told me he wanted to do." And then Jenny had slapped him. *Well done, me.*

"Well, at least you would know about it going into the relationship." Ellen raised one eyebrow at Jenny, as if to challenge this thought.

"So neither of you think Ghaith is going to leave his wife?" Jenny felt like she was going to cry. She wished this could be true, but she needed confirmation to have a renewed hope.

"I don't think he ever intended to leave her," Veronica said.

Ellen just looked at Jenny with a sad little smile and shook her head. She knew Jenny well enough to know that Jenny was on the verge of a meltdown.

Jenny nodded her head firmly, digesting all of this information. Taking a deep breath, she then rolled back over on her side and looked out the "window." The cow gave Jenny a bored look and started to chew on a piece of cardboard.

Reality was finally sinking in. The reality that this might *not* work out. The reality that Ghaith was never going to come and rescue her and their child. The reality that she had a really rough road ahead of her.

CHAPTER 61

Rage. Jenny's strongest emotion was rage—followed closely by abandonment, depression, anger, and extreme hurt. But nothing drove her insomnia the way rage did. She tried to blame her inability to sleep on delayed jet lag from the long flight to Guam, but she usually traveled across time zones the way other people drove to their eight-to-fiver every day.

It didn't feel right, being awake this late. But there she was, lying in bed at two in the morning and practically blistering with raw emotion. Jenny tossed and turned, everything either too scratchy or too soft, the sheet slipping off or bunching up every time she moved. Her head was pounding. Eventually she tossed the blankets aside, turned on the lights, walked around the outside of the house, and headed toward the kitchen— the best room of the house.

Storming into the kitchen, Jenny looked at the time on the microwave. *Two thirty in the morning. Fuck.* She took out the Cheerios and ate them angrily by the handful. The idea of marrying Ghaith in Guam felt like a farce now. They had barely even spoken on the phone since she left the Middle East.

In her anger toward Ghaith, she couldn't even taste the cereal she was eating. Veronica's words kept going through her mind. "Jenny, I don't think he ever intended to get a divorce." Veronica had said that again at the airport when they hugged goodbye. But she had added, "If you marry him, he's gonna make your life hell. You can do *way* better than him."

Jenny had needed to hear those words. They must have been buried deep in her subconscious under all this rage.

Jenny knew, now, that it was true.

Fuck him, she thought, not for the first time that night. She didn't need him, she didn't need his money, and she certainly didn't need to know about the triumphs or failures of his business. Suddenly, resolved to action, Jenny walked back to her room and opened her laptop. She knew the mood swings were caused mainly by her pregnancy, but she couldn't help herself. She sat down and began to draft an e-mail.

If only your sweet whispers had been holistic—true from every corner. I took your words as smoke from a genie's bottle, mystical and even tangible, the smell and the sight powerful to wish upon. But I cannot grab hold of smoke. Our cultures speak different languages in the same way we literally speak different languages. "I miss you" in English, to a lover, means "I miss your smell and your taste." In Arabic, when you say it, it means "Goodbye."

I thought we were making our own religion. And I forgave you, and believed you, and we conceived a miracle. But there's no magic left, no genie's smoke—just a baby. What can I do now? I'm alone, breasts rounding, thighs thickening, belly softly protruding. Where is your handful of sweet whispers now?

CHAPTER 62

Ghaith hesitated. He wanted to hear Jenny's voice—if it was going to be sweet. But he knew that, even if she started speaking nicely to him, her voice would turn venomous within twenty minutes. He put his phone back down.

He had ten missed calls from her and two messages that *sounded* nice: "I'm sorry. I'm pregnant, alone, and emotional" and simply "I miss you."

He had received several e-mails from Jenny over the last week, and each one stung him in a different way. He really could not take much more of this.

The cool day allowed him to wear one of the suits that Jenny bought him. He wanted to feel close to her, but he didn't know how besides wearing these clothes. He imagined her fingers touching these clothes softly and choosing them so precisely. He had become more and more accustomed to dismissing her from his mind, but today was different.

Walking up the stairs to a large building, Ghaith looked for the sign. "Dr. Yousef Azazi, Psychologist." Taking a deep breath, he smoothed out his pink button-down shirt. He was going to give this a go.

Dr. Azazi surprised Ghaith by opening his door. *Maybe he's a psychic, too.* He was a slight man, Egyptian, and wearing trendy glasses. Shaking Ghaith's hand firmly, he smiled broadly. Ghaith immediately liked him.

"Salam," Dr. Azazi said, and opened his door to let Ghaith pass him.

"Good morning," Ghaith said, walking into the office. Sitting down on one of the couches, he looked out the windows and toward the city traffic below. The room was a bit cold, so he crossed his legs and his arms.

"May I smoke?" Ghaith asked.

"Sure, but I will have to open the window."

Ghaith nodded. "The fresh air might make it warmer in here." He got out his cigarettes and lit one as Dr. Azazi walked across the room to open the window.

"So, tell me. Why are you here?" he asked, returning to his seat across from Ghaith.

"Well, I've got myself into a bit of a sticky situation, and I can't really talk to anybody." Ghaith took a deep drag off his Marlboro and then exhaled.

"Go on."

Suddenly Ghaith felt vulnerable and wondered if Laila was having him followed. He would have to think of some reason why he needed to see a shrink. Stress from work? Family issues with his sisters?

Dr. Azazi cleared his throat and brought Ghaith back to his senses and his real reason for being here.

"It's just that I am married and my wife is pregnant, but the woman with whom I am in love is also pregnant."

"So the woman with whom you are in love is not your wife, I take it?" The psychologist adjusted his round glasses and looked at Ghaith in what seemed a nonjudgmental manner. In fact, he appeared almost bored with Ghaith's confession.

"That's right." Ghaith felt relieved, as though just telling his secret took a weight off his shoulders. "But she won't marry me because I am already married, and now she has moved far away."

Dr. Azazi continued to look at Ghaith in the same bored manner, so Ghaith continued to talk.

"And now, well, I just don't know what to do. I know I should stay with my wife and try to persuade Jenny to marry me, but I no longer think she will agree to do that."

"If she conceded to marry you, how would that be, with two wives and different families here?"

"It would be hard." Ghaith put out his cigarette and immediately lit another one. "I know they would eventually get used to it, but I just don't know how it would all work out. They both need me right now, and I don't know how I can juggle all of it—not to mention running a growing business, on top of everything else. And they both yell at me! Laila screams at me because I am not having sex with her, and Jenny yells at me because she says I am sleeping with my wife! I can't take it anymore!"

"I see. Let's take a step back. How would you feel if—ah—*Jenny* didn't consent to marrying you? If she stayed where she is now, and you focused on your family here?"

Ghaith took a couple of drags off his cigarette as he thought about this. "It would be easier in many ways. It actually already is much easier logistically, but emotionally it is and will continue to be very hard."

"Do you think you could manage through those feelings?"

Ghaith knew the answer to that. He put out his cigarette and looked out the window. The sun was now shining in and warming up the room.

CHAPTER 63

Three weeks later, Jenny still had not heard back from Ghaith. No e-mails, no calls, no texts. She couldn't stand being ignored. Even though she had written him a Fuck Off letter, she was experiencing the crazy emotional flip-flopping of pregnancy. So now she was missing him.

Picking up her phone, Jenny called Ghaith and let it ring. No answer. She sent him a text. "Baby, I'm sorry for the e-mail, but I'm going crazy here." A few minutes later her phone rang.

"Hello!" she said in a surprised voice.

"Hey, baby. How are you doing?"

Jenny was happy that he didn't bring up the e-mail. "Well, I've seen better days." She exhaled and her voice softened. "What are you doing?"

"I've just been really busy, and I'm on my way home now. You know, my work has doubled since you left."

She felt her anger start to surge when he mentioned his home, imagining him going home to his wife. "Okay, so why the hell am I pregnant and over here by myself, Ghaith?"

"Ah—"

Jenny cut him off. "This whole thing with your wife needing to be sponsored is a load of shit, and you know it. So why are you abandoning your child and me? Tell me the truth!"

Ghaith took a deep breath. "You aren't going to like this, Jenny." He sounded deflated as he exhaled his confession. "My wife is pregnant, too."

Jenny felt like she had been punched in the stomach. As she sat down on the ground and leaned against the door, a strange yelp escaped from her mouth. "Are you fucking kidding me?"

"I'm so sorry, Jenny. I am going crazy over here, and I don't know what to do."

Jenny did not really hear what Ghaith was saying, because suddenly everything made sense in a tragically perfect way. "How far along is she?" she asked flatly.

Another ragged sigh. "Eight months."

Hanging up the phone, Jenny stared at the wall for a minute and then had a meltdown. She screamed, cried, and then yelled at the wall with the most imaginative cussing that had ever come out of her mouth. As she leaned back against the door, exhausted cries left her body in little shakes and tremors. How was she going to make it through this? She had never felt this low and out of control in her entire life.

The tears began again as she realized that she would never know what it felt like to have her child's father feel their baby move in her rounding tummy. She had wanted to be with Ghaith so much that she had been willing to give up everything for him, but now that would never happen. Her entire world was crashing down around her.

Now she would have to be the strong one. The one who carried this child. The unemployed one who had to take care of everything.

Jenny screamed again.

ȣ

The local agent's name was Ron. As they followed his truck around the island, Jenny noticed Christian stickers on his bumper. It had been nearly two months since Jenny had arrived on Guam, and she needed—no, she required—a place where she could be comfortably pregnant. Veronica had tried to help her find a place when she had visited, but Jenny had barely been able to leave the house because of her morning sickness. She would only have ended up puking on Ron's shoes.

The thing was, she still sometimes imagined that Ghaith would arrive at the airport, frantically call her, and beg her to forgive him. She would catch herself visualizing their reunion, and sometimes even let herself carry the daydream further—Ghaith's hand on her rounding tummy, her head on his chest, and him on one knee offering her a diamond ring and a stable future.

But then she would shake her head at her desperate situation and try to shrug off the pain that accompanied the daydream. She knew it was only a dream. Her heart was still trying to accept the tragic truth, but her logical self somehow went on, completely disconnected from her heart, and started to make plans. These plans involved commitment—but not to Ghaith. Jenny was ready to sign a lease and thus commit herself and her baby to Guam, half a world away from Ghaith.

When she and Ron got to the next available apartment, Jenny shifted from one foot to the other, trying to ease the slight swelling in her ankles. "So Ron, where do you go to church? I'm looking for a church to start attending."

As the child in her belly was growing, Jenny's relationship with God was being resurrected. She found herself repenting daily for the mistake of dating a married man—a married *Muslim* man. She didn't chastise herself like the Filipinos did on Good Friday, whipping themselves as they carried crosses up mountains and marked the path with their blood. Jenny's was a gentle repenting, although no less sincere, and she felt forgiven anew every day when she repented. This love must have been from God, because she could never have been so kind to herself.

Ron pushed his sunglasses on top of his head, and his light brown eyes shined. "It's called Glory Fellowship. It's a nondenominational church geared toward people in recovery, so it's a little different. But you said you were looking for a job too, right?"

"Yeah, pregnant and unemployed isn't the best position I've ever been in," Jenny said dryly.

"Oh, that sounds like the perfect thing, actually," Ron said and laughed. To her surprise, Jenny laughed too. "What's your work background?" he asked.

"I'm a grant and contract writer."

Ron's eyes lit up. "Seriously? You should come by. The church also runs a women's center, and I know the pastor is looking for a grant writer. Seriously, I mean it."

"I'll stop by the church tomorrow, okay?"

"Great! Now, tell me what you think of this place. Do you like it?" Ron gestured toward an apartment that had modern accents. The large kitchen had new appliances, and the white walls seemed to smile at Jenny.

Jenny nodded as Ellen's eyes opened wide. Jenny would pay the difference from her saved bonus, because she was desperate to get out of the shop-house. The only reason she had put up with the house this long was that she had been hoping Ghaith would magically appear and rescue her.

"I'll bring the payment tomorrow." Jenny put her hand on her tummy. *I'll raise you myself, precious baby.*

℅

Church was—*What was the word Ron had used?*—chaotic. As Jenny sat in a folding chair, a kid ran up the aisle past her and almost ran into another pregnant woman who was standing in the aisle. She was a beautiful local girl with long, dark hair and a naturally stylish look. Watching the woman rock back and forth drinking coffee, Jenny loved that she seemed so comfortable with her pregnancy.

Ron had come over and given her a hug and kiss on the cheek, apparently the status quo greeting for Guam, much like in Abu Dhabi. Then he sat down in a different row, looking handsome in a long-sleeved, white, button-down linen shirt and khaki shorts with Birkenstock sandals. Yesterday Jenny had not thought him particularly good-looking, but she really hadn't been looking at him because she had been so pleased with the apartment. But today, in nice comfortable clothes, he was much more appealing. Apparently he was also one of the church leaders, because he quickly stepped up to help collect the offerings and adjust the sound system.

Jenny made it a point not to go over to him, even though he was sitting alone. She did not want him to feel like he had to keep her company or that she had come to church because of him. She was there of her own accord, and she was going to prove that. So she sat there behind the rocking pregnant mom, with children running up and down the aisles, trying to pay attention to what the pastor was saying.

The pastor was a tall, bald white man with a friendly face and bright blue eyes. With his big nose, he wasn't particularly attractive, but there was something about him that Jenny liked immediately. She looked around at the throng of girls and noticed their hard faces. A couple of them gave her friendly smiles, but Jenny felt intimidated by these tattooed local girls, many of whom were toothless and had probably seen better and worse days.

As she looked around the room, it was pretty clear to Jenny that a lot of these people were in recovery. One of the white girls in front of her kept twitching every so often. Jenny was not sure that this was the church for her, but she wanted to see about the job that Ron had mentioned.

When church was over, Ron introduced her to the pastor. He wanted her to start work the next day, because they had two grants due at the end of the upcoming week. So Jenny accepted a freelance position and told him she could start the next day.

As Jenny walked out the front double doors of the church, a single tear of happiness slid down her cheek. The relief that washed over her was so powerful that she practically stumbled to her car. As she sat down, she knew everything was going to be all right. It was such an unfamiliar feeling, after the months of agony and uncertainty.

There must be a God.

ೞ

A month later, the song "Stereo Love" belted out of Jenny's phone, startling her. Sure enough, it was Ghaith. She quickly calculated the time difference and realized it was three in the morning his time. Since their last conversation, she had experienced the pregnancy crazy cycle a couple more times. They had talked sweetly one moment and angrily the next, with more anger than sweetness on Jenny's part, since she was still trying to process the entire situation.

"Hello?" The word came out like an unfinished question. Jenny wondered why Ghaith was calling when he should have been sleeping.

"Hey, baby." His voice was filled with exhaustion.

"Is everything all right?"

"I am on my way home from the hospital. We just had a beautiful baby girl. It was a hard labor, though. Laila bled so much afterward. She did not do that with the first two births."

A sense of numbness overwhelmed Jenny, and everything turned hazy and gray. She sat down without thinking about sitting down. "Oh, uh … Congratulations, I guess," she mumbled.

At that moment, her feelings about Ghaith as a lover disappeared. He was only a close friend telling her about this celebration of his life. The question of how she was supposed to handle this as a Christian became very real to her. She no longer hated him and she didn't feel sad—she felt only compassion for Ghaith and his family. Or maybe that was the best way that she could handle it, by separating herself from it and looking at the situation analytically.

"I thought about you the whole time," Ghaith continued.

And—*zap*—just like that, her compassion evaporated and her anger returned. "Why would you do that?"

"Just think about it, and you will understand."

"Um, I am thinking, and I don't get it *at all*."

"Well, we are going to have a baby together too. I was just thinking of how it would feel to be next to you." He said this as though it was a good answer and made any sense whatsoever.

Jenny immediately launched into a soapbox speech, because she simply could not process the idiocy of it at all. "I mean, how could you think about *me* when your wife is in labor and you guys are having a child together? That is so wrong to her."

"Shut up! Just shut the fuck up! You are making me feel terrible!"

Jenny sucked in her breath. She wanted to disobey his bitter demand, but she was so angry that she was at a loss for words—which made her even angrier.

"I am just so tired." Ghaith sighed again. "I am so sorry I am not there for you."

Jenny remained quiet and tried to process what had just been said.

"Are you okay, Jenny?"

She finally found her vocal cords again. "I don't know how to feel. Really, Ghaith, congratulations. I am glad that everything is okay. Get some sleep."

"Okay. I will try, baby."

As Jenny hung up, she looked at her phone and felt numb. Soon the numbness was replaced with a sorrow so soulful and hopeless that she erupted into sobs. After a few minutes, she tried to calm herself by holding her breath in little waves.

∞

Jenny woke up feeling more restless than rested. She shook her head, unsuccessfully trying to erase the dream that woke her up. The phone on her bedside table was still turned off. Turning it back on, she saw that Ghaith had called but hadn't left a message, as usual. An hour later, she called him back.

"Hello," he said. His Arabic accent made it sound more like "'Ello" in a slightly irritating manner—the gulf dialect typical greeting on cell phones. "What's up?" He quickly switched to a Midwestern American accent.

"Hey, uh, yeah. I saw you called."

"Yeah, just wanted to know how you were doing," he said, instead of asking directly.

"Yeah, fine." She paused. "Anything else?"

"Uh, no. I just figured I would call. You know, Jenny, I miss you."

All Jenny could think of was how convenient he was playing all of this. She had not heard from him in three days, and the last conversation they had was the "my wife just gave birth and I thought about you and shut the fuck up" conversation.

Jenny had, of course, sent him two texts since then. One was when she felt like she should be his friend, and to some extent, she could understand his craziness. She was glad that he could share this intimate life moment with her—that life he had always kept separate from her. In some strange way, she understood why he would call her right after he had been through this experience.

She did not agree with or understand anything else he had said to her, but she had sent him a text. "Really, congratulations. I am sure she is a beautiful little girl."

The next day, Jenny sent Ghaith another text because, for the first time, a complete stranger had asked her how far along she was. Her bump had been noticed! No more *maybe she's fat*. Now she was a bona fide pregnant woman, and that thrilled her. She wanted to share that moment with him, especially because he had not seen her since the baby was the size of an acorn.

Ghaith had not replied to her during those three days, however, so she went back to turning off her phone at night. She was consistently waking up at two thirty and four o'clock in the morning. And when she woke up and did not see a text or missed call from Ghaith, she would imagine him sleeping next to his wife and she'd write him an angry letter in her head. As her eyes adjusted to the darkness, she would stare in a rage at the ceiling, then at the wall next to her bed, and then at the other wall across the room, tossing and turning relentlessly. An hour or so after that little involuntary mental exercise, hunger would set in and she would need to pee. After another hour of sleeplessness, exhaustion would hit her and she would pass out, usually just as the sun was starting to rise.

Since that was absolutely no fun and caused her relentless stress, Jenny had resorted to just turning her phone off. Even though she knew in the dark recesses of her mind that there was no text or missed call from Ghaith, at least now her phone couldn't flaunt that fact in her face. And Jenny could go back to sleep without writing a marathon of hate letters and enduring hours of insomnia.

Three days and two phoneless nights later, Ghaith called her and acted as if their last conversation had gone just fine. This made Jenny angrier—not red-bolt anger, but the kind of anger where numbness just settles in.

"Look, I need to know what's going on," she said, after he rambled about his business for twenty minutes.

"Oh, okay. Well, I need to get some things done, and I will call you back."

She hung up and stared at her phone. Twelve thirty in the morning. She shut it off. She knew he wouldn't be calling back tonight, but she didn't want that sad fact displayed on her phone in two hours—when she was sure to wake up.

CHAPTER 64

"Ghaith is coming," Jenny said to her mom. It was nearly Easter, although it didn't feel like it since Guam had only two seasons, rainy and rainier.

Ellen eased on the brakes, trying to avoid the astronomical number of potholes on the coral-paved roads. She wasn't successful.

"Ow," Jenny said, as she was jostled in the car. Being in a car while pregnant reminded Jenny of being on her father's waterbed in the eighties. Any little movement would rock the entire bed and make her queasy.

"Oops, sorry." Her mom laughed a little. "When will he be coming?"

"Well, he hasn't exactly given me a date. He said he has a lot of business deals to finish up first."

"Oh, I see." Ellen let out a small sigh.

"Ahh, this air-con sucks." Jenny started fanning herself with a piece of paper she found in her purse. The humidity was extreme today, as it was every day on this tropical island. "This place is so hot." Jenny rolled down the window to try to get some more air in, even if it was hot air.

"So, what do you think about Ron?"

Jenny realized that Ellen was changing the conversation to something more positive, or maybe just trying to get Jenny's mind off the heat. Ellen worried about all the negativity that Jenny seemed unable to put down—and its potential effect on the baby that she was carrying.

"Well, he is nice and kind of cute, and the best thing is that he's a

Christian." Jenny smiled for the first time in a couple of days. "He asked me out to a fashion show fund-raiser next month."

Immediately the air seemed to lift. Jenny felt fortunate that Ron had been their real estate agent, and she was happy that she had a good job. She was also happy that she had found a group of Christians who didn't judge her, but instead prayed for her and told her she had been brave to leave the Middle East and Ghaith.

Unfortunately, Jenny usually felt more idealistic than brave when she thought about the move. Moreover, she was sad for the little girl growing inside her—Ghaith's fourth daughter. If she had been pregnant with a boy, Ghaith would be here with her right now. But Jenny was going to have a little girl, and she smiled at that thought.

"That's great! I think you two might make a really good pair," Ellen said.

"Yeah, I don't know." Jenny felt her softness slowly return.

"You never know." Ellen parked the car at the beach park, and they got out for their evening stroll on the beach. The sun was setting, casting beautiful orange and pink colors into the sky. "I'm just so glad you are here. It's such a beautiful calming place to be pregnant." Ellen snapped a picture of the sky.

"Yes, it is pretty." But Jenny frowned. She could *see* the beauty of this place, where the aqua water seamlessly stretched to a soft horizon of orange and gold, but she couldn't *feel* the beauty. She felt empty inside, even though she was literally more full of life than ever.

CHAPTER 65

Jenny thought she had picked out the perfect dress at the maternity store. Even her mother's gay coworker had approved of the beautiful plum-colored dress when Jenny showed him the pictures on her phone earlier that week. But now, at the fashion show, she was surrounded by gorgeous skinny people and she just felt like a fat cow. Of course, she was thirty-seven weeks pregnant, but she knew she hadn't gained weight only from the baby.

To make it worse, her platform shoes were pinching her swollen feet painfully, even while she was sitting down. She could smile only by gritting her teeth, and she was convinced that these gorgeously skinny people must be able to see the pain in her desperate, clenched smile.

Rose Espinosa, the hostess of the event, teetered around gracefully on four-inch heels and leaned over as Ron kissed her on the cheek. Sometimes Jenny hated that greeting. Rose had an hourglass figure with long, straight, beautiful, black hair, and Jenny hadn't been surprised when Ron told her that Rose was a former Ms. Guam beauty queen. Wearing a tight, short black dress, with a pair of diamond studs in her ears, she was the exquisite Asian beauty about whom most men probably fantasized. The very air seemed to buzz around her as she fluttered from person to person, a perfect social butterfly.

Jenny looked down at her own floor-length cotton plum dress and her clunky wedges. *To think he could be interested in me.* As if things couldn't get worse, Jenny began to sweat.

The fashion show started, and a slew of Ms. Guam models strutted onstage in the cutest Asian clothes—clothes made for their skinny Asian bodies. Ron, who was the photographer for the event—a fact he'd left out when he invited Jenny—lifted his camera and began to snap away. She didn't know why he'd invited her if he was going to leave her to sit by herself the whole night.

Usually, Jenny was fine going to new places by herself, but not when she was so pregnant. She felt like a social outcast. The only thing any of these gorgeous skinny people asked her about was the baby—although she did like the fact that on Guam, guys asked these questions too.

Annabella moved around in Jenny's belly, and she couldn't help but smile. She liked being able to physically see her baby moving inside of her as her stomach swayed around.

"Hey, do you want a drink?" Ron asked. Finally, it was intermission, so he had wandered back over to Jenny. Leaning on the back of her chair, he looked down at her with a smile on his face.

"I would love a glass of wine."

Chuckling, Ron looked at her belly. But when Jenny didn't laugh with him, he sobered up and nodded. "Red or white?"

"Red—and make it a large glass." Jenny smiled.

Ron raised his eyebrows slightly, but then a sly smile came over his face. He put his camera on the chair next to her and walked over to the bar.

People all around Jenny were getting a little drunk, and she needed something strong. It made her happy when a very good-looking guy started slurring into the microphone, praising his wife's wonderful efforts. *Rose's husband.* Jenny smiled.

"Here you go," Ron said as he walked back over and handed Jenny a glass of merlot.

"Thank you." She glanced at the drink in his other hand. "What did you get?"

Ron leaned over her chair again. "A screwdriver, but I hope everyone else thinks it's just orange juice." He picked up his camera and sat down next to her. "After all," he said, "we do work at a recovery center."

"I don't care." And as though defying anyone to object, Jenny raised her glass to Ron's. "Cheers." Sipping her wine, Jenny wondered if people were judging her, but she really didn't care anymore. She just wanted to numb herself. The occasional glass of wine or two wouldn't hurt Annabella, so these people with their judgmental opinions could kiss her ass.

ଚ

The truth was that no matter what kind of dress Jenny wore, she couldn't hide the fact that she had gained forty-five pounds—and most of it was *not* baby. She wrestled on a short, eggshell-white dress with funky lace at the edges, but then she had to pull on leggings because her large belly made the front of the dress hang about six inches higher than the back.

Today the doctor had almost kept her at the hospital to induce labor because her blood pressure was so high, but she'd begged off until Monday. If they induced labor, she'd have to give birth in a moldy, gross hospital. Instead, Jenny was determined to have natural labor at the birthing center.

So whatever it took, this weekend Jenny was going to self-induce her labor. Ellen had already given her some tips, and Jenny had diligently taken notes: (1) stimulate nipples until contractions start; (2) take warm baths and do visualization; (3) eat pineapple, kiwi, and/or mango; and (4) put evening primrose oil on cervix once per day.

Feeling somewhat overwhelmed, Jenny started fantasizing about Ron stimulating her nipples while feeding her pineapple in a warm bath. That wasn't going to happen, of course, but he had asked her out to dinner that night, and she was glad just to get out of the house. She put on a pair of comfortable red shoes and matching red lipstick. At least her hair was shiny, although as soon as she walked outside, the humidity attacked it and left it frizzy and poufy.

Jenny fell in love with the restaurant where Ron took her. It was a small local microbrewery with wooden mermaids of varied shapes and sizes shoved into every place imaginable.

"What would you like?" Ron asked her, looking at the menu.

"Let's order a beer sampler. It might help induce this labor," Jenny said with a grin.

Laughing, Ron nodded. "Sure thing."

Even though Jenny had known Ron more than four months and he had invited her out once in a while, this was the most private time they'd had. Usually they saw each other in public, at church or work, at lunch with people from church or work, or at very busy fund-raisers. Ron talked quickly and in a low voice, so Jenny really had to lean in to hear him—not that she minded.

"So what else do you have going on this weekend?" he asked, after the waitress came over and took their order.

"Well, I am determined to have this baby." Jenny told Ron about the day at the hospital and then about her mom's suggestions, leaving out the nipple stimulation and cervix oil rub. As their conversation fell into a natural flow, the waitress brought out their food and Jenny wondered … *Is he the one?*

Ron looked concerned when she mentioned it would be a natural labor and not at the hospital, but then he seemed to relax when Jenny went back to sipping her beer.

Jenny felt giggly, like her heart was starting to take shape again. All the anger was still there, but it had shifted to the background in her mind. As they drove home, Jenny felt Annabella start to do flips in her stomach. Maybe the beer and the momentary lack of stress would help induce this labor after all.

When Ron parked his car at Jenny's apartment, she was surprised that he got out of the car and ran around to open her door. As she tried to slide out gracefully, he just laughed and helped to pull her out.

"I'm so graceful," she said, laughing at herself. A slight buzz from the beer, combined with exhaustion, continued to make her feel giggly and sloppy.

"You're about to have a baby, Jenny. Relax and let me walk you up."

Jenny walked in front of Ron up the three flights of stairs, with two thoughts on her mind. First, *Catch your breath, Jenny.* And second, *Is he going to kiss me?*

When they got to her door, she took a deep breath, turned, and looked at him. "Thanks so much for dinner."

Ron smiled at her. "No problem."

Then Annabella started to do somersaults in Jenny's belly again, and Jenny looked down at her belly with wide eyes. "I might have this kid tonight. She's moving like crazy. Hey, do you want to feel her move?"

"Ah, sure." Ron awkwardly held up his hand, hesitating until Jenny giggled, grabbed his hand, and pressed it against her belly. "Oh, wow! She's really in there, hey?" There was a light in his eyes, and he kept his hand on Jenny's stomach even after Annabella stopped moving. "That's amazing. I've never before felt a baby move, not even my nieces or nephews."

Behind her, the door swung open and Ellen said, "Hey, you guys! Are you coming in?"

The magic in the air instantly vanished, and Ron quickly snatched his hand off Jenny's stomach.

"Ah, no," he said. "I've gotta run, and Jenny needs to get some rest." He smiled at Jenny, gave her a quick hug, and kissed her cheek. "Good luck on having that baby," he whispered.

CHAPTER 66

Four minutes and forty-five seconds—that had been the time between her contractions for the last four hours. Jenny packed her labor bag and then woke up her mom. It was early still, only seven in the morning.

The contractions had started only a couple of hours after she went to sleep. At first they woke her up every ten minutes or so, but they soon intensified so that she couldn't go back to sleep.

"Breathe," Ellen said.

The room at the birthing center was gently framed with pale pink walls, and the queen-sized bed reminded Jenny of a room at the Ramada Inn. But obviously it was also a medical facility, with a heart rate monitor and an IV beside the bed to prove it. This fusion of comfort with safety calmed Jenny's nerves, but it did nothing ease the pain of her contractions, unfortunately.

Her mother happened to have gotten injections the previous day, so her lips, usually nice enough, were now swollen and strangely fish-looking. It was driving Jenny crazy.

Letting out a groan, Jenny cringed but then relaxed as soon as the contraction stopped. "They're so intense, but then I feel completely normal when they're over." She had been experiencing contractions consistently for eight hours, although she was still at only two centimeters.

The contractions were getting more intense, though, and Jenny was using guttural noises to lessen the pain—which freaked out anyone who happened to be visiting with her in the room.

Just then, the pastor's wife, Cecilia, came into the room with some saltine crackers for Jenny and a sandwich for Ellen. "Okay, here's your break," she said, smiling at Ellen.

"Thank God," Jenny said, after her mom left the room. "Someone I can look at seriously."

Cecilia smiled, obviously understanding that Jenny was referring to Ellen's fish lips.

Jenny noticed that Cecilia had a splint on her pinky finger on her right hand, and she gestured toward it. "What happened?"

"Oh, I just jammed it a bit last night and broke it," Cecilia answered calmly.

Jenny groaned to herself. She wanted fully capable people around her right now, not Fish Lips and Broken Finger. But with her next breath a contraction hit and her mouth fell open with a groan. Cecilia threw the crackers on the bed and ran over to Jenny. Holding her hands, she coached Jenny through the contraction.

Fifteen hours later, Jenny finally entered the transition phase—seven centimeters and three-minute contractions every seven minutes. This was a longer labor than any that Jenny had heard or read about, but she didn't have time to think about that. She just thought about breathing, one breath at a time.

Ellen couldn't push on Jenny's back because of a slipped disc in her own back, so Cecilia took over that responsibility, despite her broken finger. And Jenny needed pressure—like the weight of a sumo wrestler—because she was suffering intense back pain. So it was Cecilia with the broken pinkie finger who pushed with all her might, for three minutes straight, off and on for six hours. As soon as a contraction ended, Cecilia's hands would go limp and she would fall asleep on Jenny's shoulder behind her.

In those moments, when Jenny's mind was crystal clear, she thought about Ghaith and how he wasn't there. How he didn't even know she was in the throes of childbirth, struggling to bring their daughter into the world.

As Jenny groaned, her mother's grip retightened and Cecilia started pushing. Then Jenny's pain overtook her and her deep guttural sounds turned into screams.

ℚ

Thirty-two hours after Jenny's labor started, a healthy five pound, ten-ounce baby was born. Annabella Hope Richert. No father was listed on the birth certificate. She was given her mother's last name.

CHAPTER 67

Jenny awoke with a start and sat up, in that small moment that always seems so long. *Where am I? Where am I supposed to be? What am I missing?* And then, *Did I drop the baby?* She looked around in a panic and saw Annabella, fast asleep and rocking in the automatic swing.

The living room was drenched in sunlight and the walls seemed to glow a deep yellow. Jenny looked at her phone—it was nine o'clock in the morning. Even though she had slept only two hours, she felt somewhat refreshed, and her momentary panic was replaced by joy to see Anna sleeping and safe. Her mom must have put her in the swing before she left.

Jenny hadn't given a thought to the swing all night long. *Wow, it really is true. Having a kid doesn't mean that you know how to be a parent.* In the first three days of Annabella's life, Jenny felt highly inadequate and anxious. Of course, the sleep deprivation did not help.

Every time she looked at the baby, she saw Ghaith. Ghaith's nose, lips, and eyes. This is what she had dreaded, that she would see Ghaith every day of Annabella's life. Her mother had said Annabella would develop her own look as she got older, but Jenny wasn't so sure. She was the most beautiful baby Jenny had ever seen, but it pained her heart and made her really miss Ghaith.

Nevertheless, Jenny wasn't going to contact him. Quite the opposite. She was seeking legal advice to terminate his parental rights. Of course, that meant he would also have no responsibilities. But short of going back to Abu Dhabi, where a judge was more likely to order them to get married or give Ghaith custody, there was nothing else Jenny could do.

She had spent months writing a manifesto and trying to figure out what her rights were. Her lawyer had been in shock when the manifesto had landed with a *Bam!* on his desk. After she thoroughly educated him on the countries that were not part of The Hague Convention and the results of the sampling interviews that she had with lawyers in UAE, he had quickly recommended that Jenny herself become a lawyer, or at the very least a paralegal.

The bottom line was that Sharia law is very different from a democracy. Under Sharia law, it was Jenny's fault that she became pregnant out of wedlock. Furthermore, she couldn't raise a child with the gender bias paradigm that permeated the Middle East. It took two to tango, and she wouldn't bear the burden of a mutual decision.

Jenny's heart soared as she watched little Annabella swinging so peacefully. *This is a mother's love,* she thought, and then began to cry. There was no way she was going to risk losing her perfect little girl.

৪০

Jenny's first day back to work included lunch with Ron and a meeting at a local coalition—both of which would, by necessity, include Annabella. Jenny spent the previous night praying that everything would be okay. She still had issues breastfeeding with a cover, and she was nervous that Anna would cry all day. It felt like a bad decision to have planned so many outings in one day. And then, to add to the stress, Ron arrived early.

"Hey," Jenny said as she let him in. "Give me five more minutes."

Ron gave her a hug and kiss on the cheek. "Okay, you get changed and I'll watch Annabella."

Jenny paused, then looked down at herself. She was already dressed for the day. Three weeks out and she had lost maybe twenty-five pounds, but it was still a far cry from the amount she had gained. She was sick of her maternity clothes, most of which weren't nursing friendly anyway, and she was still too big for her prepregnancy clothes.

To make matters worse, she regretted her shopping trip with Cecilia because they had totally different styles. And while they were shopping, Annabella had pooed through her diaper onto Jenny's shorts—her white shorts, of course. Jenny had panicked and just bought whatever came to hand, including the stretchy top and khakis she was wearing now.

But Ron was probably right—they were too casual for work. Jenny went back into her room to grab a thin blazer to go over the camisole and added a fake pearl necklace for accent.

Ron was holding Annabella in one arm and his phone against his ear with his other hand when she came back into the living room. He smiled when he saw Jenny, and she wondered if the one she gave him in return looked as embarrassed as she felt. The wrinkled blazer and necklace didn't make a huge difference to her outfit. The loss of twenty-five pounds had made a difference overall, but her stomach was still big and her breasts were heavy with milk.

Ron motioned for her to leave ahead of him, so Jenny grabbed Annabella's carrier and her purse, making sure her nursing cover, diapers, and blanket were all hidden away before walking out to the car. Before Annabella, Ron had never held such a young baby, just as he had never felt a baby move in the womb. But the moment he picked her up and she opened her eyes, he completely lost any nervousness. Jenny loved the fact that after only a few weeks, Ron was now juggling Annabella along with his phone.

Sitting in the plastic booth at the Japanese restaurant, Annabella got cranky before they'd even finished their appetizers. Jenny sighed, *Here goes public breastfeeding.* Later, after an awkward session of fumbling underneath the nursing blanket, Annabella finally fell asleep and Jenny was able to put her back into the carrier. Jenny had spilled water on herself when she was adjusting Annabella under the breastfeeding cover, and her makeup was beginning to feel tired. She felt deflated and exhausted, still waking up every two hours when Annabella cried to be nursed or held or rocked back to sleep.

"You ready for the meeting?" Ron took another bite of sushi.

"Yep, it sounds like so much fun," Jenny said sarcastically. She waved the waiter over and ordered a coffee.

Ron smiled at her. "Are you feeling all right?"

"Yes. No. Actually, I'm exhausted." She tried to open her eyes wider to muster up a sense of alertness, but it didn't work. "How's your mom?"

"Ah, good. Thanks for asking. She asks about you and Annabella all the time."

Ron's mom had walked up the three flights of stairs to Jenny's condo with her bad hip to see the baby. When Ron had been on the other side of the room holding Annabella, she leaned toward Jenny and stage-whispered, "Is that my boy's child?"

Jenny had shaken her head and blushed, pretty sure Ron had overheard the question. The way he was acting with Annabella, though, it did almost look like she was his. He and his mom had brought over bags and bags of presents for Annabella. Jenny was still a bit stunned by all of their affection for her daughter.

Ron changed the subject, maybe because he was remembering that same moment. "So have you heard from Annabella's dad?" This was the first time Ron had brought up Ghaith at all, so it surprised Jenny. Of course, she had told him the situation, so he knew what happened in a general sense, but he had never pushed for additional information.

"Ah, no. No, I haven't," she said after a moment, when she'd had time to collect herself. "I actually haven't spoken to him for a long time, since months before I had Annabella." She tore open two sugar packets, dumped them into her coffee, then reached for the cream.

"Oh, so what are you going to do about him? As far as Annabella, I mean." He looked at her evenly.

"Well, he's not on the birth certificate, if that's what you mean, but I've actually been meeting with a lawyer. I want to send him paperwork to relinquish his parental rights." She set her coffee cup down, splashing coffee out onto the table. She hadn't realized that she still shook when she talked about Ghaith.

Taking his napkin, Ron leaned across the table and wiped up the spill. When he looked up, she could tell he was trying to suppress a smile.

"That's good. It'll be easier that way," he said. He motioned for her to pass him Annabella.

Jenny reached into the carrier and picked up the sleeping baby. She paused to gaze at Annabella for a moment. Then she handed the sleeping baby over to Ron, who took her gently into his arms.

PART IV

CHAPTER 68

It had been nearly a year since Jenny had seen Ghaith, but little memories still floated through her mind every now and then, like a submerged wreck giving up pieces of itself. A subtle picture, smell, or dream would snag a memory, resurrecting it, and suddenly it would be so real that she would look around for Ghaith. Sometimes nostalgia could be the worst form of pain.

This time it was a place. Dusit Thani. Jenny was pushing Annabella's stroller down the corridor of a new mall, looking for a restroom. Rounding a corner, she saw a sign advertising the new hotel that was being built on Guam, Dusit Thani. One look at the curvy modern letters and there she was again, back in a skyscraper in Dubai.

Ghaith had taken her there to break the fast during Ramadan. It had been a good day—the day she forgave him for the affairs—and for some reason they finally felt like a normal couple. They'd spent the day walking around the Chinese mall, getting prices for bulk materials and trying to hold back the "Ramadan giggles," the silly and weak feeling from not eating all day.

Ghaith had mentioned going to the Thai restaurant at the Dusit Thani for Iftar, the feast that marked the breaking of the fast. Jenny knew the place only from driving past it, a majestic skyscraper with large Asian calligraphy boasting *Dusit Thani* across its front, glittering against the sun or lit up at night.

So that was where they had gone and been greeted by one of the largest buffets Jenny had ever seen. Almost two years later, it was still the biggest spread she'd seen. The place was empty, so they had taken the best table in the room, right beside the window. Jenny had felt dizzy from it all—the smell of food, the waiting, and the height when she looked out the window from the twenty-fourth floor. She and Ghaith looked across the freeway into the intricate maze of spiraling skyscrapers, toward the ocean, and watched the sky turn from a soft yellow to a haze of reds. The light changed Ghaith's skin from light olive to a soft red, and their eyes had met just as the muezzin sounded the call to prayer. That was when they seemed to have their own language, their own rhythm, their own religion.

Jenny shook herself from this memory, quickly letting it fall back into the depths. She was irritated that something as silly as a sign could stir these memories and emotions. Walking into the restroom, she turned on the faucet, splashing cold water onto her face and willing the memories away.

CHAPTER 69

Jenny gathered up her last reminders of Ghaith—his pajamas, his shirt, a gold bracelet he'd given her, and a few other things. Getting out a black trash bag, she started throwing things away, while tears rolled down her cheeks.

"Motherfucker!" she yelled when she threw the pajamas in the bag. "Fucking asshole!" when the shirt went in. She held onto the bracelet for a moment, hesitating. After all, it was Chanel and it was real gold—but eventually she tossed that in, too. Then she hugged the bag to her chest and let the sobs shake through her.

For a year, she had spent endless nights planning how to get back at Ghaith. But now she had to leave that in God's hands.

Walking down the hallway, Jenny put the trash bag near the door. She would throw it away when her mom got home, since she couldn't leave Annabella alone in the house three flights up.

When she peeked into her room and saw Annabella still fast asleep in her swing, Jenny smiled involuntarily. Her daughter really was so beautiful and innocent. Jenny couldn't imagine life without her, and she was pissed that her daughter's father was such a horrible person. She quietly shut the door and ran her hands through her hair.

Despite the trash bag full of Ghaith's things by the door, Jenny still didn't feel closure. She still felt this soul tie, as though she could smell his scent and feel his touch lingering on her bare skin. "How do I break this connection, God?" she asked aloud.

Should she make a list of men with whom she had been—and burn it? This would at least be a physical ritual to break all soul ties and free her up to meet Mr. Right, wherever he might be. She wondered if Mr. Right could be Ron.

Jenny began by writing out a list of what she wanted in a man.

✓ Witty
✓ Funny
✓ Likes to travel
✓ Good-looking
✓ Responsible, but spontaneous
✓ Successful
✓ Wonderful daddy to Annabella
✓ Spiritual
✓ Amazing chemistry

That's not asking for too much, she thought sarcastically. After a moment, she flipped through the notebook and began writing about a different topic—all the guys with whom she had been and little bits about each one of them.

It was somehow cathartic, putting each memory onto paper and seeing it for what it really was. This was her past. It felt good to give each person a little written memorial, but the cremation was the truly liberating part.

She took the paper outside to the balcony, along with a glass bowl and lighter. As she lit the paper, Jenny watched the names disintegrate quicker than a first kiss. Instead of the ashes falling neatly into the bowl, a strong wind kicked up and carried them around the corner of the building and beyond, to a resting place she would never know.

CHAPTER 70

Annabella Hope *Richert.* Ghaith definitely had mixed emotions about that. Attached in an e-mail was a parental rights relinquishment form from a lawyer in Guam. *Well, well, well, she actually did it,* he thought. She had taken a step to completely remove him from her life.

Ghaith was furious. There was no way that he would give up his child. He had thought about Jenny in August, when the baby was due to be born, but then he had put her out of his mind. He couldn't contact her, not when he couldn't be there for her. She would contact him when she was ready.

But now they had a baby girl! He wondered what she looked like. Did she have Jenny's green eyes and blonde hair, or his dark skin and kinky hair? Then he became angry all over again. Jenny had not even given Annabella his last name, even though she was his child too. Annabella was a part of him.

Ghaith sent Jenny a text: "I am not signing these papers. I want to see Annabella."

It was the first direct communication they'd had in six months, since Jenny was about seven months pregnant. When she stopped e-mailing him, it had been a relief because Ghaith was running out of excuses not to visit her. He knew that if he saw her pregnant, his heart would drop and he would have to stay, at least for a while. Then everything would get complicated again. Instead, he drew closer to Haifa, his youngest, and pretended that she was Jenny's baby. Somehow, this made him feel closer to her but without the chaos. It also made Laila very happy that he was showing so much interest in their third daughter.

Ghaith waited a few minutes, and then relaxed and softened his tone. "I bet she is beautiful like you."

Several hours later, Jenny texted back, "She is beautiful."

"Please e-mail pics," he texted.

Over the next few days, Jenny sent a ton of pictures. Annabella *was* beautiful, with Ghaith's dark hair and eyes. In fact, she looked more like him than any of his other girls. Jenny had cropped herself out of the pictures, so that he only ever saw her hand or shoulder. The focus of the picture was always Annabella, in every picture except one. Jenny was holding Annabella and she was smiling, and she looked exactly like she had before. Beautiful.

"Look, if you want to be a part of her life, then you should come and see her," Jenny said over the phone, a week after they had started communicating again.

"I'm trying, habibti."

But he had things he had to figure out at home, such as telling Laila a good excuse for why he was leaving. And telling Carmen, his newest girlfriend, a good reason for leaving. Of course, there was some work stuff to figure out, too.

"Inshallah, I will be there next month."

He also needed time to come up with a plan for what to do about Jenny and Annabella. Right now they were hidden away like a secret, but this journey alone would make a bold statement. Sticking to his original plan, he could still try to house them in Doha, where he was expanding his company. His father could still persuade his friend in the ministry of foreign affairs to change the date on the marriage certificate. In Doha, Jenny could run that side of the firm, and he could see Jenny and Annabella every month. He rubbed the side of his head. *If only she would marry me.* But they had fought their way through that conversation too many times.

Ghaith heard Jenny sigh and say, "Sure, I've heard that one before."

"Look, baby, it would be so much easier if you just came over here and worked for me in Doha. Then I could see you both all the time."

"Are you seriously bringing that up again? Why would I ever work for you again, after you fired me when I was pregnant with your child, and then offered no financial assistance at all? And stop calling me baby." She was clearly still angry at him.

Ghaith laughed and said, "Oh, come on. That was so long ago." Then his voice turned serious. "I'm sorry, babe—um, Jenny. I was so confused." And he had been confused. His emotions had wrapped around his heart so tightly that he'd been impotent for months. Once he'd dreamed he had hundreds of baby girls and they were all crying. No matter where he ran, they clustered around him. That's when he was still seeing Dr. Azazi, the psychologist, on a regular basis.

"Look, come and visit. We can try to straighten a few things out," Jenny said, with a flicker of hope in her voice.

Ghaith had known all along that he would have to go out there to convince her. He was also pretty sure that, as soon as they saw each other, things would click back to the way they used to be. Ghaith nodded to himself. It was a plan.

CHAPTER 71

Even though Jenny had spent two hours doing her makeup and hair, and a good thirty minutes choosing an outfit, she still felt unprepared. *I can do this,* she told herself. Taking a deep breath, she knocked on the hotel door. The sound echoed down the corridor of the eleventh floor. As her heart pounded in her throat, she leaned over the stroller for strength. Annabella looked up at her and gurgled, and Jenny was still smiling when the door opened.

This was the moment for which she had waited more than a year now. Quickly stepping behind the stroller so Ghaith would see Annabella first, Jenny sacrificed this moment—and it had truly been a sacrifice.

Ghaith stood there in the doorway as if paralyzed, looking from Jenny to Annabella for what felt like a full minute. His pupils dilated, and it was a beautiful thing to see him so in awe, looking so intently at their daughter. He then backed up to let them in, and Jenny pushed the stroller past him. The initial moment past, Jenny caught her breath and felt slightly unprepared for what would follow.

Ghaith looked like he had just stepped out of an Abercrombie & Fitch advertisement, and Jenny felt her heart leap. She wanted to feel his arms wrap around her. *Crap, I should've prepared better for this.*

As if reading her mind, Ghaith said, a bit awkwardly, "Well, I haven't even said hello to you yet." Then he let out that deep, throaty laugh she'd missed so much.

It still warmed her like it had the first night they had met in that sports bar, sending shivers involuntarily down her spine. *He's married, and he abandoned me for over a year.* Jenny kept repeating this to herself as they embraced. But Ghaith's arms around her were warm and strong, just as they had always been.

"Hi," he said.

"Hi."

Thankfully, Ghaith then stepped back and picked up Annabella. "Mashallah, she is beautiful," he said, staring down at her and then whispering to Anna in little snippets of Arabic.

Something settled deep in Jenny's soul when he held Annabella. There was something so natural about it. This was what she'd wanted to see and feel, what she had fantasized about, and now it was filling her with billowy drifts of contentment.

Spread out on the bed she was sitting on, which was next to the bed he had been sleeping on, were several baby outfits, including cold weather jackets and snow pants. Obviously Ghaith hadn't realized that Guam is in the tropics, even though she had told him that and he had booked his ticket here.

"So how have you been?" Ghaith switched from his Arabic baby talk and looked over at Jenny.

"Busy, you know, being a fulltime working mom and all." She did not want this visit to turn into a battle, but she couldn't help herself. She was just being honest. Still, she didn't like hearing the hostility in her voice, so she backpedaled. "How about you? How's everything?"

"Good, good," Ghaith said. "Work is good and the company has really grown."

"And how about your family?"

"Wonderful. The girls are getting so big."

He then started telling her stories about his kids, and Jenny immediately chastised herself for asking him. "You know, maybe just the one story is all I can handle. Sorry, not trying to be mean, but it's just a little too much."

He looked back at Annabella and held her high in the air. "Yeah, I get it."

Settling on the bed, Jenny pushed her head back onto the pillows, but kept herself propped up so her figure would look appealing. She watched as Ghaith kissed Annabella, who smiled back at him, but within a few minutes Annabella got fussy. Looking confused, Ghaith quickly walked over to Jenny and put the fussy baby in her arms.

Jenny lifted her shirt. For a moment, she thought about turning away from Ghaith, but then thought better of it. He had seen her naked many times, and she could latch Annabella on quickly, so she did just that.

Ghaith stared at her in awe. "You're still breastfeeding. That is good."

"Of course." She felt the prickling of milk starting to flow, and for the first time that day, she relaxed and smiled at Ghaith.

He smiled back. "I can't believe it's been more than a year."

"Yes, it's been awhile."

"You look beautiful. Motherhood suits you well."

"Thank you. You don't look so bad yourself." Jenny gave him a crooked smile.

Ghaith walked over to the bed and sat next to her. Putting his arm around her waist, he kissed her tenderly on the top of her head, leaving his lips nestled in her hair as if transfixed. His other hand came to rest on Annabella, and they sat like that for a moment. Even before Annabella was born, Jenny had wished for them to sit together like this—Ghaith with one hand on Jenny and the other on their child in her womb.

"I missed you." Ghaith put both hands on Jenny, hugging her shoulders and kissed her neck slowly. She savored the softness, letting the sensation seep into her memory and the very cells of her body.

"Annabella's nursing," she said, shifting away from him.

"I know, I know." Ghaith's laugh sounded shallow and, adjusting himself, he walked away. "I just missed you so much." He picked up his pack of cigarettes on the end table and tapped one out. As he held the cigarette in his hand, suddenly Jenny craved a smoke and a drink—and then inwardly rebuked herself for the sentimental craving. He walked over to the balcony and opened the curtains. "Yes, I still have this little habit," he said, as if reading her mind, and winked at her. He then looked back out the window at the cliff line, which was covered in tropical foliage. "So much green."

Jenny gazed at his muscular shoulders and back, as he opened the French doors and went out onto the balcony, shutting the door behind him. Through the glass door, she could hear him singing softly in Arabic, as he stared out over the island. Jenny remembered how she'd felt when she first arrived back on Guam—that shock of so much green vegetation massaging her eyes, after more than a year in the Middle East.

Annabella's suckling became less and less intense. As she fell asleep, Jenny reached for her phone and dialed Ron. She needed major support right now. He answered on the second ring.

"Hey, how are you doing?" he asked right away. He knew that she was seeing Ghaith today.

"Well, he's outside smoking. But—okay, thanks."

"Are you sure? How's Annabella?"

"Yes, we are fine. I just wanted to hear someone else's voice for a minute. This is a lot tougher than I thought it would be."

"I'm here, Jenny."

"I know. I really appreciate all your support and prayers."

"Of course. So what are you guys going to do today?"

"Um, I think we will probably go get a bite soon."

"Okay. Well, let me know if you need anything."

"For sure. Thanks, Ron."

"Any time."

They hung up just as Ghaith was coming back in, still singing his song. Pulling her shirt down, Jenny walked over to Ghaith's bed to lay Annabella down. Ghaith sat down next to Annabella and watched her sleeping for a few minutes. Then he nestled up next to her, shut his eyes, and dozed for a while. Jenny lay down on the other side of Annabella and looked at the two of them. There was something so special and satisfying about Ghaith being there. Reaching across Annabella, Ghaith held Jenny's arm while resting his arm gently on Annabella.

Jenny closed her eyes, feeling warm inside and out. Here was that sense of completion that she had so desperately lacked during her pregnancy and Annabella's entire life. She had dreamed about Ghaith holding her and Annabella, aching for it so deeply. Now it was here. So differently, yet the feeling was just as she had imagined.

∞

The next day, waking up at home, Jenny felt more optimistic than she had on the previous day. She had a conference call at ten that morning, and Ghaith had told her to come to the hotel room so that he would watch Annabella for her.

Jenny had tried to bring up their future co-parenting plan over dinner on the previous evening, but Ghaith had had a few drinks and kept changing the subject. Obviously he didn't have a plan, or if he did, he didn't want to share it with her. But when she had dropped him off at the hotel, he had tried to talk her into coming up.

She had refused. "If I came up right now, I would be tempted to be with you." After a couple of drinks herself, she meant it.

"All the more reason to come up," Ghaith had said, with a laugh. Then he had looked at her for a long moment—and abruptly given up. "Okay, yalla, I'll see you in the morning." He kissed Jenny hard and fast before she could say anything else. Then he climbed out of the car and walked into the hotel, without looking back.

Jenny had held her lips as she watched him go. The quick, perfunctory feeling behind the kiss had reminded her of the shallow goodbye kiss at the airport when she'd left the Middle East. She cringed at that memory, at the abandonment. And yet, he'd offered to watch Annabella and seemed to dote on her. Wouldn't he agree to pay child support for a little girl he loved?

"Hey," she said when he opened the door. Ghaith was in sweatpants and a T-shirt again, and Arabic music floated out of the room behind him.

"Good morning." He reached for Annabella and smiled at her. "Daddy missed you."

After Jenny's conference call, they decided to go down to the pool to enjoy the weather. Jenny changed in the bathroom, putting on her black and white striped bikini. Her breasts were a bit swollen, and her belly was rounder than the last time she had seen Ghaith, but she had no stretch marks. She sucked in a breath, nervous, but confident too. She had been running nearly every day for the last couple of months, preparing for her first full marathon. This year, she was going to actually do it. She looked good, all things considered. She slid her sundress over her bikini just as Annabella began crying in the bedroom.

"Hurry up, habibti. Someone's hungry," Ghaith called, and laughed sending warm rushes of vibrations throughout her body.

"Coming!"

There were only a few other people at the pool, so Jenny put Annabella in her carrier in the shade. She had fed her while Ghaith changed, and now the child was sleeping. Jenny nervously took off her sundress and laid on her back on the sun chair next to Ghaith. He had his aviators on and looked pretty much as he had the first time they'd met.

"Hey." He smiled at Jenny, sizing her up.

"Aww, this is better." Jenny stretched her arms over her head and clasped her hands behind her head, trying to push out her chest and flatten her stomach.

"Wow, no stretch marks," Ghaith commented, and she could feel his gaze run up and down her body. "You look really good."

"Thanks." She paused, then went on, hoping to leverage some of the sexual tension. "So let's just get this out on the table. What are we going to do?"

"Relax."

"You know what I mean. About this situation." She let out a half smile. "Are you going to be involved in Annabella's life? Are you going to visit occasionally, or—?"

"Habibti. You know how complicated this is for me."

"And it's not for me?" Jenny sat up, suddenly angry again. "You haven't given me a dime and I've had to do this all on my own. I get absolutely no help. It's not just about you and your wife and *your* life anymore, Ghaith."

Ghaith exhaled deeply. "I know, I know." He propped himself up on his elbow and looked at her. "Why don't you just come to work for me in Doha? Then you can be close by, and I can help out financially."

"I would be working for you and earning well-deserved money. That's not how child support works." Every time he brought up Doha, she felt more and more frustrated. He had mentioned it on the phone before he came out, too. Jenny was his lucky charm, and he needed her help to expand his empire. But he wasn't thinking about Annabella at all—only about himself.

"It's perfect," Ghaith was saying. "You guys would be close, and I go to Doha every month. I could help out, and you could have a house and a nanny. You never know, we might end up together again."

Jenny shook her head. It was all about him. Again. He wanted everything to work out the way *he* wanted. "Look, I need help here. You know I'm working my ass off, and it's expensive here. I'm staying with my mom right now, but if she leaves, it'll be a disaster."

"Then you could come to Doha. You'll make way more money than you would here."

She'd forgotten how stubborn he was. Jenny swung one foot down onto the concrete, feeling the heat of the sun on her skin. "Look, we need to talk about what you're going to do with things as they are now. I'm happy here. Annabella is happy here."

"Annabella will be happy wherever you are."

"Well, it would be nice to have some financial support. Do I need to bring up that I don't trust you?"

CHAPTER 72

Even though the air-conditioning was on full blast, Ghaith was still hot and uncomfortable in his office clothes. The lawyer was dressed more casually, and Ghaith began to understand why men on Guam did not wear long-sleeved, button-down shirts.

"So you're not on the birth certificate," the lawyer said. He was a tall man and looked whiter than local, which Ghaith supposed must have helped him move up the ladder here.

"No, I'm not."

"Then you'll need to have a paternity test done to prove you're the father." He rested his elbows on the table, hands clasped under his chin.

Ghaith gritted his teeth, then gripped the chair to stop himself from getting up and pacing. "I know that. Just tell me what all this entails financially."

"Well, if you want to be on the birth certificate and get any kind of custody, you'll have to pay child support."

"I see."

"It's not too difficult, but it can take some time. Maybe a couple of months, depending on how quickly we get a court date."

"A couple of months?" There was no way he could stay on Guam for that long. "I don't have the luxury of that kind of time."

"Well, think about it and let me know. You can always travel back and forth, but ultimately your ex has a good case against you. You don't live on Guam and you haven't given her anything so far. But if you're interested, you can always send me the retainer, and I can start working on your case even if you're in Abu Dhabi."

Ghaith stood up. He took a Kleenex out of his pocket and wiped the perspiration from his forehead. "Thank you," he said, and shook hands with the lawyer.

Out in the lobby, he took out his phone and called his dad. "Baba, it's more complicated than I thought."

∞

Taking another drink of vodka, Ghaith enjoyed the warmth that spread into his belly. On his computer, Erykah Badu's melodic, sultry voice sang "On and On."

It was one of the songs Jenny had put on a CD for their road trips, and he loved how sexy this music was. It always reminded him of that perfect honeymoon period that he and Jenny had shared, before everything got so out of control. Behind him, the door swung open, and Ghaith turned to see Jenny coming in.

"Hey," she said, "my mom's waiting downstairs."

Ghaith patted one thigh. He was sitting just in front of the open balcony doors, his legs kicked up on the desk. He had a drink in one hand and a cigarette in the other.

"Baby, come sit with me for a minute." The nostalgia of the music and booze made him want her to hold him. He wanted to relive a minute of the past, and smell her hair, feel her body against his.

"Didn't you hear me? My mom's waiting for us in the car. She has Annabella with her."

Why couldn't everything be different? He wished he'd left Laila— that he *could* have left Laila. "Just one drink, habibti, for old time's sake." He stood up and reached for her, but she crossed her arms and glared at him.

"Okay, okay," Ghaith said, and reached to turn off the music. "Let's go." He kicked back his drink and put out his cigarette.

He had traveled halfway around the world, only to learn that Jenny hadn't even put his name on the birth certificate. *Hurt* was a completely inadequate word. Ghaith was crushed and angry. He'd thought this was going to be a happy reunion, but it hadn't turned out that way at all.

CHAPTER 73

As soon as he saw Jenny's car pull up outside the hotel, Ghaith felt a great wave of sadness. This might be the last time he would see her and Annabella, at least for a long time, and it was breaking his heart. Jenny was probably bitter or angry too, when all he wanted was a pleasant goodbye.

Annabella was awake in her car seat, and she looked at Ghaith with big eyes as he opened the back door to give her a kiss. She had his cupid lips and his well-defined nose. She would look like her father for the rest of her life.

Letting out a sigh, Ghaith sat next to Jenny.

"So," Jenny said, "I'm taking you by the notary to sign the parental rights relinquishment form."

Ghaith felt like he had been punched in the stomach. "Baby, why do you have to keep bringing that up?"

"Are you fucking serious? You won't pay a cent in child support, and you think you can still be Annabella's father?"

Ghaith felt his anger start to rise. If Jenny hadn't put all those restrictions on their relationship, and she had actually given him a real chance, his time here would have been very different. He would not be leaving alone right now, for one thing. But his anger and sadness affected his ability to articulate these points—and frankly, he was tired of fighting.

"I mean, you didn't even offer to pay for anything when you were here, not even diapers."

That did it. Ghaith reached into his wallet and took out all the money he had on him. "Here's about a thousand dollars," he said, tossing the money into Jenny's lap. "Go buy some diapers."

She didn't take her eyes off the road, or even acknowledge the money. It just sat in her lap like an unloved pet, but he noticed that her jaw relaxed a bit.

When Ghaith had called his father after his appointment with the lawyer, his father told him, "If you don't get married, you will always be fighting about money and time with your daughter. There will be no peace."

That, at least, seemed to be true.

"Are you sure this is what you want, habibti?" he asked.

It was all happening too quickly, and he knew that his pain had made him screw this up. But when Jenny looked at him, there was no love in her eyes—only pain and irritation. Maybe, he thought, he was never going to be a good parent.

Then Jenny's eyes softened slightly, and she looked over the seat at Annabella. "I don't know, but it's what needs to happen."

Ghaith grabbed the paperwork that Jenny had pulled out and looked at her again. Tears began to well up in her eyes and she looked away from him briskly, as though she might break if she kept looking at him. He knew that she was right, and that his dad was right. But *he* did not feel it was right.

There were only a couple of pages, but within those two pages and two signatures, he would be completely giving over his rights as Annabella's father. Someone else could adopt her, once Ghaith signed this. Annabella would grow up, live her life, and never know that he'd been in it. These papers would remove any right he had to spend time with his daughter—but he also wouldn't have to pay a dime for anything. He would be fully and truly free from any kind of responsibility or even shame. A done deal.

There was a measure of relief in that, but the only thing Ghaith felt was emptiness. He just wanted to forget Jenny and Annabella and this terrible feeling.

He got out his ID, walked over to the notary, and handed over the paperwork.

"Just sign these two pages," the guy said, looking over the document and pushing it back toward him.

Ghaith took the pen and took a quick breath, then signed his name. At that moment, he felt like he had cut off his own arm, like a part of him had died. He felt like he was going to be sick.

"Where's your restroom?" he demanded. He felt sweat dripping down his forehead. The guy behind the counter was looking at him a little strangely.

Ghaith reached the toilet just in time to vomit. Signing his child away induced a deep sickness in his body and soul. Then he stood up, splashing cold water on his face, ready to face reality. When he opened his eyes and looked into the mirror, Ghaith saw that a part of him was gone. His eyes had a strange black tint that he knew would always be there.

&

"I'll mail you the papers after my lawyer can look at them," he said. They were at the airport, and Ghaith looked at Jenny holding Annabella.

"It's better if you just give the document to me now. I can process it through the courts here. Besides, if I meet someone soon, then I'll want those papers signed." Jenny had broken out the big guns. She knew that Ghaith didn't believe in adoption, but that was exactly what she was referring to.

He looked closely at Jenny, seeing how beautiful she was even when she was angry. Grabbing her, he kissed her hard on the mouth and felt her soften in his arms. Then he pulled back and kissed Annabella on the head.

"Go ahead then." Ghaith clumsily pushed the parental relinquishment forms into Jenny's free hand and then quickly walked over to the security lanes. As he felt her eyes on him, a terrible numbness spread throughout his body. He put his items on the scanner belt and felt like he was walking away from a part of himself.

Ghaith knew that out of all the women with whom he had been, he would always be in love with the one from whom he was walking away right now. Some women had changed his life by one or two degrees, but Jenny had changed his life by five degrees. He would never be able to shake her completely.

After he walked through the x-ray scanner, Ghaith turned around to see Jenny still standing there holding Annabella. They were both looking earnestly at him. A tear was rolling down Jenny's cheek, and she gave him a little wave. He knew her well enough to know she was faking bravado.

Then Jenny looked down at Annabella and smiled softly, with a gentle look that Ghaith had never before seen on her face. Annabella kept her eyes fixed on him, and he physically felt his heart weaken. Then Jenny looked back up at Ghaith, and the tear had dried. *Yes, she is a good mother.* He gave them both one last glance and returned the wave clumsily, then walked away. He knew they would both be standing there until they could no longer see him.

Ghaith's heart seemed to fracture, and the piece of Jenny and Annabella shattered. He knew it would be hard, but he could bury those pieces. Turning his thoughts back to his life in Abu Dhabi, he picked up his pace and walked out of sight.

EPILOGUE

THREE YEARS LATER

Jenny felt like she was trying to catch a handful of smoke, as though she could push the particles and atoms together to form something solid enough to grasp. But there was nothing there.

Why had Ghaith added her as a connection on LinkedIn? Maybe it had been an accident, a fleeting thought brought about by a song he'd overheard in a nightclub, or the way a girl in a tight black dress had moved. Maybe he'd seen Chloe in the mall while he was sipping a coffee with his new girlfriend. Or maybe he saw a biracial girl on the street, and it reminded him of Annabella. She didn't know.

Jenny closed her eyes and willed Ghaith to think about her and Annabella. To care. Rejection was the worst feeling. At least hate had some energy to it, pity involved some sort of care, and disgust had intensity. But rejection left her powerless. No amount of yelling, silent treatment, begging, or being nice evoked a response. She had done it all and received the same emotionless treatment. Until today …

The war in Gaza and Israel made Jenny think about Ghaith. Her daughter's relatives might be dying right now. She wanted to find out, and she wanted him somehow to know that she was thinking about him—because she *was*. Throughout the last three years since she had seen

Ghaith, she had thought about him at regular intervals. She had so many discussions with other single moms, and none of them felt the intensity of love that she still felt, which left her feeling confused and stupid.

"There is always this hope in the back of my mind that we will get back together," Jenny said to her mom—and that was part of the problem.

Jenny didn't know whether she was pitiful or idealistic, but she still hadn't gone forward with anyone since Ghaith. For the first couple of years, she hadn't thought about it much, especially since she lived in a sleep-deprived state, worked full-time, and was a single parent. She had also rededicated her life to Christ, so she couldn't just go out and sleep with someone or find a rebound—as tempting as that sometimes sounded. And things with Ron hadn't worked out. Their chemistry had waned and turned into a close friendship that seemed to fade as time went by.

Jenny wanted someone to distract her from Ghaith, but she just hadn't found anyone worthy of her and Annabella's time. But this LinkedIn notice had sent her head spinning. She began to think about Annabella growing up in the Middle East, learning Arabic, knowing her dad.

Also, Jenny wanted Ghaith to know that their daughter's third birthday was in just few days. And she wanted him to know that her mother had been deathly ill. Jenny sighed and thought about the mix of emotions that she was typing to him—*I care about you … Damsel in distress … Our daughter's birthday.* What the hell was she doing awake, at nearly midnight, wanting him to know these things?

She didn't know, and neither did she think about what messages, albeit mixed, she might be sending. She clicked 'send' before she could fully process the likelihood that Ghaith wouldn't respond.

Then she went to a tucked-away file in her computer, found his number, and tried calling him. Strangely, her heart was not beating as fast as it used to when she called him, but that was because this call wasn't calculated. As Ghaith's phone rang, Jenny realized what she was doing— and then an Arabic recording picked up saying the caller wasn't available.

As she hung up, sorrow overtook Jenny in large billowy drafts. Finally, her heartbeat twittered away, as if making sure to wake her out of her misery and fan her familiar second reaction to sorrow—rage. Rage also dried up a tear that tried to fall from her eye, and she sat there as the next old nemesis showed up—rejection.

Then Jenny remembered why she didn't reach out to Ghaith anymore, and why it was better to keep her arms by her sides, rather than trying to touch things that couldn't be touched. Since Ghaith had left Guam, they had exchanged only a couple of e-mails. In one conversation, they had planned to meet up in Japan, but he never followed through. In the second one, Ghaith had told her to go ahead and process the parental relinquishment forms through the courts. Ironically, she had just started the process a couple of weeks earlier. That was just so *final* that it had taken her a long time to commit to doing it.

Next, Jenny entered emotion number four—depression. It always happened like that. She'd experience sorrow as big and wide as the ocean, so big that she would nearly give in and drown. But then rage would roar up from the depths of her being and unwillingly save her from drowning. Then rejection would turn into depression, permeating everything she did for weeks. Each time rejection arose, she seemed to move through the process a little more quickly. She sighed. She had not felt these emotions in a long time, and she certainly had not missed them.

Jenny imagined Ghaith replying to her e-mail and missed call, and she let herself daydream for a brief moment. *If he asks me to marry him again, I just might say yes.* She was alarmed at this thought, this realization. Her daughter's biological father still had a strong effect on her. Was that because her own father had abandoned her when she was young? Was it because she wanted Annabella to know about the other side of her family? Or was it just the prolonged exhaustion of being a single mother with a young child?

In church, the pastor had preached about people going to their death in a predominantly Catholic area of Iraq because they would not give up their religion. Their children were even being beheaded because the parents wouldn't give up Christianity. Jenny knew she wouldn't give up her faith in her heart, but she would more than likely give it up verbally if it was for Annabella. And then, a strange thought entered her head and heart. *Would I give up my faith just to be with Ghaith?* Jenny knew that to marry Ghaith in the Middle East, she would have to say the Arabic confession that meant she was living for Allah. Even though Ghaith had her say it once, she hadn't known what it was. Would it be that easy when she knew what she saying? She knew the answer to that—no.

And then, in a rush, a deep sense of peace descended upon her. Giving her rest. Taking away her stress and hardship. The insomnia of thoughts. Like a wave washing over her, she began to relax and felt absorbed by a calmness. There really was no other way to describe it. *If I give my life to you, Lord, then what?* Jenny thought. Already she knew that turning to Jesus didn't mean that she got everything she wanted. It didn't mean she would be blessed a thousand-fold in this life. She still hadn't met someone to really be with. She still had freak-out tantrums at regular intervals. *That's hard stuff,* she thought.

Jenny leaned back against the couch and let out a sigh. She would probably always love Ghaith, and she knew that. Clearly, that was not a choice. No matter how hard she had pushed those feelings deep inside of her, or tried to extract them, she couldn't stop loving him. Choosing what to do with that was the only thing she could do, and now, as the paperwork worked its way through Guam's court system, she knew she had made her choice. She had released herself from what she knew would be only a bittersweet battle for money, from a lifetime of perpetual rejection, and from the sweet whispers of lies. Now, finally, she could be free from all of it.

Glancing out of the corner of her eye, Jenny saw her phone light up. She recognized Ghaith's number, a number that used to make her heart race. Turning off her phone, Jenny got off the floor and went into Annabella's room. Curling up next to her daughter on the bed, Jenny fell into a deep and peaceful sleep.

AFTERWORD

Handful of Smoke is a fictionalized memoir based on my time in Abu Dhabi, Kuwait, and Guam. Characters are not necessarily based on real people, events have been dramatized, names have been changed, and the histories of characters have been changed. This book was not written to cause a scandal or offend any person, culture, or religion. The hope is that this book will serve as an encouragement for open dialogue, while enriching a universal sharing of emotions through a unique story. If there was more trust in the world, from all sides, maybe we could really understand each other better.

A book trailer, art pieces, and music have been produced, based on the space that *Handful of Smoke* has created. To view these complements, please go to www.handfulofsmoke.com. Additionally, this book is part of a series; two prequels are in development, using Jenny as the main character in the spirit of fictionalized memoirs.

ACKNOWLEDGMENTS

This novel began in 2010, but when I got serious, actually writing it took about a year and a half. The only way I could even get serious about writing was with assistance from babysitters, coffee, wine, online accountability, and tons of support. This book would have taken another five years without the support of the following people: Jean Claude de Cayette, a huge supporter who believed in me the entire way through the process; Jason Salas, the guy who read all three separate drafts; Deborah Espinoza, who believed in me even when I doubted, and her husband, Robert, who let her be there for me; Deborah Ellen, my mother, who helped watch my daughter and did long edits; Leana Zimmerman, who always met up with me to hear about my story; Brandi Hawthorne, who helped with kid swaps so we would have time to focus on our dreams; Sarah Jacobson, my content editor, who helped "kill my darlings"; Sarah Goodridge, who knew the whole story and let me vent about it while drafting the original cover; Claudia Lamparzyk, who tirelessly redesigned the cover nine times and let her art be voted on; Chanel Cruz Jarrett, who read the story and still decided to star in the book trailer; the entire film and talent crew from the trailer; Lindsey and Bobby Cooper, who encouraged me and did my photo shoot; Crystal Moradi, my mentor, who handpicked me from a crowd and gave me confidence; all of my sponsors who committed to being part of this project; some of my virtual heroes, including Napoleon Hill, Paulo Coelho, Justin Fike, Sean Croxton, Rich

Roll, and Chase Jarvis, all of whom—through books, podcasts, and interviews—allowed me to believe in the impossible; and most of all, to my daughter, Isabella, who inspired me to continue this novel and give her a voice. She will no longer be a secret.

ABOUT THE AUTHOR

Erica Sand is a published poet who uses her own experience to tell her stories. When she is not hunched over at her laptop drinking Pinot Noir at dingy bars, you can find Erica playing tag in the sand with her daughter. *Handful of Smoke* is her debut novel.